All their vows had been made.

Nothing important remained that needed to be given voice.

Mary put her hand over Nick's sleeve, the tips of her fingers still shaded with berry juice. The crested ring he wore was briefly touched with moonlight. Seeing the glint, he slipped it off his finger and onto her thumb.

"Take it to my father if…" The sentence trailed off, unfinished.

She nodded.

"I love you, Mary Winters," he whispered. "I will always love you. Dearer to me than my own soul."

Again she nodded.

He felt the small tightening of her fingers over his forearm as she leaned to place her lips against the roughness of his unshaven cheek.

"God keep you safe," she whispered, a prayer, and stepped away, releasing him, freeing him to fulfill other vows, as compelling to his honor, she knew, as these they had made here together.…

Dear Reader,

His Secret Duchess is a heart-wrenching new Regency title from Gayle Wilson, a RITA Award finalist who is also making a name for herself with her spine-tingling mysteries for Harlequin's Intrigue line. In this month's title, a nobleman presumed dead returns home after seven years of war to discover his "secret wife" on trial for murder, and a son whom he must rescue from a vengeful merchant. Don't miss this dark and extraordinary tale of love and redemption.

Linda Castle's new book, *Temple's Prize,* features a hotshot young paleontologist who discovers that his challenge to his former professor will be taken up by his daughter instead. And popular author Suzanne Barclay returns to her bestselling series, THE SOMMERVILLE BROTHERS, with her newest medieval novel *Knight's Rebellion,* the stirring tale of the leader of a band of outlaws who finds himself unable to resist the mysterious woman whom he has rescued.

And when a homeless schoolteacher is taken in by the wealthy uncle of one of her students, falling in love is the last thing on their minds in Pat Tracy's new Western, *Cade's Justice,* the first book in her terrific series set in Denver, Colorado, called THE GUARDSMEN. Another great read from an author who always delivers a fast-paced and sexy story.

Whatever your tastes in reading, we hope you enjoy all four books.

Sincerely,

Tracy Farrell
Senior Editor

Please address questions and book requests to:
Harlequin Reader Service
U.S.: 3010 Walden Ave., P.O. Box 1325, Buffalo, NY 14269
Canadian: P.O. Box 609, Fort Erie, Ont. L2A 5X3

HIS SECRET DUCHESS

GAYLE WILSON

Harlequin Books

TORONTO • NEW YORK • LONDON
AMSTERDAM • PARIS • SYDNEY • HAMBURG
STOCKHOLM • ATHENS • TOKYO • MILAN
MADRID • WARSAW • BUDAPEST • AUCKLAND

ISBN 0-373-28993-6

HIS SECRET DUCHESS

Books by Gayle Wilson

Harlequin Historicals

GAYLE WILSON

is the award-winning author of ten novels written for Harlequin. Gayle has lived in Alabama her entire life, except for the years she followed her army aviator husband to a variety of military posts. She holds a master's degree and an additional certification in the education of the gifted from the University of Alabama. Before beginning her writing career she taught at a number of schools around the Birmingham, Alabama, area.

Gayle writes historicals set in the Regency period of England for Harlequin Historicals and contemporary romantic suspense for Harlequin Intrigue. She was a 1995 Romance Writers of America RITA Award finalist for her first historical title, *The Heart's Desire.* Her first contemporary novel, *Echoes in the Dark,* won the 1996 Award of Excellence presented by the Colorado Romance Writers, and placed third in the Georgia Romance Writers' prestigious Maggie Award competition.

Gayle and her husband have been blessed with a wonderful son, who is also a teacher of gifted students, and with a warm and loving extended Southern family and an ever-growing menagerie of cats and dogs.

For my friend and mother-in-love, Emma Lou,
who also creates heroes,
and who gave me the best.

Prologue

April 1815

The chestnut gelding, fresh and eager for the promised run, resented the sedate pace to which his rider was relentlessly holding him. That resentment had been subtly demonstrated to the man who competently, and without conscious thought, controlled the horse's brief rebellion. To an outside observer, of course, it would have seemed that a flawless connection existed between the horseman's hands and the magnificent animal they guided.

It was not until Lieutenant Colonel Lord Nicholas Stanton finally sighted the slender figure moving through the dappling shade the ancient oaks provided that he allowed his mount his head, and then only until they had closed the distance. The gelding was pulled up once again, and horse and rider sedately followed the strolling girl until, apparently hearing them behind her, she turned to look over her shoulder.

Her blue eyes, shaded by the wide brim of a style of straw bonnet that would certainly not have been seen in the fashionable city from which the Duke of Vail's younger son had just returned, openly considered the rider a moment. Her gaze then returned to concentrate on the path she had been following along the edge of the shadowed country lane.

The horseman's well-shaped lips tilted upward. Nick Stanton was unaccustomed to being snubbed. Especially by women. Indeed, the adulation of the marriageable ladies of the ton during his recent visit to London would have been enough to turn the head of many a man. Not only was he nobly born and extremely well-fixed, but he was an acknowledged military hero, as well, his exploits in Iberia having been remarked upon in dispatches by Wellington himself.

It didn't hurt his standing with the fairer sex that his profile had, on more than one occasion, been compared to Adonis and his tailor was never forced to resort to buckram padding in the making of the well-cut uniforms Nick wore to perfection. The calm dismissal in the eyes of the girl in the outmoded straw bonnet was certainly not the reception Lord Stanton had recently been accorded by the London ton.

Perhaps in response to that obvious disdain, Nick touched his heels to the chestnut and guided him alongside the strolling figure. Again, blue eyes rose to his, their gaze far too direct for fashionable flirtation.

"Good afternoon," Stanton said, holding his mount to the pace the girl had set. A finger of sun reaching through the overarching branches touched briefly on his hair, turning it gold. The fair hair was darkened now with perspiration, and slightly curling. What others of his set achieved with heated irons, nature had bestowed upon him quite naturally, another of her generous gifts for this favored son. His uniform jacket set off broad shoulders and a narrow waist, the tight pantaloons emphasizing the muscled strength of his long legs.

At his greeting, the girl's eyes lifted again, slowly appraising both horse and rider. Her upturned face was classically heart-shaped, but her mouth was too wide for the current fashion and her nose straight rather than retroussé, and there was nothing the least bit simpering in her manner. Her assessment was unflinching.

The sprigged muslin she wore was at least two years old, its skirt rucked up in the country style to protect the fragile material from briars, revealing underneath a plain white petticoat. She carried over her arm a wicker basket almost half-full of red currants.

"My lord," she said simply, and then the blue eyes returned to the lane before them.

Again, that upward tilt disturbed the line of the rider's mouth, as his gray eyes, also, sought the shaded path that stretched ahead of them. The silence lasted for several moments as they moved side by side.

"Berrying?" he asked finally—a ridiculous question, given the evidence in the bottom of the basket.

The girl's mouth, more used to laughter than to primness, flickered dangerously, almost losing its determined sternness. "Indeed," she agreed.

Again silence descended, broken only by the plodding hooves of the gelding. The horse had finally relaxed into the pace his rider was keeping him to.

"May I give you a ride?" Lord Stanton offered, holding out his hand. His fingers were long and deeply tanned, despite the months he'd spent in England and away from his regiment. That had not, of course, been his choice, but the ball he took at Toulouse had proved to be far more troublesome than anyone suspected it might. There had even, at one juncture, been talk that he might lose the leg, but, thankfully, that danger was long past. Despite a slight, persistent stiffness in his right knee, Nick considered himself in fighting trim, and that had been the point of his recent trip to London—to convince his superiors at the Horse Guards of that.

"Thank you, but no, my lord. I'm sure you're far too busy with your own affairs to bother with mine."

"I promise I should be delighted to assist a lady."

The girl's eyes rose to linger a moment on the handsome face. "But surely you can see," she said, "that I'm not—"

"A lady?" he said, interrupting her, his mouth controlled and his face a politely inquiring mask.

"In need of assistance," she finished, without apparent rancor at his insult. She changed the heavy basket to her other arm, and from that sleeve removed a scrap of lace with which she touched the dew of perspiration on her upper lip.

"Making jam?" Stanton asked pleasantly, his eyes following the dabbing movements of the cloth along the beautiful bow of her upper lip.

The girl glanced at him, her dark lashes sweeping upward to reveal some emotion dancing in the depths of her eyes.

"Pies, I believe," she answered.

"For your sweetheart?"

"I have no sweetheart, my lord."

"For a lass so beautiful, I find that difficult to believe. Are all the men here blind?"

"Perhaps. To my charms, at least. It seems there are always...other pleasures that distract them."

"Then they're fools," Nick said softly. Unthinkingly, he slipped his right Hessian out of the stirrup and eased it into a more comfortable position, straightening the aching knee.

"So I've often thought," she agreed, watching the procedure until he glanced down again. Then her gaze deliberately shifted from its focus on the man who rode beside her to the lane ahead.

"Do you have a name?" Stanton asked.

"Of course, my lord."

This time Nick lost the battle to control his amusement, and the smile that had charmed the feminine half of the beau monde was unleashed in full force. Remarkably, it seemed to have no effect on the girl.

"Might I know it?" he urged.

"You might," she said calmly, removing from her basket a berry that had apparently, on closer examination, proved unworthy for inclusion in the proposed pies. "And then, you might not. I'm sure I don't know *what* you might know, my lord."

"Has no one told you not to be pert with your betters?" Nick asked, laughing.

"No one but you, my lord. But I'm sure that was simply an oversight."

"Gertrude," he offered.

"I beg your pardon?" the girl said, but it was obvious, even to Stanton, that she didn't.

"Since you seem so reluctant to share the information, I was attempting to guess your name."

"My name is Mary Winters, my lord."

"Do you live here in the village, Mary?"

"With my father in the vicarage, my lord."

"The proverbial vicar's daughter?"

"Indeed, my lord."

"And have you finished gathering your berries, Mary Winters?"

"Oh, no, my lord. The very best spot, you see, is just through here."

As she spoke, the girl stepped off the apron of the road

and, pulling aside a limb that had blocked a small footpath, she disappeared into the shadowed undergrowth, the branch she had pushed aside returning to cover the hidden opening, as if by magic.

Horse and rider were left alone in the sudden quietness of the lane. Almost before the leaves had stilled, Stanton had dismounted. Displacing the same branch, he led the gelding into the clearing into which the girl had vanished. Once shielded from the road by the intervening hedges, he looped the horse's reins over a branch and ran his hand soothingly over the shining chestnut of the horse's neck.

Then the man's gray eyes lifted to seek the girl. Surprisingly, she was standing on the gnarled trunk of an oak that had forked early in its existence. Something had bent the branch she stood upon, so that it now formed a natural platform about a foot off the ground. The basket rested on the grass beneath the other side of the trunk, which had grown straight and true. She balanced herself by holding on to a limb that protruded from the undamaged trunk of the tree. She had removed the straw hat, releasing a cascade of dark brown curls that seemed to lure all the leaf-diffused light of the clearing to glint in their richness. Her blue eyes watched as Nick Stanton crossed the clearing.

"You appear to be limping, my lord," she said.

"I've just spent three days successfully *not* limping," he answered, smiling, "so I should think you might try to be less critical."

"A war wound, I suppose."

"An honorable one, I assure you. Taken in the front."

The girl's mouth quivered, almost a smile.

"And heroic, no doubt?" she asked tauntingly.

"Not particularly."

"Lord Wellington seemed to think so," she said challengingly.

Smiling, Nick shook his head in denial, but his steps didn't falter. Inexorably, he continued his approach to the oak.

"And foolhardy? Incredibly brave?" she suggested.

"A matter of opinion, I should imagine," he said dismissively.

He stood now directly below her, his height enough that their eyes were almost on a level. Blue met gray and held a moment, and then she touched him. She had turned her hand so that her knuckles trailed against the curling golden hair at his temple. He put his left hand up to catch her fingers, bringing them to his lips.

His mouth drifted slowly over the slender fingers, stained at the tips with the juice of the berries she'd gathered. Her free hand found his shoulder, the thumb caressing along the fine wool of his uniform and then upward along his neck until her palm cupped behind his head, her fingers lost in the warm silk of his hair.

Nick released the hand he'd captured and, putting his on either side of her slim waist, he lifted her from her perch into his arms. There was no resistance. She melted against his body, arms clinging around his neck, her mouth automatically opening and lowering to his. Familiar and practiced, his tongue slipped inside, as intimate as a lover's. And as welcome.

The kiss was long and unhurried. Despite the limp with which he'd crossed the expanse between them, Stanton held her without effort, her body resting trustingly along the hard, masculine length of his. Slowly he lowered her until the toes of her kid slippers touched the ground, and still their mouths clung, moving against one another, cherishing, reluctant to let go. Finally she broke the kiss, her palms resting on either side of his face.

"Tell me that they refused you," she entreated.

Smiling, he shook his head. "You know better than that, Mary. The Beau needs every experienced officer, every veteran, he can find. I told you that before I left."

"And you convinced them you were fit."

"To be truthful—"

"To be truthful, you lied about your leg," she said accusingly.

"They were too glad of my offer to think of refusing. I suspect they'd have accepted me if I'd lost the leg," he said, still smiling down at her. "Don't be angry, Mary, my heart. That's where I belong. It's where my men will be. My regiment. It's where I want to be."

"Not again," she whispered. "I can't let you go to that hell again." There was no answer for that plea. No comfort. Men were the warriors, and women those who wept. "How long?" she asked, and watched his lips tighten.

"Three hours. Less. I had to change horses. There were things I needed at the Hall, and I had to say goodbye to Charles and my father, in case..." His voice faded at the pain in her eyes, suddenly glazed with tears. "I came as fast as I could. But I have to be back in London to board the transport at dawn."

"You just arrived. Surely—"

"Three hours, Mary," he reminded, his mouth finding the small blue vein at her temple. "Shall we spend it arguing?"

"No," she whispered, her lips lifting to his, her tongue seeking, fingers tangling through the golden curls. "No," she said again as his mouth shifted over hers, turning to meld, to possess what was his. And always would be.

Nick had taken his cloak from his saddle pack and laid it on the ground, and now they lay together, watching dusk darken the sky they could barely see through the sheltering branches above their heads. He had removed his uniform jacket, and Mary's fingers had long ago found the buttons of the soft lawn shirt he wore beneath it.

She had unfastened them, daringly, first one and then another, her lips exploring each inch of the hair-roughened chest as it was revealed. Her mouth had finally touched the smooth skin of his flat belly, tracing at last down the line of gold that disappeared into the top of his pantaloons.

His breathing had changed as she touched him, but he'd not protested the tentative exploration, except occasionally, his fingers locking suddenly in the spill of dark curls when her mouth found some previously unexamined area. Tortured by the sweetness of her lips, he was beyond conscious thought, beyond any remembrance of right and wrong. This was Mary, and it seemed that he had loved her so long. There was nothing about the gentleness of her kisses on his body that profaned what he felt for her. What he had felt almost since the first time he saw her.

He had come to service that Sunday morning only because his father insisted he leave the Hall, where he'd been secluded since his arrival from Spain. He'd been embarrassed then by the clumsiness of the crutches, by the villagers' sympathetic stares and interested questions about his military exploits.

He and his father had taken their places in the ducal box pew, which was raised above the congregation and directly across from the pulpit. Nick's eyes had remained downcast as he fought the humiliation of his body's unfamiliar awkwardness. It was only when his father's elbow admonished him that he'd looked down onto the congregation, his gray eyes rebellious, and found Mary.

She was sitting in the first row, her face rapt, listening to her father's sermon, totally unaware of the fascinated attention of the Duke of Vail's younger son. It was an experience that was new to Nick Stanton, and perhaps that was her initial appeal.

If so, it was soon overtaken by other, more conventional elements of attraction: the beauty of blue eyes fringed by long, dark lashes, the incredible clarity of her skin, the shining coils of brown hair demurely hidden under her Sunday bonnet. Stanton, long considered as one of the catches of any Season fortunate enough to find him spending a few months in London, quickly fell under the spell of a country vicar's daughter.

Apparently, however, Mary Winters had no interest in his existence. Indeed, she seemed to be totally unaware that such an illustrious figure as Lieutenant Colonel Lord Nicholas Stanton had deigned to grace her father's simple parish church that morning. And so, of course, motivated at first simply by boredom and his enforced inactivity, Nick set out to change that situation.

In the next few weeks, his father grew suspicious of Nick's desire to attend service. The duke began to fear that the recently passed dangers of his wound or the disastrous influence of some Methodist evangelist might be responsible for his son's unprecedented religious zeal.

It did not, however, take Vail long to realize that something more in keeping with Nick's normal temperament had occurred. He had only to focus his lorgnette in the direction the straightforward gray gaze took each Sunday to find that the object of Nick's devotion was not the promise of celestial paradise, but something more tangible, more earthly, and far more apt to cause trouble. He spoke sternly to his son and was surprised by the tenor of his answer.

"Trifle with her?" Nick repeated, incredulous at his father's fear. "Good God, sir, look at her. Who would dare to trifle with Mary Winters?"

Recognizing the serenity of spirit and the cool intelligence in the girl's blue eyes, attributes that Lord Stanton had already acknowledged, the duke was forced to agree.

"Mary," Nick whispered finally, more plea than protest. But her lips lingered only a heart-shattering moment longer over the coarse hair that arrowed toward his achingly responsive body. He closed his eyes tightly at the sudden desertion of her mouth, knowing that her retreat was far wiser than his acquiescence had been.

Having spent three years on the battlefields of the Iberian Peninsula, he had come to find Mary today, well aware that he might never see her again, might never be allowed to make her his. Even now, he should be on his way to rejoin his regiment. He had told her three hours, and under the untutored tenderness of her slender hands and the sweetness of her lips, those moments had slipped away, melting from his possession like snow in summer.

He lay, eyes still closed, listening to the sounds of approaching evening, the coo of the doves, the rising breeze disturbing the stillness of the leaves above his head, all the while desperately trying to will his body back to control.

"Nick," Mary said softly, her voice coming from above him now. He opened his eyes, and then, despite the knowledge that there was only madness in the act, he found himself unable to close them again, unable to deny what she offered.

Mary had lowered the bodice of her gown and her chemise, holding the soft muslin protectively over her breasts with her fingers, the stains at their tips almost startling next to the pale delicacy of the fabric. Her eyes held his, her lips unsmiling, a tangle of dark curls over the bare ivory of her shoulders.

Then, as he watched, she lowered the garments, exposing for him the flawless perfection of her breasts. He lay un-

moving, his breath stopped by wonder. Slowly, her eyes
never leaving his, she raised the fingers of her right hand
and placed them under one rose-tipped peak, her thumb
stroking downward over the swell of smooth skin.

He was not aware of consciously directing the movement
that brought his mouth to replace her trembling fingers. It
was not planned or ordered by his brain. Something far
more primitive was responsible for the placement of his
lips over that small captive. Her breath shivered out against
his hair, stirring in the golden softness, sobbing with the
movement of his tongue, drawn slowly over and then
around the nipple she had so trustingly given to his worship.

She hadn't known that his mouth would feel like this,
hot and moist and demanding, his teeth teasing the hardened bud his tongue created. Something was happening inside her body, moving, too, reaching toward him now, as
her breast had sought out his caress. Unfamiliar and unknown, it responded to the incredible sensations of his
mouth suckling the sensitive area no man's eyes had ever
seen before. No one but Nick. She was his, and it was right
that he know before he left.

His tongue floated across the valley between her suddenly aching breasts, her heart fluttering underneath its heat
and moisture, the trail it left branded on her skin by the
very air. Her hands held his head, pulling it down against
her chest, wanting his touch inside, where she ached. She
made no protest when he turned her, laying her gently on
his cloak, the coarseness of the wool against her bare back.

He leaned above her, propped on his elbow, the gray
eyes studying the slender body before him. He touched the
base of her throat, finding the small pulse. His long fingers
were dark against her paleness, hard and callused against
the soft translucence of her skin. They feathered lower, un-

til, as hers had earlier, they stroked over the rose nipple that centered the milk-white globe.

Watching his eyes, she put her hands on his shoulders to urge him downward until the golden hair on his chest grazed over her too-sensitive flesh. Instinctively he moved above her, never allowing the hard muscles to contact her softness, choosing instead to torture them both, almost touching and then not, so close she could feel the heat of his skin beneath the softly tantalizing brush of hair.

It was not until her small hips arched upward into his, shockingly intimate, that he allowed his arms to close around her, locking her against the straining wall of his chest. She arched again, her body into his, demanding, this and more. Far more than she knew. Far more than he had ever intended. But not more than she wanted. And now, more than he could deny.

Her fingers, caught between their bodies, found, as he held her, the flap of his trousers, and frantic with need, she sought to free him from their restraint.

"Mary," he said, his voice denying, but she didn't listen.

He was leaving, and she, too, knew the dangers he'd face. Hers was a conscious decision, undeterred by all she had been taught, by all that she had truly believed until the reality of his danger intruded. Nick was hers, and her body demanded the fulfillment of that ownership, despite the denial of society's mores, of her religion. This was hers and his. And might never be again.

She touched the unfamiliar contours of his body, desperate, urging him to finish what they had begun. What could no longer be denied.

"Mary," he whispered again, his voice hoarse and agonized with need, with want, with pain.

"Yes," she whispered. "Yes."

Again, her small hands entreated. Country-bred, she had

no sophistication and no longer any hesitancy. She could taste the salt on his skin as the strong brown column of his neck rested over her lips. And finally, after she had touched him a long time, his hands joined hers to help with what she sought, to guide and to direct.

The air was shocking against her uncovered body, cold and invasive, but she wanted it, as she wanted the invasion that followed. Painful and tearing. She gasped her shock into the shoulder that strained against her mouth and heard his voice again whisper her name.

He turned his cheek against her face, the slight roughness of his beard burning her skin, his movements frenzied and uncontrolled. His hips drove above her a long time, and from within her pain, from its dark center, something began to form, to open like the tight-furled bud of a rose releasing into the afternoon's sun.

She wasn't sure of the feeling at first, at the edge of pain, and then beyond discomfort. Into something else. Pulsing and growing at the heart of his body's driving caress. Expanding like the silk of the balloons she had watched them fill that summer in the London pleasure gardens. Filling with heat that couldn't be denied, that couldn't be contained by the pull of the earth's gravity, until all at once, whatever had been there floated upward, soaring as the balloons had, out of her control.

She heard her own voice, crying out as the center released, and then Nick's mouth was over hers, capturing the echo of the cry that had shattered the twilight stillness around them. His own release followed quickly, hot and powerful, roaring into the receptacle of her body like a torrent, shattering in its intensity. His body convulsed under her caressing hands. Once. Twice. And then was still. As still now as the clearing where they lay, still entwined. One.

Finally he moved, raising his chest away from hers on

hard brown arms that trembled. He looked down into her face, which was touched with this great mystery, softened and exposed by what had happened.

"Mary," he said again, the afternoon's litany, and thinking that, she smiled at him. "I'm so sorry," he whispered.

Her smile widened, blue eyes moving over the strong lines of his face. Beloved. *This is my beloved.* She watched her fingers touch his cheek, feeling, as she had felt before, the dear roughness. Too intimate and too private. Only hers.

"Oh, dear God, Mary, what have I done?" Nick said, his tone choked with despair.

"Hush." She comforted him, her voice that of a mother whispering from the darkness of the storm's rage to her frightened child. "It's all right," she promised. Her thumb moved against his lashes, which were gold tipped and darker at the root. Beautiful eyes. She had never really seen them before. Their color now was the same slate as the afternoon's sky in winter. "I love you," she said, and watched his face change again. Realigning. Finding the direction he had lost, the sure course of honor she had stolen from him.

"Where is your father?" he asked, and for a moment she couldn't remember. Or think why he would want to know.

"With the dean. On visitation."

"Will he be home tonight?"

"Not until Tuesday," she said, thinking suddenly about her dear, frail papa. Of his unfailing gentleness with those who fell short of the grace so generously given. And thinking, finally, of the reality of what they had done.

"Come on," Nick said, rising in one smoothly athletic movement and then reaching down to pull her to her feet.

Standing, she was embarrassed for the first time by their undress. She watched, unmoving, as he rearranged his garments, the action a matter of seconds. When he turned to her, the long fingers dealing competently with the last button on his shirt, his hands stilled at what was in her face.

"I have to go," he said, trying to imagine what she must be feeling. "If I don't, then I'll be a deserter. It won't matter that I'm Vail's son. My regiment is going into combat, Mary. I have to go. I've been recommissioned."

"I know," she whispered, wondering why he was explaining. She had always understood he had to leave. That was why...

"Mary?" he said.

She would never see him like this again, she knew suddenly, the surety of her premonition so strong it took her breath. And so she let her eyes glory in him as he stood before her, young and strong and so beautiful. So alive. His hair disordered by their lovemaking, by her fingers. His tanned skin clean, its taste sweet and warm, salt-kissed under her tongue.

She closed her eyes, imprinting his image on her brain. To last forever. Nick. For one instant of time, he had belonged only to her, and she would cherish that in the dark future that lay ahead.

"Mary?" he said again, his tone questioning.

Her eyes opened, and she forced herself to smile at him. He crossed the small distance that separated them. He gently guided her hands through the openings in her chemise and then through the sleeves of the bodice of her gown, his fingers dealing with the intricacies of feminine dress with an ease that argued long familiarity. She wondered how many other women...and knew that it didn't matter. Whatever they had been before, they were no longer. There was only now.

She stood and let him dress her as if she were a porcelain fashion doll. Or a child. It was not until his thumb had lifted to wipe away the tears that she even realized she was crying. She caught his hand, to lay the dampness of her cheek against its warmth.

"I didn't mean to hurt you," he said, feeling her smile begin against his palm in response to that apology.

"I know," she whispered.

"Is it very bad, my heart?"

"No," she answered, looking up to comfort his concern. His eyes were too serious, worried, a crease forming between the golden brows. "It doesn't hurt." A lie, but there was no need to add to the burden she'd already given him to bear, a guilt he would carry with him onto some battlefield in a place whose name she wouldn't even know.

"We have to go," he urged again.

"I know."

But when he led her from the clearing, the gelding following as placid as a shepherd's dog, and lifted her onto the animal, careful of her discomfort, it was to take her to a destination she did not expect.

The stones of the ancient monastic chapel blended into the fall of night's shadows, almost hidden from the road. This was the oldest part of the benefice, seldom used since the newer church, much closer to the village, had been commissioned by the old duke, Nick's grandfather. Built as a penance for his many sins, some had said. This small chapel was peopled now only by the ghosts of those who had prayed beneath its roof through so many centuries.

She didn't question when Nick lifted her off Comet's back and, taking her hand, pulled her toward the wooden doors. They creaked protestingly when he pushed them open. The interior was darker than the outside twilight, and they were forced to wait for their eyes to adjust to its gloom.

There was a tall stained-glass window behind the chancel, and in the light filtering through its gemlike panes they were finally able to see the simple stone altar in the shadowed darkness. The faint scent of incense seemed to permeate the silence. Nick again took her hand, leading her across the nave toward the altar. It was only at the realization of his intent that she shrank back, struggling to free her hand from his determined hold.

"No," she said, her recoil from the sanctity of this place instinctive. "Not here." She could not come here, could not stand in this place with him, her body wet with their lovemaking.

"Yes, Mary. Here."

Wondering, she shook her head. Nick held her eyes a moment, and then turned to face the figure depicted in the central light, below the flowing tracery of the window.

"Here," he said again. His eyes still raised to the image in the window, he began to intone the familiar words, "I, Nicholas William Richard, take thee, Mary…"

His voice faltered, and his gaze came back to the tear-streaked beauty of her face, lifted almost reverently, not to the window, but to his.

"Elizabeth," she whispered. His gaze rested on her features a long time, and then returned to the figure portrayed in the stained-glass window above their heads.

"…take thee, Mary Elizabeth, to be my wedded wife. To have and to hold, for richer, for poorer, in sickness and in health…" The soft words faltered again. He was unable to remember the rest, and so he finished. "From this day forward. Forever more. Amen."

He turned to her again, waiting, and fighting tears, she raised blind eyes to the jeweled lights of the window.

"I, Mary Elizabeth, take thee, Nicholas William Richard, to be my wedded husband. To have and to hold, from this day forward, in sickness and in health, to love and to cherish, until death us do part. And thereto I plight thee my troth.''

"Amen,'' Nick demanded. A talisman, perhaps, a charm to make the spell complete.

"Amen,'' she echoed obediently.

He released her hand. There was no kiss. She shivered suddenly, and he pulled her against the heat of his body, tall and strong, enclosing her in his strength.

"Where's the register?'' he asked, his lips against her hair.

"I don't know,'' she said truthfully, leaning back, sniffing, wiping her cheeks with the back of her hand.

"We have to find it,'' he said, no longer the tender lover of the clearing or the ardent maker of vows. He was again the arrogant nobleman, Wellington's officer, confident and demanding.

"Why?''

"To record the marriage.''

"But—''

"Think, Mary.''

Instead, again obeying him without question, she moved behind the altar to the small vestment cupboard. She struggled a moment with the stiffness of the clasp, and when she had succeeded in opening the door, she found only an ancient leather-bound register. Its vellum pages were filled, she knew, with the scrawling signatures of previous village priests recording the important events of the parish when this building had served as its spiritual heart. The current register, where any marriage should now be recorded, rested in the chancel of the new church.

"Everything was taken to the new sanctuary when it was consecrated,'' Mary said, shaking her head. "There's nothing here but the old.''

"Is there room, Mary?'' Nick asked.

"Room?" she repeated, puzzled.

Stanton strode to the cupboard. Without hesitation, he lifted the massive book from its resting place and brought it to the fading light of the window. He laid it on the stone altar, opening it to the last page.

"Here," he said, pointing to the blank space at the bottom. "Now all we need is pen and ink."

"Nick..." she protested again, knowing in her heart that this was wrong, against all the church held sacred.

He didn't listen. The point of the pen he found in the cupboard was sharp enough, but the blackened smudge of dried powder, which was all that remained in the well, was unusable.

He carried the pen back to where Mary stood, still watching. He smiled at her before he pushed its point into the pad of his thumb, squeezing the flesh to encourage the welling crimson drop.

Following the pattern of the previous entries, Nick began to inscribe the circumstances of this marriage that was no marriage. His signature first. Then he handed the pen to Mary, his eyes compelling her, and almost against her will she obeyed, carefully inscribing her name.

"This isn't a marriage, Nick. There've been no banns and no clergy. We can't marry ourselves. And there must be witnesses."

"Of course," he agreed, the gray eyes calm, and again he began to write, using still his own blood.

She watched, horrified because she knew the penalties for what he was doing—counterfeiting a church record, falsifying the required documentation of a marriage.

"No, Nick," she said, catching his hand as he finished the scrawling signature of his father, an arrogant hand he could copy out as well as his own, having seen it a thousand times. "This is felony."

"Who will charge us? My father would never deny me, Mary. Nor Charles," he said, freeing his hand from her clutching fingers to add the name of his brother, and then his title. "They would suffer a traitor's death rather than betray me."

"And the priest's signature. Will you forge that, too? My father won't lie. He would never agree. You don't know *his* hand," she added, glad she had thought of something to stop what he was doing.

"But you do," Nick suggested softly. It was true, of course. She knew she could produce a reasonable facsimile of her father's scholarly penmanship. "Would he deny you, Mary?"

Would her father condemn her to the cruelty of the courts if she falsified this record? Into her mind came the image of his well-loved face. "No," she whispered, certain of the truth of that, no matter what the cost to his conscience. "No," she said again, more strongly.

"For me, Mary, my heart. Have I asked you for so much?"

The words hung between them like the perfume of the incense. He had asked for nothing. What she had given him had been offered freely, born of her own love and her need.

"You have asked me for nothing," she whispered.

She took the pen from his hand, and fingers trembling, dipped the point again into his blood. *This is my beloved.* She added her father's name, another lie, to go with the ones Nick had already written on the page.

She stood silent when it was finished, the enormity of all they had done weighing down her soul. Gently he took the pen from her hand and closed the book. He returned them both to the cupboard where they had lain undisturbed for so long and would lie again.

He walked back to her, the heels of his boots echoing

across stone floor. He took her hands in his, enclosing their trembling coldness in his warmth. "Tell your father when he comes home. Tell him what happened." Looking into the troubled blue eyes, he knew what he had tried to do here had not been enough and knew again the guilt of the clearing. "There wasn't time. Not enough time to make it right. We've done the best we can, Mary. I'll write my father and explain."

"But it can't be legal," she argued, wondering why he had been so determined on this farce. It almost made it worse, she thought. A mockery of all that should have been.

His eyes rose once more to the lines of the figure crudely delineated by the colored panes in the window behind her. She turned, and her gaze found the blessed hands, outstretched to sinners.

"Intent, Mary. This is our intent. *He* understands what's in our hearts. Our vows are real, signed in my heart's blood. Those are what is important, and in them there is no deceit."

And finally, wordlessly, she nodded.

It was dark now, only the crescent moon silvering the earth below. Mary stood beside him in the stillness. They had not spoken after they left the chapel. There had been nothing to say. All their vows, physical and verbal, had been made. Nothing, then, of any importance remained that needed to be given voice.

She put her hand over his sleeve, the tips of her fingers still shaded with the juice of the berries she had picked a hundred years ago. His fingers, long and brown and restless now, for he was eager to be off, closed around hers. The crested ring he wore was briefly touched with moonlight. Seeing the glint, he slipped it off his finger and onto her thumb.

"Take it to my father if…" The sentence trailed, unfinished.

She nodded.

"I love you, Mary Winters," he whispered. "I will always love you. Dearer to me than my own soul."

Again she nodded.

He felt the small tightening of her fingers over his forearm as she leaned to place her lips against the roughness of his unshaven cheek.

"God keep you safe." She whispered the prayer and stepped away, releasing him, freeing him to fulfill other vows, as compelling to his honor, she knew, as these they had made here together.

He mounted, the movement smooth and practiced. Comet circled, dancing with the familiar weight. Nick controlled the gelding long enough to place warm fingers against her cheek and then, removing them, he dug in his heels, racing the sun toward London.

Mary stood in the shadows of the chapel a moment, listening to the pounding hoofbeats fade into the distance. Finally, when the silence was as deep as the darkness that surrounded her, she, too, turned away and reentered the chapel.

It was there that dawn, seeping redly into the shadowed sanctuary, through the ruby panes of the window, found her. The sun finally rose high enough to gleam in the tangled curls of the girl whose head lay pillowed on her arms, still on her knees, but asleep at last, on the altar steps where she had poured out through the long night hours the first of the countless prayers she would say for Nick Stanton.

Chapter One

February 1822

"When will my father be home?" the child asked, carefully placing the wooden soldier, brightly painted with the smart blue-and-red uniform of the Royal Horse Guards, back in its box.

The woman seated in a chair turned to the window in order to catch the fading light of the winter afternoon looked up from her embroidery to watch the childish fingers complete the task. Although she failed to ply her needle again, Mary Winters's eyes returned to the piece she was working on before she answered.

"Perhaps tonight. Depending on the state of the roads."

"I wish he might bring me another soldier," the child said, almost plaintively.

"If wishes were horses..." Mary reminded him softly, looking up to smile at him.

The boy finished the familiar admonition. "Then beggars might ride."

He should certainly have known that was a fruitless wish, Mary thought. His father had never brought home any present for the child after one of his numerous business trips. She herself had given him the toy soldier.

She was twenty-five, long past the first bloom of youth, serenely handsome rather than pretty. Her coloring was not fashionable, and she was too slender for the current mode that demanded softly rounded curves. The glowing dark curls were severely restrained, hidden under the lace cap she habitually wore.

Her dress of brown serge was free of decoration, deliberately fitting loosely over her body. Only the blue eyes would have found favor with the fashionable world she had no desire to enter. Her feet were firmly grounded on country soil, and she no longer dreamed of any other existence. And if once she had...

Resolutely Mary banished memory and took up her needle. If only the light would last a little longer, she could finish the mending today, she thought. She had gotten a great deal of it done. The household ran more smoothly when its master wasn't home. She and the boy were content to sit before the warmth of the winter fire and talk, tell stories or discuss the past summer's exploits. There were no demands. No uncomfortable tensions. No arguments.

Her eyes lifted again to the child's small head, lowered over his toy. They closed briefly, dreading the renewal of the arguments. There seemed to be nothing she could say to convince the man whose arrival they awaited that what he'd suggested could never be. She shivered suddenly and, although the room was not chilled, she pulled the soft warmth of the woolen shawl more closely around her shoulders. Unconsciously, she sighed, and the boy looked up at the sound, the soft, childish lips moving into his beautiful smile.

"What's wrong?" he asked, his slate-gray eyes resting on hers.

"I'm losing the light," she said.

His eyes fell, his fingers touching the gilt paint that had been applied over the blue of the soldier's uniform.

"You don't like him here," he said. "You haven't wanted him here since my mother died."

The realization that he so clearly understood her feelings took her unawares, and Mary hesitated, trying to think how to answer. At the continued silence, the gray eyes lifted again.

"It's all right," he said, forgivingly. "Sometimes I don't want him here."

She knew the times he meant. The discipline was harsh, but the man argued that much was expected of his son, and so he must be taught to be above reproach. Knowing her protests only made it worse, Mary had bitten her tongue to blood the last time, although the boy hadn't made a sound under the repeated blows of the small cane.

"You mustn't say that," she corrected, laying down the needlework and allowing herself to place a hand on the down-fine softness of the child's hair. "He's your father. And you must love him." Her voice had softened to a whisper, but the child's eyes never left her face. "Do you understand?" she asked when he didn't respond.

The gray eyes fell, back to the toy his hands still rested against. The small shoulders heaved with the depth of his sigh, but he said nothing else.

"I think it's time for tea," Mary said, making her voice strong and pleasant. "Are you hungry?" She waited, unsmiling, her eyes on the downcast head until finally he nodded. "Good," she said, rising. "So am I. I think that as a treat we shall have currant scones and cream."

The childish fingers brushed again along the wooden figure. The light from the fire played over the boy's curls, touching them with the same gold the painted soldier wore so proudly.

It was long after dark when the master of the house returned. Mary had forced herself to wait up, keeping the fire in the parlor alive and the lamps lit. Unkindness was not in her nature, and no traveler should be forced to return to a cold, dark house in the dead of a winter's night. She had no wish to see him, no wish to greet the man whose arrivals she had grown to dread more and more with each passing week.

Marcus Traywick was a merchant, successful, certainly, by the standards of the district in which his sturdy brick house stood. He had ordered the dwelling built to his own specifications, untrusting of the architect he had sent to London for. There was, therefore, nothing of the aesthetic about the structure, but simply the same stolidness and lack of imagination that colored the character of the man whose home it was.

It was Mary who unlatched the heavy oak door and let him in. No other servant slept within the house. Traywick employed a man to tend to the coarser tasks demanded by the household, a grizzled veteran whose military service had returned him to the village missing an arm and who was pathetically grateful for the job.

Mary suspected Bob Smithers's employment was the result of neither kindness nor patriotism on the part of her employer, but rather the realization that given the ex-soldier's impairment, the merchant could more easily justify the pittance he paid him. All other tasks fell to Mary Winters, who did them willingly, grateful still.

"A cold night, Mary," Traywick said, brushing the snow off the top of his beaver, letting it fall to puddle on the gleaming boards of his entry hall. "It's not fit out for man nor beast."

Mary made no response as she helped him out of the greatcoat and hung it to dry on the hall stand. She had found in the long years she had spent here that there was no need for an answer. The merchant expected none, and if one made a response to the familiar comments, which were always the same or were said with some slight variation, it disturbed the even tenor of the homecoming. So she was silent, respecting what she had come to understand was merely ritual.

Divested of his outer garments, Traywick crossed the hall to the parlor and the warmth of its welcoming fire. Mary waited, watching from the doorway as he spread his broad hands before the cheerful blaze, their chilblained redness visible even in the shadowed room. He never wore gloves, often mocking the virility of those who did. "Simpering fops" was his most frequent sobriquet.

Although she never responded to his comments or made her own, Mary had come, through the years she worked for Traywick, to despise the vulgar coarseness of his hands. She had at first prayed for forgiveness for whatever was in her nature that would allow her to feel about his hands as she did.

Now she no longer bothered to seek divine intervention for this evidence of her ingratitude. She tried to ignore the feelings those rough, cracked fingers created in her mind, but sometimes she dreamed of his hands, seeing them in her nightmares as separate from the man himself, having their own almost animalistic life.

Clearing that ridiculous childishness from her mind, Mary waited until he had turned from the fire to face her before she asked, "Is there anything I can get for you, Mr. Traywick, before I retire?"

Often it was bread and a piece of cheese, some nights a glass of the strong port he kept in the decanter on the sideboard. Sometimes he dismissed her, and she was always thankful for those rare occasions, grateful to escape.

"Nothing, thank you, Mary."

She had already turned to go when he added the rest, and she felt the tight bud of the fear she had fought during the three weeks he was away blossom sickeningly in her stomach.

"Except your answer to the question I told you must now be considered," he said.

She hesitated a moment, seeking control, before turning back to face the man standing before the fire. This was a discussion they had had with increasing frequency during the past two months. Always her response had been the same. And always he had pretended to believe she simply needed time to better think through the proposal he was making.

"I cannot wed you, Mr. Traywick. I thought you understood."

"You are living in my home, Mary. Already there's talk about the unseemliness of our situation."

"There will always be those willing to gossip. And those willing to listen. I have *lived* in your home, sir, for more than six years. I am your son's governess."

"Indeed you are," Marcus Traywick said, his thick lips moving, almost in a sneer. "However," he continued smoothly, controlling his amusement at her argument, "until two months ago, my wife was also living in this household. There was then no reason for tongues to wag. The situation has changed. Surely you understand that."

Mary Winters had held the fragile, reedlike body of Abigail Traywick as she breathed her last, her health stolen first by the too-frequent miscarriages and then by the illness whose evidence had grown large and mocking in her womb, a malignant growth rather than the child she had so fervently pined for, a growth whose only outcome could be death.

Long an invalid, unable at the end even to leave her bed, Abigail Traywick had died as she had lived these last years, with only the company of Mary Winters and the small fair-haired boy who sat contentedly for hours on the bright coverlet of her bed.

The laughing conversations of the three had been almost a conspiracy, quickly hidden when Mr. Traywick returned from one of his frequent business expeditions into the outside world. At those times, Mary and the boy had sought the dim, fire-warmed isolation of her small room, removed from the sounds that always accompanied the master's return.

"I need a wife, Mary. The boy needs a mother. It is up to you if you wish to be the one to fulfill those roles."

He wanted someone who would satisfy his carnal needs. Not just someone, she acknowledged. He wanted her, and she had been made aware of that for a long time. He had made the first approaches even before his wife's death. The unwanted brush of his hand against her arm or her hip. The sly, inviting smile. The slide of his eyes across her body.

Not that he had stopped his conjugal visits to Abigail, not even when her body was so wasted that it made almost no disturbance of the bed's smooth coverings, except for the grotesque swelling of the tumor in her belly. Mary knew the reality of his continued visits too well, having seen the evidence of his passions clearly revealed in the dark bruises on the dying body of the woman she cared for, gently bathing the thin limbs and dressing her, at her instruction, in a pretty nightgown, pitifully awaiting her husband's expected return.

When Mary finally found the courage to ask, Abigail's eyes had not met hers.

"Because he's my husband," she had said softly. *"It's my duty. I cannot deny him, Mary. It is his right."*

Mary Winters had nodded, placing the skeletonlike arm tenderly under the warmth of the quilts that she piled around the dying woman.

"There are others, Mary, more than willing," Traywick reminded, pulling her thoughts back to the present, to the question for which she could not imagine an answer.

She knew the truth of what he said. He was rich, prominent in the affairs of the district, tall and stout, his thick body taken as a sure sign of his prosperity. It would be thought that spinster Mary Winters had made a match far above her expectations. Traywick's florid complexion and the slightly protruding, mud-colored eyes were not flaws serious enough to put off the women who would be more than willing to take over the running of this house Mary had entered more than six years ago.

In those years, the reins of its management had slipped slowly and yet inexorably from Abigail Traywick's fragile fingers into Mary's capable ones. She could not imagine anyone else living here.

Nor could she imagine sharing the upbringing of the boy with another woman. Certainly it would not be with the instantaneous, sisterlike rapport she had found with Abigail.

"You may go or stay. That is your decision, Mary," Traywick went on. "Your right. But if you choose to stay, it must be, given the change in our circumstances, as my wife."

"Go?" she repeated unbelievingly. Surely he couldn't mean—

"I don't think another woman will be willing to share the management of the household with you, as Abigail was.

Her health, you know, almost forced that surrender of her duties, but another woman..."

He let the sentence trail off, its implications clear. Another woman would perhaps demand sole control. Not only of the house, a task she would gladly surrender, but also of the child.

"What of Richard?" she asked. The central question, of course. She watched his thick lips move again into that knowing smile.

"There is Richard, of course. Did you think I had forgotten Richard, Mary?"

"Even if you remarry, sir, he shall still need a governess. A new wife might not be so willing to take on the raising of a child from a previous marriage."

"Especially if she has sons of her own," he suggested.

The idea was one that she had not considered. How stupid she had been that the realization of what he really wanted did not cross her mind. She had done everything he demanded. All these years, knowing that she was entirely at his mercy, but knowing also, in her heart, that Abigail Traywick's body would never produce the son her husband's vanity demanded.

They had been married five years before Mary came to live here. Even then, there had been eight small markers in the churchyard of the village, all the stones bearing the name of Traywick. A few of the babes had been stillborn, carried long enough for hope, she imagined, to flourish in Abigail's breast that this time, this time at last, she might produce the son her husband wanted so desperately. And his obsessive desire for a son to carry on his name had been Mary's protection.

"Besides," he went on, "Richard is old enough to be sent away to school."

"He's still a baby," Mary argued, but suddenly she

knew what he intended: to ease aside the child he had been so willing to claim as his own six years ago, and to put into his place a son of his own loins—now that the convenient death of his barren wife had freed him to marry again. She could be his new wife and could bear the sons he wanted, sons of his own seed. In that position, she would be able to care for and protect Richard. Otherwise...

"Your decision, Mary. Shall you become my wife and continue here in the household you have surely come to think of as your own? To care for Richard as if he were your own son..."

Again he allowed the sarcastic suggestion to fade away. There was no reason to voice the truth. They both were aware of it. She had given him her son, and in exchange she had been allowed to live in this house, to care for the baby and for the woman who willingly pretended she had finally carried a living child within her womb, carried it this time to term.

There had been nothing but a strong mother's love evidenced for the baby by Abigail Traywick, but her spirit was generous enough to share "her" son with the slender, too-quiet girl who had come to live in her home and who had come, also, eventually, to be her friend.

"You know I can't leave Richard," Mary said.

"Then the decision seems simple. You will find me an indulgent husband, Mary. Abigail wanted for nothing. You must be the first to admit to that."

Still she hesitated, remembering the bruises, and the noise that had sometimes reached even to the sanctuary of her room. Involuntarily she shuddered, but then she wondered why she hesitated. She had already given up so much. There would be the physical surrender, and no matter the painful reality of that, she would willingly sacrifice whatever discomfort it involved to protect the child. She could close her mind to the reality of his body straining above hers in the darkness.

With that thought came the memory of the clearing, and the strong, young body of the man she had loved. So long ago. And of the shadowed chapel where she had spoken vows that bound her then and had bound her since.

"I cannot," she whispered.

His hand, the fingers broad and spatulate, was suddenly against her cheek. His palm was smooth, softer than her own hands now were, hard worked with the many tasks of the household. She had not felt she had any right to complain. There had never been bitterness in her heart about her role, only gratitude that she and the boy were warmly dressed, sheltered from the cold cut of both winter wind and cruel gossip, and well fed. He had never begrudged their care. Despite his cruelty, he, too, it seemed, kept to his bargains.

"You think about it, Mary," he suggested, his fingers sliding slowly over the smooth white skin of her neck, coming to rest over her shoulder, his thumb making caressing movements just over the swell of her breast.

She could not prevent her shiver, and again his lips lifted into that suggestive smile. "Think very carefully about what you want. And about what you are willing to give up. I think Richard would have a hard time adjusting to the rough-and-tumble of school. So many do, you know. I even heard of a child who hanged himself. Too sensitive, they said, but if Richard had brothers... Perhaps a tutor might be the solution, if there were other children."

Mary said nothing, her eyes held with deliberate courage on his, unprotesting of his hand's caress. He smiled again, at whatever was revealed in her rigid features.

"Be sure you bank the fire, Mary," he said. His hand squeezed her shoulder, the pressure painful with the brute strength of his fingers. He stepped beyond her, stopping only to pick up the crystal decanter of port. Unmoving, she listened to his footsteps fade down the hall, to the room he had shared with Abigail.

Only when she heard the door close did she allow her body to sag, almost gasping for air as would an exhausted runner. She moved slowly to the fire, but instead of tending to the task he had assigned, she watched the golden flames blur and disappear behind her tears. She blinked, determined to clear the unfamiliar moisture.

Her hand trembled like an old woman's when she put it against the small mantel. Suddenly, though she had never wavered in the path she had chosen, or been forced by fate to choose, her proud head bent, her forehead allowed to rest against the back of the hand that gripped the narrow mantel.

Her father had often promised that one was never given more than there was courage to bear, but for the first time Mary Winters wondered if the strength of her resolve and the level of her endurance would suffice.

The cold disturbed her, so she turned, trying to find the familiar warmth of the piled quilts. The fire must have gone out, she thought drowsily, her fingers searching for the bed-clothes that somehow had become so disarranged as to leave her shivering, uncovered to the winter's draft.

She was not yet awake, so when her fingers encountered the unexpected solidness of a body above her, she screamed.

She was dreaming, she thought. Only a nightmare. Like Traywick's hands, huge red spiders fluttering over her body in the darkness. And then his hand moved upward, pushing against the bunched material of her cotton rail, thrusting his knee between the two of hers, his hand under her gown, cold against the bed-warmed skin of her thigh. She was awake now, awake enough to think that she must not scream again. It would frighten Richard, sleeping in the nursery next door.

"No," she said, pushing downward against those blunt fingers with both her hands. She held her knees together, one pressed tightly on either side of his, but then she could do nothing about his mouth, descending over her breast. His lips fastened over her nipple and, reacting to that invasion, she turned her body, fighting against his massiveness, against his sheer bulk. She felt his mouth lose contact, and the hope that small victory gave her added strength to her will. He must not, she thought. He must not.

With his free hand, he caught her wrists and wrenched them above her head. The hand that was under her gown, tracing coldly over her thigh, continued inexorably to its destination.

"No," she said again.

"Hush, Mary," he whispered, his lips on her cheek. She could smell the sweet-sick odor of the wine on his breath, hot and fetid against her skin.

"No," she begged, her slender body bucking under his weight, trying to push him off.

"You'll wake the child," he warned hoarsely. His mouth found hers, and he pushed his tongue inside, the soured taste of wine sickening. His tongue was too large, too strong, like the body that strained above her. It was choking her. Moving inside as the spider hand was moving now against her lower body, his fingers painfully digging into the soft flesh of her thighs. Not a caress, but a punishment. And she thought of the bruises that had always marked Abigail's frail body.

Unbidden and unwanted, as weakening as the realization of how little control she had over what was happening, came the image of Nick Stanton's fingers drifting with sensuous grace across her body. This was not lovemaking. This was assault, and Mary knew suddenly that if she agreed to what he urged, no matter whether anyone else ever knew, *she*, at least, would always know the desecration of those vows she had made. *Till death us do part...*

She bit the tongue that pushed vilely against hers, bit hard and tasted his blood, and felt the bile rise in her throat as the blessed air rushed in where there had been only the hot stench of his breath.

"No," she said aloud. Fighting more strongly, determined now that he should not take what was not his. "Get off," she ordered. Her right wrist suddenly came free from his hold, the pain of her teeth perhaps having surprised him enough that he loosened his grip. She put her palm flat against his chest and pushed, and then her legs came up, knees struggling to get under his weight, trying to throw him off her.

The blow that smashed against her mouth and nose was casual, not delivered in anger, but as unthinking as if one were swatting at a summer's fly, brushing aside something that dared to annoy. His strength was enough, however, that her face went numb with the force of it, and she tasted blood again, her own, her lips cut against her teeth. There was no pain, not yet, only shock, and unthinkingly she cried out. She had never been hit in her life, not even as a child. The unexpectedness of it was more painful than the physical force.

Neither was aware of the opening door.

"What are you doing to Mary?" Richard's treble piped from the doorway.

Mary felt the momentary hesitation in Traywick's hands. He lifted away from her chest, turning to look over his shoulder in automatic response to the boy's presence.

Would he hurt the child? she wondered, and the hated image of the descending cane came into her mind. Panic made her strong, and some primitive instinct for survival taught her what to do. She raised her legs, their slender whiteness a flash of motion in the darkness of the bedroom. Her bare feet made contact with his body, and she kicked with all her strength, somehow throwing his huge body off hers.

Traywick had not been expecting it, but he was more agile that his bulk suggested, and somehow he managed to land on his feet. He was off balance, however, and he took several staggering steps backward in a futile effort to right himself.

They watched, child and woman, as almost in slow motion Traywick began to tumble backward, toward the small light of the nighttime fire, carefully banked before Mary had lain down to sleep. His head cracked with a force that was audible against the edge of the mantel and then Marcus Traywick fell, the back of his skull landing hard again on the stones of the hearth.

His head bounced with the force of the blow so that, unconscious now, he came to rest with his cheek against the black metal of the andiron that held the banked fire. The scent of singed hair and the sickening aroma of burning flesh pervaded the tiny chamber.

Mary was stunned by the unexpectedness of his stillness, and then she realized what the smell meant. She jumped up from the disordered bed and rushed to kneel beside the man who lay unmoving on the hearth. She grasped his hair, pulling his face away from its contact with the searing metal. She found she was panting with the exertion of the fight.

The only thought that moved through her brain was that she had done murder. She had killed a man. Not just any man, but one who had given her and her child refuge through these years. On her knees, her slight body swaying over the massive one of Marcus Traywick, the smell of his burning skin and hair filling the cold, still dimness of the room, she felt her son's hand on her shoulder.

"Is he dead?" the boy asked.

"I don't know," she whispered, wondering what she could say, how she could ever explain away what he had seen.

"I shall hit him if he's not," Richard said fiercely, and, glancing up for the first time, she saw that he was standing beside her, his small fingers fastened with his father's strength around the handle of the nursery poker. "I shall kill him for hurting you."

Her throat closed with the force of her love, and both arms enclosed around the small warrior standing beside her.

"No," she said, her mouth moving against the fair curls, touched with gold by the flickering light of the flames. "It's wrong to kill someone, wrong even to wish someone dead," she breathed.

This was her punishment, she knew. For her pride. She had wanted Marcus Traywick dead, and now she had made it happen. The price for her sin. Perhaps for all her sins, she thought, hugging Richard more closely to her. She wondered how much more she would be called upon to pay.

Chapter Two

The Duke of Vail's long fingers lay relaxed against the smooth surface of the gaming table. Despite the amount of the wager involved, his demeanor was one of polite disinterest as the points were totaled. Most of the other patrons of White's had quickly abandoned their own pursuits this evening in order to watch the high-stakes game His Grace was engaged in winning.

The gentlemen assembled around his table were all aristocratic and wealthy, but not nearly so much so as the man whose presence had attracted so much attention tonight, even among this elegant throng. Although long a member, by virtue of birth and reputation, of the foremost gentlemen's club in the capital, the reclusive Vail did not often come to London now, and when he did, it was certainly not to participate in the games of chance to which the members of the ton were addicted.

No one was sure why the duke had come tonight, or why he had agreed, when invited, to take a hand, but the event was unusual enough that those who watched knew they would be able to dine out on the story for weeks to come. They could not know, of course, that they were about to be provided with a far juicier bit of gossip than they had any right to expect.

"That's sixty points and the hand," the Viscount Salisbury said, the words forced through lips suddenly gone numb with the realization of the sum he had just lost. He could imagine his father's reaction. A season's rustication, at the very least.

"My game, as well, I believe," Vail said. His face was carefully expressionless, but there was a glimmer of sympathy in his gray eyes. He was well aware of the situation of the young Corinthian whose pockets he had just emptied. There was the fleeting thought that he might return the winnings he certainly didn't need to the man seated across from him, but he knew that, given the constraints of their society, the attempt to do that would be far more humiliating to the young nobleman than the loss itself had been.

"Gentlemen, I thank you for the game," the duke said, instead of making the offer he had briefly considered. Vail began gathering up the wagers, stacking the notes into an untidy pile. Forty years ago a man such as the Duke of Vail might have been accompanied by a dwarf or even a small Indian boy appropriately attired in rich Eastern garb, whose job it would have been to perform such a task for him. Times had changed, and title or no, a gentleman collected his own winnings. One might, however, as Vail certainly was, do so with an air that proclaimed the task to be hardly worth the effort.

"I was told that without your efforts in the House today, Wellington's bill might have failed," one of the players commented as they watched the unhurried movement of those elegant fingers. It was difficult for these young aristocrats to believe that this man could truly be interested in the dull Tory agenda.

"Although we don't always see eye-to-eye on political

matters, I agreed to speak in support. In return for a favor of long standing, if you will." His Grace acknowledged the correctness of that information without glancing up.

"A very great favor, I should think," Essex ventured. "I understand you returned from France to take part in the debate."

"Family business had occupied me there for the last few months. That was finally completed, however, and I was very glad to be able to return in time to put myself at Wellington's disposal."

"But you've missed most of the Season," someone said sympathetically.

The duke's eyes lifted, gleaming suddenly with an unexpected amusement, to the speaker's face. "Indeed," he said, a trace of humor also clear in that single word. It was somehow made obvious by his tone that the charms of the famous London Season were certainly lost on him. "I am so sorry," he said, although it was also obvious to them all that he was not.

No one knew whether or not to laugh. That was the trouble with Vail. One was never certain whether his quietly sardonic comments were intended to evoke amusement. The silence stretched uncomfortably, until the duke, as if suddenly becoming aware of their discomfort, raised his storm-gray eyes and allowed his gaze to skim the circle of faces surrounding him.

"Was there something particularly entertaining about *this* Season?" he asked, allowing one brow to arch slightly in question. His brows and lashes were several shades darker than the gold of his hair, which shone now almost silver-gilt in the soft glow of the chandeliers. The fine lines imprinted on his handsome features were not those of dissipation, of course. Given his family's tragedies, it was not surprising that the face of this man bore the marks of suffering.

The slightly patronizing question reduced the social highlight of the London year to the most inane of activities—at least as far as His Grace the Duke of Vail was concerned. They were well aware that the duke seldom left his vast country estate, disdaining the society they adored. So they racked their brains for some town event that might prove he had, by his voluntary seclusion, missed a great deal that was entertaining.

"Lucy Sanderson produced a new brat to add to her brood," someone ventured. "And, of course, no one may be sure of his patrimony—other than that it is certain *not* to be Sanderson's."

A poor choice of topic, since there was nowhere to go with the story. Although there had been heavy wagering posted in the betting books on the outcome of that pregnancy, the child had proved remarkably ordinary, and no one had been certain enough of the father to claim to have won.

The polite boredom in His Grace's eyes did not change.

"Cheatingham's youngest eloped with a fortune hunter. The earl chased them halfway to the Border, but a broken axle delayed him long enough that the wicked deed was done by the time he arrived," Lord Alton added.

"More than *one* wicked deed had been accomplished by the time of Cheatingham's arrival," another corrected archly, and appreciative laughter greeted the sally.

"Since the girl has spots and a squint, besides her ten thousand, she's lucky someone was willing to suggest the anvil," Alton said.

The story was greeted with silence by the man they were attempting to entertain. Vail apparently found the petty scandal exactly that.

"And then there is the ongoing rustic sensation," someone suggested. "That entertaining morality tale of Mary Winters and the merchant."

It was a story with which they were all familiar. The interest with which the ton had followed the unfolding events, was rather amazing considering that the scandal involved no one who had the remotest connection with the beau monde. Their fascination, however, was characteristic, bred from the same ennui that caused them to worship the latest opera dancer or prizefighter, or to choose the worst of the numerous highwaymen who plagued the countryside to lionize and applaud, even as the man dangled on the gallows, as inevitably he did.

The story of Mary Winters contained the sordid elements that titillated the jaded imaginations of London's elite: sexuality and violence. The tale had circulated for weeks, and as her trial approached, one still might find animated arguments in the clubs on aspects of the case that had not been brought to any suitable resolution and might never be.

"Mary Winters?" Vail repeated the name softly, his tone subtly different from the gentle cynicism of a moment ago. The deep voice had expressed the merest hint of interest in what the speakers had said, but since it was the first he had shown in any of the gossip they had offered, they hurried to enlighten him.

"A serving girl who tried to murder her master," Alton began to explain, only to be silenced by several protesting voices.

"Governess," someone corrected. "She was the child's governess."

"There's no proof she was attempting to kill him." Another voice came clearly through the hubbub. "*She* claims she struck in self-defense."

"Of course," someone else said derisively. "What else could she say, given what she had done?"

"Apparently the merchant discovered the woman had been stealing the household moneys, as good as taking food out of the mouths of his dying wife and his son while he'd been away on business," Alton continued, over several protesting voices. "Naturally, Traywick was horrified, angry enough to upbraid her, even to threaten legal action. The thought of prison must have frightened her to death. Later that night, she attacked him with the poker and knocked him unconscious into the fire. He suffered the most abominable burns to his face. It's said his visage is permanently marred."

"That's the merchant's version," the viscount said dismissively. "The few villagers who had contact with the woman, however, are openly doubtful of that sequence of events. For one thing, it doesn't explain the blow to her face."

"And what do they believe?" Vail asked. His eyes were not on the speaker, but rather on his fingers, which, despite the sudden pounding of his heart, still appeared relaxed, idly playing with one of the cards from the now forgotten game. Ironically, he noted, the card was the queen of hearts.

"That Mary Winters was defending herself from Traywick's unwanted sexual advances," Salisbury said succinctly. "His wife had recently died, and the merchant is deemed to be a man of strong and...somewhat strange sexual appetite. He has an unsavory reputation for cruelty among the local prostitutes. Despite the death of the wife, the governess was still living in his home. She has no family, no one to offer her protection. Maybe he thought he could get away with assaulting her, or that a spinster in her situation would welcome his advances in the hope that eventually, if she pleased him, they would lead to an offer of marriage.''

"But she was dressed," someone reminded him. "Remember that. She was fully dressed when she came into the village to get help.''

"With a torn nightgown left behind as proof of his attack.''

"Which she could have torn herself to back up her version of events.''

The excited babble of argument grew and expanded, each speaker repeating assertions that had already been made innumerable times since news of the country scandal reached the capital. No one could have explained why, but the circumstances surrounding the case had fired enough interest that the trial of Mary Winters had become something of a *cause célèbre*.

"Consider that the child cannot speak," Alton said. "Sure evidence that something untoward occurred.''

"Perhaps evidence that he had watched his beloved governess being attacked by his drunken father.''

"Traywick *had* been drinking. There's no doubt of that. The constable found the empty decanter of port overturned in his room.''

"The woman poured it out to give weight to her version.''

"Why was she fully dressed?''

"Would you have her run into the village naked? Use your head, man.''

"And no one knows whether or not the child is capable of verifying either story. Traywick won't allow anyone to question him.''

"And the outcome?" Vail asked. The quiet authority in the duke's voice broke through the confusion. There was silence for a moment as they considered the surprising question, but after all, they gradually realized, Vail had been out of the country. He could not be expected to know the details they were so familiar with.

"Well," Alton admitted, "there has *been* no outcome. Not yet, at any rate. The charge of attempted murder was too serious for the local magistrate to hear, so it's been put over until the assizes. The trial is to convene..." He paused, uncertain.

"This week," someone supplied.

"The location?" Vail asked. The gray eyes lifted to the speaker who seemed to have more factual knowledge than the rest. Somehow the duke's face had changed, its planes reset into granite, as cold and as hard as the gaze he was wont to direct at those who had dared through the years to encroach upon his fiercely protected privacy.

"Penhurst," Harry Caldwell supplied. He was better versed in the controversy than anyone, since his father's manor house was the largest in the district where the assizes would be held.

The duke's mouth moved slightly. It was a location less than forty miles from his own estate. Despite the failure of the searches he had launched, Mary Winters had not traveled far in the intervening years.

"Then, gentlemen, if you will forgive me, it seems I have a journey to undertake."

The duke rose. Despite the hours he had sat at this table, the black coat and trousers, the silk waistcoat and the snow-white stock were perfect, just as they had been when he left his valet's hands. He adjusted his sleeves, and then glanced up to find shocked curiosity manifested on the faces of the gentlemen who had sought to entertain him.

"Journey?" Harry Caldwell repeated carefully.

"Penhurst, I believe you said," Vail affirmed.

"To the trial? You plan to attend Mary Winters's trial?"

The question was one they all had, but only Alton had the presence of mind to give voice to it.

"It seems, gentlemen, rumor has erred in asserting that Mary Winters is without protection," Vail said simply.

He inclined his head politely, at the same time fighting the urge to smile that their slack-jawed shock had evoked. He could imagine, given the ardor with which they had argued the case, how his declaration would be bandied about over dinner tables and hands of whist in the days to come.

Let them gossip and be damned, Vail found himself thinking. Perhaps it would add some semblance of importance to the meaningless chatter with which they usually entertained one another. Of course, none of them would ever know the real story.

"Again, gentlemen—I bid you good-night."

They watched in stunned silence as His Grace, the Duke of Vail, made his unhurried exit from the club.

Mary Winters had been told what to expect only because she was persistent enough to ask and ask repeatedly. She had had no idea how such affairs were conducted, and when it was all explained to her by the local constable, her intellect had easily seen through the flaws in the process, but, of course, the fact that she found them to be vastly unjust would have no effect on the proceedings.

She was the accused, which meant, as it had been explained to her, that she would not be called upon to give testimony. Indeed, she would not be allowed to tell her version of the story at all. She had been accused of a crime, and it was assumed, therefore, that a crime had been committed. The only investigation of the events in question would be conducted on that premise. She had been asked if she wished to engage a serjeant-at-law to represent her, but since she had no funds with which to hire counsel, she had simply shaken her head in bewilderment.

There would, therefore, be no one to speak on Mary Winters's behalf, and she would not be allowed to speak for herself. The justices could be trusted, everyone assured her, to get to the bottom of the affair, but since only three people knew the truth of the matter, and since, it appeared, only one of those would be allowed to give testimony...

Mary had found her mind running in the same fruitless circle in the weeks she was confined, waiting for the justices to arrive to hear her case. She had been accused by Marcus Traywick of attempted murder, and he would be allowed to prosecute her, but she would not be allowed to defend herself.

So startling did she find the information that she had forced them to repeat the parameters of her situation several times. They had explained patiently, but with no understanding, seemingly, of her concerns. This was the way English justice had been conducted for hundreds of years. It was the job of the judges to get at the truth, they repeated, and Mary had been assured again and again that she might trust them to do just that.

She had been confined in the small county gaol since the winter dawn when she stumbled into the village to seek help for her master. That morning her face had already begun to darken where he had struck her and her nose had been grotesquely swollen, but her concern had been all for the man she had injured, lying near death, she believed, in his tall brick house.

She had not understood at first what they were saying when they returned. Out of some mistaken sense of gratitude, perhaps, she had made no accusations against the man who had sheltered her and her son for six years. And she could never have imagined, of course, the story Traywick had devised to explain away the events of the previous night.

She had had three long months to contemplate what a fool she had been not to blurt out the shocking truth when she first confronted the sympathetic women who ministered to her injury. By the time their menfolk returned from the errand of mercy on which she had sent them, it had been too late.

During her imprisonment, she had been allowed her needlework and her Bible. She had been visited by the vicar of the parish church, who apparently felt obligated, despite her crime, to offer her what spiritual comfort he could. He knew nothing of her story, past or present, and Mary did not choose to enlighten him.

She had not, of course, been allowed to see Richard— not since she left him in the cold darkness, standing watch over the body of the man whom he believed to be his father. The possibility that she might never again be allowed to see her son was a constant weight upon her spirit. All else she might bear, but the thought of Traywick's control over the boy was like a spear through her heart.

She knew the nature of the merchant too well to expect that Richard would completely escape his wrath at what she'd done. Her best hope for her son was that Traywick would carry out the threat she had once feared above all others. She hoped desperately that he might marry again and send the boy away to school. There alone might the child be safe from the merchant's vindictive spirit.

So she had prayed through the remaining days of the winter and in the weak sunshine of the arriving spring for her son's safety. The prosperous merchant who had been injured in the incident and who had brought the indictment against her was certainly her social superior, even if he was engaged in trade. There was no one she could turn to for help against his accusations. She had made her appeal for help once before, and it had gone unanswered. There was no one to speak for Mary Winters—and, of course, there never had been.

The hall where the trial was to be held was crowded with curious spectators. The sensationalism of the testimony about the attempted rape had lured onlookers from miles around, it was even said from as far away as London.

Mary had spent a sleepless night attempting to prepare herself for the ordeal of listening publicly to the lies Marcus Traywick had devised. Although at one time she had hoped that Traywick's appearance to prosecute his claim might allow her a glimpse of her son, she had come to recognize that the merchant's refusal to allow the child to be questioned was far better for Richard—and, of course, damning for her own cause.

Richard, had he been allowed to give evidence, would undoubtedly have corroborated her version of the events. But having her son forced to sit in open court and listen to the proceedings would be horrifying. If she could not devise a plan to free him from Traywick's control, it would be better that she suffer whatever punishment the courts might give than to have Richard exposed to that sordidness.

She had not expected the size of the crowd. Although she attempted to remain outwardly composed, she could feel the avid eyes of the curious examining her features. Finally the proceedings began and then swirled around her, voices coming at her as if in a dream.

She allowed herself no outward reaction to the sight of Marcus Traywick's brutally scarred profile. He had lost weight, his wool suit fitting loosely over his thick body. His yellow-brown eyes flicked over her once with contempt, and then he listened to the proceedings without again glancing her way. He never even looked at her as he repeated the same lies he had been telling since the morning the constable arrived at the house to find him fully conscious, suffering agonies from his burns, and insanely furious.

There were no witnesses to give testimony other than the constable, Traywick, and the doctor who had eventually been called to treat the merchant's injuries. As she had been led to expect, Mary was not given an opportunity to speak.

When it seemed that they were done with questioning the witnesses the prosecution had presented, Mary attempted to address the judges, splendidly robed and wigged, whose job it was, she had always supposed, to bring English justice to the district. She was quickly and harshly instructed by the chief justice to cease speaking. She was even informed that it was not in the interest of the proceedings to listen to the accused.

"But surely, my lord Justice, it is in the interest of this court to hear the truth," Mary avowed calmly, despite his orders. "Have you not come here to seek the truth?"

"We have come here to hear the testimony of your accuser, and you would do well to remember that you are not the injured. *You* are not the one seeking justice in this case."

"Since it is *my* freedom that is at stake, my lord, I am indeed the one seeking justice," Mary argued reasonably. "Which, if you listen to the lies that have been told here today, I shall not find in this court."

"If you speak again, I will be forced to ask the constable to remove you."

"Then at least I should not be made to hear Mr. Traywick's spiteful inventions against my character."

"Silence!" the justice roared. Apparently he had never been challenged in a session of the assizes before—certainly not by a criminal. To his mind, her boldness seemed to argue the truth of her prosecutor's allegations better than any testimony that had been given against her. "We are not interested in anything *you* may have to say," the lord chief justice continued, imbuing his tone with all the authority his position gave him.

"Then perhaps you might be interested in what *I* have to say." The deeply masculine voice came from the back of the hall, and in the silence that had fallen after the justice's outburst, its calmness gave the words a power they might otherwise not have had.

Heads turned and eyes shifted to find the man who had spoken. Mary Winters alone among the throng did not attempt to see the speaker. From the first syllable out of his mouth, there had been no doubt in her mind as to his identity.

"And you, sir? Who are you to disturb the proceedings of this court?" the lord chief justice asked. His question was as harshly demanding as when he had spoken to the accused.

"Forgive me, my lord Justice. My name is Vail," the tall, golden-haired man in the back of the courtroom announced calmly.

The words might have been a thunderclap, for the effect they had. The chief lord justice's mouth sagged, and an excited buzz of comment wafted through the assembly. It was a name that was familiar to all in this district, one of the oldest titles in England, and the man who bore it now was both enormously wealthy and powerfully influential, especially given the makeup of the current government. There was no doubt in anyone's mind that he would, indeed, be listened to.

The Duke of Vail was dressed in his customary black, the somberness of his attire broken only by his spotless white cravat. The stickpin that nestled in the starched lawn appeared to be the only piece of jewelry he wore. Not even a signet ring gleamed on the long, elegant fingers that rested, relaxed, on the gold head of an ebony cane.

"It seems, my lord," Vail said, "that there has been a mistake."

"A mistake," the judge echoed, attempting to find again the authority that had been stolen from him by this interruption of one of the most mysterious members of the nobility.

"Not only are the charges against the accused patently ridiculous, but this court has no jurisdiction to hear any accusation that might be brought against this woman."

"May I ask why not, Your Grace?" the judge questioned, more comfortable now that the argument seemed to have moved onto legal grounds. Perhaps Vail was suffering under some delusion about the situation.

"Because this court has no authority over Mary Winters."

"Indeed, Your Grace? And may I be so bold as to ask again—and why not?"

A smile disturbed the firm line of the Duke of Vail's well-shaped mouth. His gray eyes sought for the first time the heart-shaped face of the accused, and despite her intent, Mary Winters's eyes met his.

"Gentlemen, I have the honor of presenting to you the Duchess of Vail."

Had he confessed to carrying out the attack on Traywick himself, the effect would have been less startling.

"The Duchess of Vail?" gasped the lord justice, in the midst of the resulting uproar.

It was noted by very few that the proud head of Mary Winters was, for the first time, allowed to lower, and her eyes closed briefly. It might be supposed by those who had thought to gauge the reaction of the accused that she was praying, giving thanks for this miraculous intervention. That was not, of course, the case.

Nick was well aware of Mary's reaction, because he had been watching her. And in spite of his belief that he had steeled himself to ruthlessly carry out this desperate plan, he found that he was shaken by that small gesture. *Be brave, Mary, my heart,* he thought, but nothing of the sudden emotion he felt was revealed in the classically handsome features.

"We were married in her father's church in April of 1815," Nick went on. "I am afraid that, like most husbands, the exact date of that ceremony has slipped my mind."

Unlike the London aristocrats, this crowd had little trouble reading the duke's tone, and there was open laughter at the confession.

"Indeed?" the chief justice said faintly.

Marcus Traywick was on his feet, the first to realize the implications of this disastrous turn of events. "Surely, my lord Justice, you don't intend to entertain this nonsense," he shouted. The puckered and discolored scar on his cheek had flushed with unbecoming color, almost pulsing with the force of his anger.

"Since I am unaccustomed to having my word called nonsense, I suggest that Mr. Traywick might wish to...reconsider his objection," Vail suggested. It was clearly a warning. It was apparent that His Grace believed that no one, not even the king's justice, would need to verify the accuracy of any claim he chose to make. Mary Winters's mouth moved slightly, almost a smile, and then was still.

Vail was perfectly correct in his reminder that one did not challenge such a nobleman's word with impunity. Traywick might be rich by the standards of the district, but he was a pauper compared to the Duke of Vail, and in the arenas in which this man functioned, the merchant was powerless.

"I demand to see a record of this wedding. Mary Winters has been my servant for more than six years, and this is the first I've heard any claim of marriage," Traywick blustered.

"I am not surprised," Vail said calmly. "I so seldom discuss my affairs with provincial nobodies."

Traywick blinked. His mouth opened and closed like that of a dying fish, but it seemed he had trouble thinking of some suitable comeback for that biting comment.

"Surely, my lord Justice," the merchant said, turning to plead his case to the judge instead, "you cannot possibly entertain the notion—"

"I give you my word as a gentleman," Vail interrupted, "that this marriage occurred, exactly as I have stated."

"But even so, Your Grace, I am afraid that without some existing record—" the lord chief justice began.

Vail turned his head slightly, and in response his London barrister moved from behind the duke, walking toward the table that had been set up for the justices. In his hands he carried an enormous leather-bound volume, whose age was obvious.

"If I might, my lord Chief Justice, I would be pleased to show the court the record of the marriage of His Grace, then Lord Stanton, to Mary Winters, the accused," the lawyer said deferentially.

With the Duke of Vail standing at his back, he might well have spoken to the king himself, but his courtesy was appreciated. Here, at last, was someone skilled in according the king's justice the deference with which he should be treated. Mollified, the judge inclined his head.

The barrister laid the book on the justices' table, and then opened it to the last page. None of them appeared to notice when Traywick moved to peruse, as they did, the record he presented.

"And the dates?" the lord justice questioned. With one long white finger he traced the date of the entry above the marriage record in question. "How do you explain that there are more than thirty years between the previous entry and this?"

"Apparently, the vicar who officiated recorded the marriage in the older of two parish registers. Irregular, perhaps, but perfectly legal, I assure you, my lord Justice."

"Then, if the witnesses are here present to verify—" the judge began, only to be interrupted, most respectfully interrupted, by the duke's lawyer.

"It is unfortunate that both witnesses are now deceased, my lord Justice. Tragically deceased when their yacht sank in a storm while crossing the Channel."

"And the priest?" the judge questioned, the first hint of doubt creeping into his tone.

"Alas, the vicar has also passed to his deserved reward."

"How convenient," said Traywick, his voice vicious with sarcasm. "Surely, my lord, you must see that this is all a hoax designed to trick the court. Improper register, all the witnesses dead, and yet these two would lead us to believe that a true marriage took place seven years ago and has been kept a secret since. This is mere trickery, my lord," the merchant said. "An attempt to allow this woman to escape justice."

The judge pursed his lips, obviously swayed by the argument, but he was not given long to consider its merits.

"I would remind my lord Justice of a legal point about which he is most certainly informed," the London lawyer said smoothly. "The entire purpose of recording marriages began as an attempt to put an end to the legal entanglements caused by the clandestine unions so frequently entered into by our ancestors.''

"Of course," the justice agreed.

"It was found that actions brought by one party against the other in such a union tied up the court's time, which might better be spent on more important judicial matters."

Again the judge inclined his head in agreement. All of this was commonly known legal history, and although he was not certain of the barrister's point, it was intellectually entertaining to find a well-informed mind in such a provincial proceeding.

"But since that is not the case in point, therefore—"

"Not the case—" The justice interrupted, having lost the thread of the argument somewhere, only to be cut off himself.

"Both parties were of legal age, and neither is *denying* that the marriage took place. Indeed, both will testify to this court that vows were exchanged. Therefore, there should be no impediment to the recognition of its legality."

The lord chief justice was momentarily silenced by the logic. Everything argued was true. If, of course, both parties agreed. He turned to the accused.

"And will you so testify, Mary Winters, that the exchange of vows recorded here did indeed take place?"

Mary looked up at his question. Her eyes moved back to consider the man standing in the central aisle of the hall. The crowd was hushed in expectation. There was some emotion, some silent communication between Vail and the woman he had claimed as his wife, and then the justice found Mary Winters's remarkably clear blue gaze focused again on his face.

"I will, my lord," Mary said, her voice calm, despite the aura of breathless anticipation with which they had awaited her answer. An answer that was not a lie, considering the wording of the question that had been posed.

Vail drew a breath. That had been, all along, what he feared most. That Mary's honesty would force her to deny what he had claimed.

"And you considered those vows to be binding on you both, a true marriage?" the justice continued.

There was, this time, no hesitation. "I did, my lord," Mary Winters assented truthfully.

"Then, if the banns were read—" the judge began, relieved, only to be interrupted again by the persuasive voice of Vail's barrister.

"I must inform you that there were no banns, my lord Justice." He had to raise his voice to continue to speak over the murmur that resulted from that startling information. "*But* as you are well aware," he went on, "it is always the priest's prerogative, as an officer of the Archbishop of Canterbury, to grant dispensation for special causes."

"And the special cause in this case?"

"To facilitate this marriage in order to allow His Grace's attendance on that field of battle now commonly referred to as Waterloo. Despite having been grievously wounded during the Peninsular Campaign, he had appealed to Whitehall to recommission him so that he might assume command of his men to give support for the glorious victory of the Duke of Wellington against the Corsican monster."

The words were carefully chosen, reminders of Vail's role in that defeat and the cost of his unquestioned heroism in other battles, a blatant admonition that the justices should remember the distinguished military career of the man standing in appeal before them and a less-than-subtle remonstrance to their patriotism.

"Indeed," the chief justice said faintly.

"Therefore," the barrister went on, speaking more strongly, surer now of his audience, "you must see that whatever action Mr. Traywick is so foolish as to try to prosecute against Her Grace, the Duchess of Vail, it should not be conducted in this court."

"Again, I protest that this woman—" Traywick began, only to be cut off by the whiplash of Vail's voice.

"If you profane my wife's name with another of your vile accusations, be warned that I shall kill you."

The gray eyes were cold and calm, but there was suddenly no doubt in Traywick's mind that the nobleman meant exactly what he said. The merchant's lips closed against the savage rejoinders he longed to make against the woman who had turned him into a monster. He looked for the first time fully into the threatening eyes of the man who had claimed Mary Winters as his wife, and for some reason was reminded of her son. And then, of course, Traywick realized why the remembrance of the child he so seldom bothered about now had come into his head. Of course.

Suddenly Marcus Traywick threw back his head and laughed, the sound chilling and disturbing. Peal after peal, hysterical with delight, his laughter rang through the room, eventually silencing the whispering crowd.

The shock of distaste at the merchant's display was briefly seen on the controlled face of the Duke of Vail before he turned away. Only one person in the courtroom realized the reason for the insane laughter. Again, Mary Winters bowed her head. And this time those who believed her to be in prayer were not mistaken.

Chapter Three

Those who continued to watch the elegant Duke of Vail after the lord chief justice summarily dismissed the proceedings were perhaps surprised that the person he sought out first was not the woman he had claimed as his wife or the lawyer he had brought from London to plead her case. Instead, Vail walked over to a small, undistinguished man, his clothing the same as that of the simple village folk who had come to witness the trial. He had stood in the back of the courtroom, quietly watching the drama Vail had just enacted unfold.

"Congratulations," John Pierce said to his master, his voice low enough that, in the hubbub of comment occasioned by the abrupt ending of the trial, only the duke might hear. "The enemy's routed, and it seems the field is yours, Colonel."

Pierce was the only one who ever called Vail by his military rank, and since the duke had immediately resigned his commission when he tragically attained his present title, it was, of course, an anachronism.

"Did you see her eyes, Pierce?" the duke asked. "I thought for a moment she intended to deny me."

"You always knew that was a possibility. And the greatest danger of this whole implausible scheme."

"But it worked," Vail reminded him. "That's the important thing. It succeeded."

"I think what happened this morning was the easy part, Your Grace," Pierce said softly. His dark eyes sought the stout form of the merchant, who had apparently decided his continued protests to the justices were having no effect on the decision they had just rendered. "I wonder why he laughed," Pierce said, watching Mary Winters's scarred accuser rudely shove people out of his path to the door. "I wonder what the bloody hell he found so amusing in being beaten."

Mary didn't resist when the Duke of Vail's barrister came to hurry her from the courtroom. He pushed through the throng with a city dweller's disdain for the bumpkins who had come to ogle the participants in this now aborted trial.

Mary held her head high, ignoring their comments and their plucking fingers. Despite the fact that, almost like a miracle, she had been freed, the far more important problem of obtaining her son's freedom still loomed. She knew she had no power to force Traywick to give up Richard, who was still legally *his* son.

There was, however, someone who did, she had finally realized. Someone who had chosen, despite his silence through the long years of her struggle, to speak today. She might not understand the reasons behind Vail's sudden decision to claim her as his wife, but she had just watched a potent demonstration of his influence. His authority in the world in which she had none could not be thrown away.

Richard was also his son, and the man who had once been Nick Stanton was now her only hope of recovering him. Thinking that it might be possible to speak to him now, to convince him to undertake that task immediately, she turned back to the barrister to ask, "Where is the duke?"

"His Grace will wish to thank the lord chief justice, I'm sure. A matter of courtesy, and probably politic, as well. We shall certainly want his goodwill when this story is repeated in London." He took her arm, encouraging her to move forward again. "And now, we really must be on our way."

"Of course," Mary said, without the least understanding of what he was talking about. What could it matter what the lord justice said? Did that mean there would be a London trial, as well? Another ordeal of sitting silently, forced to listen to Traywick's lies?

"His Grace's valet will see you home."

"Home?" Mary repeated, wondering if she was expected to return to Traywick's house. The remembrance of the triumph in the merchant's laughter sent an involuntary shiver through her frame.

"Why, to Vail, of course. The duke has opened the Hall. They're expecting you."

By then, they had reached the black coach marked with the ducal crest that she still associated with Nick's father. The slight, gray-haired man standing beside the carriage opened the door for her and pulled down the steps.

"Thank you," she said, taking the hand that he offered to help her in. The support of his callused palm was steady, its grasp far stronger than she would have expected, given his build. Her own fingers were still cold and trembling from the ordeal of the trial and from the shock of Nick's unexpected rescue. The solid grip that closed around them was very welcome.

"Don't you worry now," Vail's valet said, tucking the

lap robe securely around her after he had settled her into the carriage. "*He's* not going to let anything else happen to you. You're safe now, Your Grace. You let him worry about the rest."

The title was so unfamiliar that she wondered for a moment if he might have mistaken her for someone else. She met his eyes, which were dark brown and filled with compassion. Seeing her confusion, he squeezed the back of her hand as it rested in her lap, a quick gesture of comfort very much like one her father might have made. She supposed it was a familiarity she should not allow from a stranger, but she didn't resent his touch. It was the first kindness anyone had shown her in a very long time.

"Thank you…?" she said.

"Pierce, Your Grace. My name is Pierce. He told me to look after you, and I've found through the years that it's wise to do exactly what he says. It saves wear and tear on the ears and on the nerves."

The smile that accompanied those words was almost conspiratorial, leading her to believe that this man had little fear of displeasing his powerful employer. And there was no doubt, of course, to whom he had referred. In Pierce's world there was apparently only one "he." As there had once been in hers, she thought.

"Is there anything I should arrange to be sent from the merchant's house?" Pierce asked. "Anything there that belongs to you?"

Only my son, she realized with despair, but that was not, of course, an issue that could be discussed with a servant, no matter how kind or trusted he might be.

She had learned from the gaoler's wife that Traywick had had her few possessions burned—very publicly burned. Bob Smithers, the ex-soldier the merchant employed, had been instructed to carry out that destruction on the village green. Further humiliation, she supposed, for what she had done to Traywick.

There had been little enough of value there. The only meaningful thing she had left behind at the merchant's tall brick house could not be retrieved by this man. There was only one person who could rescue Richard, perhaps as easily as he had accomplished her own release, but still she heard in her mind the echo of Traywick's almost insane laughter. "There's nothing," she said finally.

Pierce nodded and closed the door of the carriage that would take her to the estate of the Duke of Vail.

The house was enormous, its furnishings richer than any Mary had seen in her life. The sturdy brick dwelling where she had once been so grateful to have found sanctuary for herself and her child was, she now realized, a pauper's cottage in comparison. It seemed there were miles of wide corridors, their walls hung with portraits in gilt frames and their scattered tables crowded with priceless objets d'art. She tried not to stare, tried to concentrate instead on the route to the bedchamber that she had been told would be hers. Despite her efforts, by the time Thompson, the duke's majordomo, had personally conducted her to the suite of rooms, she knew she was hopelessly lost.

The bedchamber itself was dominated by a vast canopied bed. Its hangings and the matching draperies were of ivory-and-coral silk, repeating the colors of the costly Oriental rug that covered the gleaming oak floor. A slipper-shaped copper tub stood before the blazing fire, whose warmth was welcome, despite the spring sunshine that flooded the room through tall mullioned windows. The scent of the rose petals that floated on the surface of the steaming water filled the room.

"This is your maid, Your Grace. Her name is Claire," the butler informed her.

The red-haired girl, hardly more than a child, looked up shyly. Her sherry-colored eyes were almost as warm as Pierce's had been, despite the quick blush that stained her cheeks. "Your Grace," she said, bobbing a curtsy.

Mary smiled at her, wondering about the proper way to greet a maid. She had never before had a personal servant, of course. "I'm very pleased to meet you, Claire," she said simply. It was what she would have said to any new acquaintance, and social status had never mattered to her before. Why should she now wonder how to treat people, simply because they were in the employ of the Duke of Vail?

"His Grace requests that you join him before dinner. He will await you in the grand salon at half past eight," the butler said, bowing slightly in preparation of leaving. He seemed to take her agreement for granted. It was *not* a request, Mary realized, but an order, issued by a man who was accustomed to having his orders carried out. A man whose help she desperately needed.

"Of course," Mary said, "but I'm afraid I'm not sure…"

"I shall send a footman," Thompson said, as if he had read her mind, and, bowing again, he closed the doors of the chamber behind him.

"His Grace instructed that a bath be prepared," the maid offered tentatively when they were alone.

Since Mary had, for the past three months, made do with a pitcher of tepid water and a cloth, always fearing the interruption of her privacy, it seemed suddenly there was nothing that could be more wonderful than a bath. She wondered how that exquisite stranger, the grand Duke of

Vail, could possibly have known how much she longed for a real bath.

He seems to be omniscient, as well as omnipotent, she thought irreverently. The man who gave orders to the staff of this vast establishment and even to the justices of the king's courts seemed very far removed from the young, recklessly courageous soldier who had once made love to her.

They were neither of them the people they had been then, she reminded herself. There was nothing left of the foolish lovers who had made those pledges so long ago. Only one thing bound them still. One thing and one alone. Richard was the only reason she had come to the Duke of Vail's home, but there was no reason not to take advantage of the luxurious hospitality it offered until she had thought how to make her appeal. No reason at all, she decided, and she walked toward the welcoming fire and the waiting bath.

The salon when she entered it that evening seemed ablaze with candles. Their costly wax scented the room as the rose petals had perfumed her chamber upstairs.

"Her Grace, the Duchess of Vail," Thompson intoned behind her. As she had in the coach, Mary almost looked around for a glimpse of that lofty personage before she remembered that *she* was the Duchess of Vail, or at least so Nick had claimed today. That particular farce would have to be straightened out, but doing so was far less urgent than the true purpose for which she had come here.

Although the salon appeared to be empty, the butler retreated back into the hall, firmly closing the huge double doors behind him. Mary did glance around at that, surprised at the finality of the sound, and when she realized she had been left alone, she turned to face the room, wondering what she should do now.

Nick was standing before the fireplace. He was attired in formal evening dress, and despite the fashion for masculine colors, it was, like the clothing he had worn in court today, almost entirely black, the somberness relieved only by his silk stockings, white shirt and snowy cravat. As they had in the courtroom, his hands rested on the top of a slender gold-headed cane.

The slate-gray eyes were focused on her face, and at the intensity of their gaze, Mary's breath faltered and her heartbeat quickened. Somehow she had forgotten what it was like to have Nick's eyes on her.

She wondered what he was thinking. Despite the becoming hairstyle Claire's nimble fingers had devised, despite the unfamiliar richness of the gold shot-silk gown she wore, she knew an uncharacteristic pang of regret—or vanity, perhaps—that she was not the girl he had last seen seven years ago. It was not in her nature or her upbringing to overvalue physical attributes, but still, she was aware that her body was no longer softly rounded or her face unmarked. The years had been hard, and that was, she was sure, very apparent to this elegant stranger who had once known her so intimately.

"Please come in, Mary," the Duke of Vail invited.

Fighting her nervousness, Mary raised her chin as she had in the courtroom and crossed the distance that separated them. Nick waited, unmoving, his eyes still on her face, until she was standing before him.

He lifted his left hand from the head of his cane and held it out to her, palm up. She hesitated, and then, willing her fingers not to tremble, she placed them over his. His strong, finely shaped hand closed around hers. The slight roughness of the horseman's calluses on his fingers was somehow reassuring. And too familiar, their movement against her skin a sensation she suddenly realized she had never forgotten.

He brought her hand to his mouth, brushing warm lips against the tips of her fingers. His eyes held hers, but his expression was unfathomable. Despite the fact that she was aware the gesture was simply ritual, at the touch of his mouth all the memories, deliberately suppressed through the years, moved unbidden into her consciousness. The force of them moved, also, in her body, jolting through her nerve endings as summer lightning splits the darkened sky.

She had given him her hand because she had no choice, but she freed her fingers as soon as possible. She knew that he was aware of her reluctance to prolong that contact. The knowledge that he knew exactly what she was feeling was in the gray eyes, in the almost stern set of his mouth.

This is not Nick, Mary thought with sudden despair. No longer the man she had loved. He had changed. But then, she was no longer the girl he had tenderly made love to in the sun-dappled clearing. No longer the innocent who had trusted so completely in the vows and promises he whispered that day. The same lies she had sworn to today, in an attempt to save the son he had never known. A child whose every gesture, every expression, every feature, proclaimed his parentage.

"Won't you sit down?" Vail invited, indicating the chair facing the one he had obviously occupied before her entry.

Mary took a breath before she obeyed, seeking her customary poise. There was no reason to be afraid. The past was dead. As was its hold over her emotions. Only the future mattered, she reminded herself. Richard's future. She had nothing to fear from her previous relationship with this man.

The silence stretched briefly after she was seated, and she felt her anxiety grow again. Nick was watching her, and the absolute calmness of his features was disconcerting. She wondered why she had believed before that she could tell what he was thinking. His face was a smooth mask, giving nothing away behind its calm disinterest. His eyes, however, had not left her face.

"Why did you come to court today?" she asked. Despite the knowledge of how much she needed his help, the words slipped out, fueled by a bitterness she had thought long forgotten, if not forgiven. Why, after all these years, had he decided to make public their association?

Something moved behind the gray eyes, and then the response disappeared, controlled. The line of his mouth shifted, realigned itself into a slight smile, unrevealing of whatever emotion had touched his eyes.

That small movement of his lips reminded her suddenly of how they had felt against her breasts, his tongue circling the aching nipples that hardened under its caress. She tore her gaze away from their sensuous curve, her mouth dry and her heartbeat again too rapid. *Dear heavens,* she thought, *is his every move to have this effect on me?*

"Someone told me Mary Winters had no protector. You and I are both aware that is not true, of course."

She shook her head, denying that ridiculous claim. Anger was an unaccustomed emotion, one that had not been allowed in the narrow existence of the past seven years. The small surge of adrenaline it produced was unfamiliar. She could feel her face flush, the hot blood sweeping upward through her throat and into her cheeks.

"Protector?" she questioned. She had not really intended the mockery, had not anticipated the sharp tone of her repetition.

His smile didn't change, but one brow arched. "I am your husband, Mary. You are, of course, entitled to my protection."

"An obligation you have only recently become aware of?" she asked, still mocking.

"I have *always* been aware of my obligations. You chose not to allow me to fulfill them."

"I chose?" Mary repeated, unbelieving. "*I* chose?" she said again, her voice rising.

"You have *always* known where to find me. Indeed, my whereabouts are extremely public."

"Are you saying...?" She interrupted the explanation, and then the question faded as she realized what he meant. The import was obvious. She could have come to him at any time.

"My residences have not changed," the Duke of Vail said. "Nor is mine a name that is unknown, especially in this district."

She remembered then to take a breath, shock having disturbed the normal pattern of her breathing. "And had I presented myself at your door, you would, I suppose, have readily acknowledged me as your wife," she said. The scorn rang clearly in her tone. *As if it had all been so simple,* she thought. *Always so simple, the situation so easily remedied.*

"Of course," Nick said, apparently dismissing as ridiculous the thought that he might have done anything else.

He was still standing, looking down on her, the long fingers resting on the head of the cane. Just as he had today, Mary remembered. She wondered suddenly if he needed its support, if the injury he sustained in Spain had grown more debilitating through the years or if he had been further injured at Waterloo.

Had he lain wounded and suffering during the months when her whole being was consumed with securing the safety of her child, a place for her son? But she knew that was not true. She would have heard the village gossip, es-

pecially as avidly as she had listened for any word, any
rumor, that might explain his absence. Or her father would
have written her at Mr. Traywick's if he later learned such
news.

"But you never came," Nick added softly, eerily echoing what she had been thinking.

She looked up. Something in his tone had been different,
but his face was still controlled, still a mask. She shook her
head in disbelief. He had to have known. *Go to my father,*
he had told her, and she had obeyed him in that, as she
had in all things. She had left the ring as her message, just
as he had instructed. Nick *had* to have been told. What he
had just said was another lie.

He was so adept at them, she thought bitterly. Why had
she not known that all those years ago? Even her father
had realized what the duke's lack of response meant when
she was finally forced to confess what they had done.

At first she had waited, hiding her nausea, praying for
help, for some word from Nick, so that she would not have
to tell her father. She had not doubted his compassion, but
she had known what it would cost him. So she had come
alone to this great house, and she had left the ring and her
carefully worded message. But as the slow weeks passed
without any response, hope had faded from her heart. Hope
and trust. *Dearer to me than my soul.*

"Of course I came," she whispered. "I gave him the
ring you had given me. Your father's butler. Whoever he
was. He told me the duke was away, but he promised to
give him the ring, to tell him I had come as soon as he
returned. I made him promise that before I left. It was so
important."

Her throat closed suddenly, as she remembered the force
of her fears. Not for herself, but for the baby she carried.
Noble bastards might abound, their place in society un-

questioned, even if their positions were not recognized by law. Peasant children born without the exchange of vows were not even a seven-days wonder, but were quickly accepted, welcomed, even, by the mother's family as another pair of hands for the fields. But that would not have been the case for her son.

She had known the record they forged in the register would not stand up. Without the same authority Nick had brought to bear in court today, no one would have believed in the legality of that marriage. Without his support, her claim to be his wife would have been far more dangerous than the situation she faced. The penalties for such a hoax were severe, just as she had warned Nick.

But bearing her child out of wedlock would have brought disgrace to her father, who did not deserve to suffer for her sin. He might well have lost the vicarage, the living given to someone else, someone worthier. No man of her class would ever, of course, have been willing to marry her, knowing she had borne an illegitimate child. She would forever be soiled goods, a ruined woman, and with her father's death, she would have been left without any means of support for herself and her child. Despite the ring and the promises, she had never heard from the Duke of Vail.

"I never knew that you came to my father, Mary."

She turned her face away from the calm gray eyes, sickened. Even if she believed that the ring and her message had gone astray, that did not explain the rest.

"You came home in August," she said, working to control her voice, to keep it calm and even, despite reliving the fear and disappointment. She had truly believed she had forgotten them, or had grown beyond their power to hurt her. "You spent some weeks in London, and then you came here, back to Vail."

She looked up, and saw that his face had not changed.

In spite of the blaze of candles, his eyes were very dark, unreadable, but he didn't interrupt or deny what she was saying. "We heard that your father and Charles had died, and that you now held the title. You were the Duke of Vail. I said it wouldn't matter, not to what was between us. I told my father you were grieving, and I waited. There was still time then. And as the days passed, like a fool, I still believed you would come for me."

She paused, trying to control the emotion that even now was so strong. "But you didn't come, Nick. You *never* came for me. My father wanted to tell you, to come here to find you. But I wouldn't let him. You didn't want me. I had appealed for your help once, and received no answer. I suppose my pride wouldn't let him come to you to beg you to make it right. I didn't want you to humiliate him by denying what had happened between us."

There had been only one other option, and so, with her father's help, she had found the Traywicks, who desperately wanted a son, and she had made her bargain. If the child she carried was a boy, he would be reared as the merchant's son. As always, his wife had been more than willing to go along with whatever Traywick planned, and so poor Abigail had pretended to be pregnant once again. When her son was born, Mary had given him away. It was the only possible way, she had believed, to protect him.

The room was silent except for the small, pleasant sounds of the fire. Vail had not moved, and he made no response to the accusations. "You were carrying my child," he said finally. It was not a question.

She smiled, bitter and without pleasure. "Your child, Nick. Do you wonder what he was like?"

His hands tightened over the worked gold of the cane's handle and then relaxed, but that small, telltale movement gave her hope that he was not as unfeeling as he appeared.

"What should I have done with the child?" she asked him. "Given the circumstances, what do you think would have been the wise decision? I considered them all, even those which are...unspeakable. To protect my father, I told myself. Perhaps, selfishly, even to protect myself. I watched my body thicken with the fruit of your seed, waiting for you, knowing that soon it would be too late. And yet...you never came." The words were almost a whisper.

"Mary," he said.

At last there was emotion in his voice. The same voice, she reminded herself, that had deceived her so long ago. That had made her believe in his lies. His promises. *Dearer to me than my soul* echoed in her heart. She had given him her soul and far more.

"What could I do with a baby? Alone. Disgraced. I have always believed that what we did, Nick, broke my father's heart. He died that winter, even before the baby was born. He never condemned me. Or even you," she admitted softly. "But the pain and the grief for what I had done was in his eyes. I was his child. If he could not teach me what was right, how could he instruct others? With one afternoon's passion, I had made his life's work meaningless. I betrayed all that I was for you. And still you never came."

It was again very quiet in the room.

"What happened to the child, Mary?" Vail asked, as if the silence had finally grown too agonizing to bear.

She had wanted him to have to ask. Deliberately she had not told him. She had *wanted* to hurt him, she realized. She had not even known through the years that she harbored that desire. Or had not admitted it. She had once believed him to be the kind of man who valued his promises, and she had been mistaken.

She raised her eyes to his face, the lucid blue locked with his as he waited. This was why she had come. To secure the Duke of Vail's influence in getting Richard away from Traywick. Vail's only son.

"I gave him away," she said, "because I thought that would keep him safe." She had finally realized the depth of her mistake in the courtroom today, and that was the only reason she had come to him tonight—for Richard.

"Where is he?" Vail asked.

His voice was still calm, still reasoned. As if they were discussing some trivial household item that had been temporarily misplaced, instead of... She closed her mind to the sudden echo of Marcus Traywick's insane laughter. Only the man standing before her had any chance of removing Richard from the merchant's control. Only this man, who had once before betrayed them both.

"I gave your son to Marcus Traywick," she said. "To be *his* son." And then she added the terrible irony. "I gave him to Traywick to keep him safe."

Nick's features changed, hardened, and she knew that he understood. The line of his lips flattened, whitened with pressure he exerted. She hated the part of her that took some perverse pleasure in his shock, but she did not deny that there was satisfaction in watching his realization of exactly what had been the result when, almost seven years ago, he broke his word.

"The son you failed to acknowledge belongs legally to the man you humiliated today, the man you mocked and infuriated. A very dangerous man to cross, as I have reason to know. You suggested this all was somehow my fault, because I didn't come to you, to the famous Duke of Vail. Well, no matter the circumstances or the time that has passed, whatever mistakes I made, whatever vows you believe *I* have broken, I come now to ask you for my son. What will you do now, Nick, for your son?" she asked bitterly.

There was no answer from the Duke of Vail. As there had been no answer to the appeal she made so long ago. She rose and stood a moment facing him. She was unaware, perhaps, of the challenge in her eyes, or that her small, bitter smile was almost triumphant. She had once known this man well enough to be sure, even now, that what she had told him was disturbing, if only to his pride, to his arrogance. If she had wanted revenge for his desertion, she could take comfort in the knowledge that she had succeeded. That much was revealed in his face, the handsome features uncontrolled enough now that she could again read the pain in them.

"You deserted him once before. And believe me, he has suffered. Will you desert him again?" she asked.

This was not what she had intended, not the method, at least, by which she had planned to secure his help. Her own emotions—emotions she had never before openly acknowledged—had played a role in the direction this confrontation had taken. Her accusations might be something she would eventually regret, but she did not feel remorse now for what she had done. Let *him* think about solutions. Let *his* mind circle endlessly, trying to find the best way to protect his son, as she had been forced to do so long ago.

"Good night, Nick," Mary said finally when he didn't speak. "Sleep well." She crossed to the double doors through which she had entered, and still the man before the fireplace did not move. She was grateful that there was a footman outside the salon, his face carefully impassive. She wondered briefly what he had heard, but his features, like his master's before, gave nothing away.

She denied her tears until Claire had undressed her and finally left her alone in the huge, lonely room. She had always known that crying would not change things. It was a worthless indulgence of the energy that had been needed instead for the endless tasks of Traywick's household, for Richard's care and happiness. But tonight Mary Winters cried, and she wept with a certain bitterness because she knew that her tears were not only for the little boy she had not seen in three months and whom, without Vail's help, she would never be allowed to see again.

When Pierce entered the salon, most of the candles had been extinguished. Only the desk where Vail sat was circled with light. The duke did not look up when his valet entered, carefully closing the doors behind him, but the two spaniels who lay curled beside the desk raised their heads and then, recognizing the familiar figure, relaxed again. Nick finished whatever he had been writing and even took time to sand and then place his seal on the document before he glanced up into his batman's dark eyes.

"How did it go?" Pierce asked. The tone of the question was not that of servant to master. There was little deference, but not a lack of respect. It was the tone a friend might have used, and indeed the relationship between these two had long ago become something closer to that than to any other. The facade of service was carefully maintained, except in private. They knew each other too well for that.

The eyes that met Pierce's were shadowed, the handsome features again cold and composed. "As you would expect from a woman brutally deserted by the man who took her virginity," Vail said.

"Didn't you explain to her—"

"What is there to explain?" the duke demanded, interrupting him. "She knows about the deaths. She knows I came home to the town house in London in August. And she also knows, of course, I never came to ask her father for her whereabouts."

"You didn't *come* home. You were carried home. I carried you home, and you were in no—" Pierce began, and was then cut off as the duke's hand was raised, palm outward, to halt the protest.

"I didn't contact her father. And I could have. We both know that. She's right. I never attempted to find her."

"Not then, maybe, but—"

"But *then*, Pierce, was when it mattered," Vail said. "When it might still have made a difference."

"It's not too late," Pierce said. "If you'll only—"

"Mary Winters has informed me that she bore a child." The calm voice again overrode Pierce's attempt to soften the self-castigation. "More than six years ago."

Shock was apparent on the valet's face. Vail's was still unrevealing, but then, he had had time to come to terms with what Mary had told him.

"A child?" Pierce repeated. "There was no mention of a child."

The cynicism of Vail's brief smile would have been familiar to those who could claim some social acquaintance, far more familiar than other expressions that had disturbed the perfection of his features tonight. "There was mention," he corrected. "Do you remember the merchant's child, from whom Mary Winters was supposedly stealing food?" There was an edge of bitterness to the statement.

"Your son," Pierce said when he realized the truth. "And she's not a stranger," he reminded Vail. That was twice the duke had referred to the woman by her full name, and this was a man who did nothing by chance.

Keeping his distance from them both, Pierce thought, *from the woman and the child. Protecting himself from what he cannot bear.* But the valet did not, of course, express the errant thought aloud. He wasn't a fool.

"But she is," Vail said. "Almost she is. There is nothing

there, it seems, of the girl—'' The soft admission was halted abruptly.

"What are you going to do?" Pierce asked finally into the long silence.

"Discover Traywick's price. Every man has one."

"You plan to try to buy your son from the merchant?"

"Why not? It seems the safest way, and what better use for my father's money? It should one day all belong to the boy."

"That's why he laughed," the valet said. Given what he had just been told, the explanation was obvious now for what had today appeared to be sheer insanity. "Somehow he realized the boy is your son."

"Apparently there is some...resemblance," Vail said.

"You think Traywick will sell you the child?"

"Everyone has his price, Pierce. We simply have to discover his."

"You spoiled the revenge he was attempting. There was no reason to bring charges against Mary, given his own guilt, except vengeance, pure and simple. You heard him today. The memory of that cursed laughter still sends chills down my spine. You're no fool, Your Grace. Never have been. Traywick isn't going to hand over the most powerful weapon of revenge a man can possess. He has Mary Winters's son, and he's going to make her pay dearly to get him back. And I don't mean money."

Believe me, he has suffered, Vail thought again. Mary had told him that, in anger and bitterness, and in the hours that had passed since their conversation, he had found himself imagining all the kinds of suffering that might be inflicted on a six-year-old child by the man he had defeated today. Even now...

He blocked the images, demanding the same control of himself that he had always demanded. The Duke of Vail raised eyes, cold as the slate of winter's sky, to his only friend.

"Whatever it costs, Pierce," Nick Stanton vowed, "I'll get my son." It was a promise. One he would keep. This time he had taken an oath he would not break to the son he had never known.

Chapter Four

Despite the events of the previous day, Mary had slept. Drugged by the release of long-buried emotions that had at last been faced, she had finally drifted, exhausted by her tears, into an almost dreamless sleep. It was Claire's entry into the bedroom the next morning that woke her.

When the maid put her heavy tray down on the table beside the bed and pushed aside the hangings, Mary knew by the quality of the sunlight flooding the room that the morning was well advanced.

"Good morning, Your Grace," Claire said, her quick curtsy perfunctory, or perhaps simply careful, considering the brimming Sèvres cup she was offering. Mary had felt a momentary confusion at her unfamiliar surroundings, but with the girl's greeting she remembered everything.

She was at Vail. She was supposedly the Duchess of Vail. It was a title she had never sought, had never imagined, even when she learned of the deaths of Nick's father and brother at sea. Given the circumstances, it was one she would very willingly deny, except for what it might mean to her son.

She took the cup and saucer from Claire, and as she sipped, savoring the fragrance of the chocolate and the feel of the fine porcelain under her fingertips, she imagined, as she had every morning since she had last seen him, what Richard might be doing. Whatever she envisioned would be only fantasy, she knew. The comforting stability of their peaceful days together had been disrupted. He was cared for now by others, and she prayed daily that they would be kind, patient with his curiosity about her continued absence. If only...

Again she denied the troubling memory of Traywick's laughter. In spite of his obsession with having a son, she reminded herself, he had almost ignored Richard. There had, of course, been the small presents on the traditional holidays, gifts strictly utilitarian—gloves or a new jacket.

Richard's only toy, the painted wooden soldier, had been her own gift, carefully saved for and purchased in London. It had taken a great deal of trouble to find someone in the village who would undertake the errand—so few traveled beyond the limits of their small world—but she had been more than repaid for whatever inconvenience she had had by the child's delight.

Her lips curved, remembering his joy and his continuing pleasure in the simple toy. She had been afraid that the merchant would disapprove of her gift, but he had never seemed to notice. As he had noticed almost nothing about the boy except his rare and occasional lapses in fulfilling the duties Traywick expected of him. It had been then that the slender cane was brought out.

The beatings were, she had acknowledged, always attempting to be fair, no harsher than the punishment dealt out to most boys, but they had seemed to her far stronger than were merited by the minor offenses that provoked them. When each punishment was over, the merchant had again ignored the child until the next time he was displeased with some small forgetfulness or misbehavior.

Now, his customary indifference was the only thing that gave Mary comfort. Despite Traywick's obvious hostility toward her, she truly believed he would not bother to take his anger out on the boy. Indeed, had she thought there was even a possibility of that, she would be at the stolid brick house, attempting to steal her son. No one, not even Traywick, was insane enough to mistreat a six-year-old boy because he was angry at the child's parents, she prayed. Such inhumanity was simply beyond her conception.

Her best hope for getting Richard was Vail. She was still sure of that, despite his lack of response to her story last night. He would not abandon his son. His desertion of her was one thing, but deep in her heart she knew the man who had been Nick Stanton would not abandon his own child. She remembered his long-ago certainty that his family would never betray the irregularity of his marriage vows, no matter how they felt about them. *They would suffer a traitor's death before they would deny me,* he had claimed.

Vail, too, would feel something of that family connection for his son—if by custom and tradition alone. Or for pride, she thought, as she had last night. He was rich and powerful enough to rescue Richard. She had only to wait. And to trust. That, of course, was the hardest part. To place her trust again in Nick Stanton.

Mary's eyes moved to the tall windows whose light illuminated the room. She remembered the ruby glow of the setting sun that had seeped through the stained-glass window behind the altar. She had been just as sure then. What if she were again mistaken in him? Her hand shook slightly with that sudden fear. She glanced down at the sound the cup she held made as it trembled against the thin saucer. Her eyes filled with tears. She could not be mistaken this time. She could *not.*

The maid had wondered before at the sadness in the

beautiful eyes of her new mistress. It was beyond her comprehension that this woman who had everything might be unhappy. But then, it seemed to her that the duke had always been unhappy, too. What possible problems could these two people have? Unconsciously she shook her head. It was not her place to understand the ways of the quality, but simply to serve them.

"Will you be needing anything else, Your Grace?" she asked.

The focus of the blue eyes shifted, finding her face, and the duchess smiled at her. "Nothing more, thank you, Claire. And thank you for bringing the chocolate," she added. "It's wonderful."

"You're very welcome, Your Grace," the girl said, surprised by the kindness. *Poor sad lady,* she thought, but she remembered to drop another curtsy before she left the room.

The blue eyes of the woman in the bed returned to their unseeing contemplation of the morning light.

It was Pierce who brought Mary the message. By the time he knocked on the door of her chamber, Claire had already returned to help her dress and to fix her hair in a less elaborate, if no less becoming, style than she had devised last night. After she had completed her toilette, Mary sat in one of the small, graceful chairs that flanked the marble fireplace, wishing she had her needlework to occupy her hands and at least some small portion of her mind.

"Come in," she called out automatically at the knock. Pierce's presence was unexpected. He seemed slightly uncomfortable in the decidedly feminine atmosphere of the room, and certainly out of place, in the leather vest and cotton shirt, his trousers tucked into worn riding boots.

How in the world had such a man come to be the powerful Duke of Vail's valet?

Pierce would be far more at home in the stables of this huge country estate, Mary thought, than in its salons and bedchambers. She almost smiled at that, but she quickly hid her amusement. He had been kind to her yesterday, and she was grateful. For some reason, she already considered Pierce to be a friend, and she knew that she desperately needed one.

"His Grace asks if you'll join him downstairs," he said.

Anxiety blossomed in her stomach. And something else. A sensation she recognized, but stubbornly refused to acknowledge. There was no longer any place in her relationship with Vail for those feelings, and she could not understand why they should resurface whenever he was mentioned. There was *no* place, she told herself firmly.

"Your Grace?" Pierce questioned at her hesitation.

It was, of course, another summons. Nick had had several hours to think about what she had told him. And she wanted desperately to know what he intended to do about his son, so she could not understand her reluctance to face him—except for those other, unexplainable emotions she didn't seem able to completely deny.

"Of course," she agreed. Her voice was too soft, too revealing of her uncertainty. The same compassion that had been there yesterday reappeared in Pierce's eyes.

"Don't you go worrying, now," he advised. "He's more than capable of dealing with the Traywicks of this world. You know that."

Mary was a little surprised that Nick had confided to his valet what she had told him, but she was also relieved at those words of assurance. She wondered if Nick would be as forthright. And then she knew that it wouldn't matter.

The certainty that Vail would tend to this matter was in the dark eyes of his valet.

"You learn a man's character quick on a battlefield, Your Grace," Pierce continued. "Those you can trust and those you can't. You learn or you die."

"You were in the army?" That was his connection, of course, she realized, to the man who had been Nick Stanton.

"For more years than I can count," he agreed, smiling.

"That seems...a strange preparation for being a duke's valet," she suggested carefully.

"Not so strange as you'd think," Pierce said. "Not for this particular duke, at least. And we prefer the term batman, Your Grace, begging your pardon."

"Batman?"

"A military term," he explained, and then, seeing her confusion, he added, "It doesn't matter, really, but that's what we agreed on, years ago. I became Colonel Lord Stanton's batman in the Low Countries."

"At Waterloo," she realized.

"Sergeant Major John Pierce, Your Grace. At your service," he said, his body stiffening suddenly to attention and his hand snapping into a salute. "And his, of course," he added, eyes twinkling as if he'd let her in on some great secret.

"What do you call him when you're alone?" she asked, smiling back at him. She really had wondered, because the valet so often referred to his master simply as "he." But Pierce had to call Nick something when they were in private, and she knew that whatever it was would be a further revelation of their relationship.

"Well, the truth is, Your Grace, I've called him a fair lot of things through the years," he confessed with a grin.

"Not many of them were said to his face, and there were few I'd repeat in front of a lady."

She laughed, the tension that had held her since Nick's summons relaxing suddenly. "I'm afraid I've called him a few myself," she said.

"But you remember this, Mary Winters," Pierce said, his voice filled with conviction. "There's not a better man to have at your back in a fight. He's not going to let you down. Not this time."

She nodded, wanting to believe that, needing very much to believe it. "Thank you, Pierce," she said.

She stood up and crossed the room, expecting him to step out into the hall before her to lead the way downstairs. Instead, he stood, waiting until she was very close before he spoke again.

"How did Traywick know?" he asked. "How did he know so quick the boy is Vail's?"

Mary's sudden remembrance of golden curls and trusting gray eyes was vivid. And painful. "When you see him, you'll know," she said simply.

"And other than his looks?" Pierce asked.

"That night..." Mary began, and then her voice faltered with the force of the memory. She was again in the cold, dark room, the smell of burning flesh sharp and frightening. She made herself go on, because he had asked, and because he had been kind. "The night Traywick tried to...assault me, Richard came to help me. He brought the nursery poker with him to strike down the man he had always believed to be his father."

Pierce said nothing for a moment, and Mary wondered if the child's defense of his "governess" seemed strange to him. "It seems, then," he said finally, "the boy deserves to know that Marcus Traywick is *not* his father. He's waiting for you," he added, and only then did he turn to lead the way to the Duke of Vail's private study.

Nick had steeled himself in preparation for the encounter he was facing. He had dispatched Pierce on his errand, believing that he had his emotions well in hand. As he watched Mary enter his study, however, he found he was still unprepared for the effect of her presence. His groin hardened, his quick arousal tightening painfully beneath the fashionably fitted riding breeches he wore. As uncontrollable as his reaction to Mary had always been.

An irony worthy of the old gods, he thought, *who were always waiting to trap you with your own bloody hubris.* Unconsciously his lips moved into a slight smile. Whatever Vail felt was usually carefully hidden. But he had never been very successful at hiding his feelings about Mary Winters. Not then and not, apparently, even now.

She was wearing the sapphire morning gown he had chosen, its low neckline and the slightly Empire waist emphasizing the proud lift of her high breasts. He had known when he ordered the fabric made up what the color would look like against the purity of her skin, complementing the blue of her eyes and the dark hair.

The fit was not perfect, his exacting gaze discovered. He had described Mary's body from memory, her graceful curves imprinted on his brain by the languid movement of his hands over them so long ago. The London modiste whose enormous fee for the rush order he had paid without question had apparently followed those instructions precisely.

But the girl he had loved, had made love to so long ago, had changed. She was a woman now, more slender, her carriage erect and uncompromising. As were her eyes, which were considering him from the open doorway without pretense or apology. The integral part of Mary Winters, that inherent honesty and dignity, would never change, no matter what she suffered.

Vail dismissed Pierce with a small movement of his head, but because he knew him so well, he was aware of his batman's reluctance to leave. *He doesn't trust me to treat her as he believes I should,* Nick realized, almost amused by Pierce's ready championing of the woman who had been a stranger to him only yesterday. He shouldn't have been surprised at Mary's conquest. She had had the same effect on him when he met her, seven years ago.

"You wanted to see me," she said.

Her tone was confident, a little challenging, and amusement again tugged at the corners of Vail's lips. He knew well enough that her self-assurance was an act, but it was an effective one, he would give her that. No one watching the performance would guess the anxiety for the child that she had revealed last night. Or the bitterness.

"Thank you for coming," he said aloud, indicating with his hand that she should take the chair facing his desk. He had not risen. He was paying the inevitable price for the hours he had spent pacing the salon, thinking about all she had told him and of the years that lay between them. Despite the growing ache in his damaged leg, Vail had been grateful when dawn's arrival finally gave him permission to send a message to the stables that he intended to ride. And the punishing gallop he'd used to escape those memories had helped his mind, if not his body.

"I didn't realize I had a choice, Your Grace," Mary said.

He gave her credit that she managed to say it almost without sarcasm. She crossed the room and sat down gracefully in the chair he had indicated, tranquilly arranging the folds of her skirt.

When she finally looked up to meet his eyes, hers were

perfectly calm, but Vail had not missed the slight tremor of her fingers as they played with the delicate fabric. Suddenly he remembered the feel of her hand yesterday, trembling against his own, the thin fingers hardened with the burdens she had carried, especially the burden of providing for his son. He blocked the remembrance of her touch to complete the business that lay between them. The task of freeing the boy required, despite her bitterness at his betrayal, that he and Mary Winters work together.

"My agents in London are investigating Marcus Traywick's holdings," he said. "They should have information for me within the week."

She said nothing, her gaze still serene, but no longer indifferent.

"As soon as I have that information," he continued when she made no comment, "I should be able to decide how best to approach Traywick concerning changing the child's legal status."

Vail realized that his fingers had somehow found the pen he had used last night to send those instructions to his bankers. They were nervously caressing its length, and deliberately he replaced the instrument on the shining surface of his desk and forced his hands to rest, unmoving and seemingly relaxed, beside it. He looked up to find Mary had been watching the movement of his hands. She glanced up into his eyes.

"What does that mean?" she asked.

Trust Mary to cut to the heart, Nick thought, as he considered how much, or how little, to tell her.

"I need leverage to use against the merchant. Without an exact understanding of Traywick's financial arrangements, any offer will be made in the dark. I need as much information about the man as is available."

"You intend to offer him money in exchange for your son?"

"Every man has a price," he said. He had, of course, considered kidnapping the boy, but there was always the danger that the child might accidentally be hurt if they tried to take him by force. And if they failed, Traywick would be angered enough to dig in his heels and refuse to negotiate. Offering him money seemed the safest solution.

Mary's quick laugh revealed her disbelief. "His price will be retribution. He won't *sell* you Richard," she said with conviction, her tone almost the same as one would use with a small child who had just said something ingenuous. "He'd far rather make me pay for what he imagines I did to him. Perhaps even for the things you said to him in court. For rescuing me. He'll *never* sell you Richard."

"He won't have a choice," Vail said. He had not intended to tell her this, had not believed it would be necessary to divulge the machinations by which he could force Traywick's hand, but she was no longer as trusting of his word as she had once been. And that was, of course, his fault.

"How can you make a man like Traywick do something he doesn't want to do?" she asked.

"There are always ways to apply pressure. Every business has debts and creditors. Notes can be bought, mortgages called due."

"Threats, rather than enticements?"

"Only if he makes them necessary."

Trying to ruin a man was not a game Vail had played before, but the strategy was no different from chess or cards, or even from battle. Discover your enemy's weakness and direct the thrust of your attack at that point. Vail knew his position and almost unlimited wealth made his hand far stronger than the merchant's. He had no doubt that he could eventually secure the man's agreement to give up his claim to the boy.

Mary shook her head, and her eyes fell. "You don't know him," she said.

"Then tell me. Anything you believe will—"

"He likes to cause pain," she said, interrupting him. "Will your agents tell you that? He enjoys making people suffer. Especially if they've displeased him. It…" She hesitated, and then she went on, trying to explain what was to her unexplainable. "Even as his wife was dying, slowly and painfully dying, he…used her. Brutally used her body. Again and again. Maybe because she had failed him, failed to give him a son. Maybe because… I don't know. I can't imagine why he would desire a dying woman. She was…"

Again she paused, and Nick waited for her to go on, knowing that this was information that might be valuable, however distasteful.

"She never denied him because she thought it was a wife's duty, but I saw…I *saw* evidence of the things he did. It was there on her dying body. And he enjoyed doing those things. I could hear him. I was always afraid that Richard, too, would hear." The disjointed narrative ground to a stop.

"Will he harm the boy, Mary?"

"No."

But she had answered too quickly, Vail knew, which meant that the idea was one she had already considered. If that was the case, then the possibility existed that he would, and Mary was aware of it. Her eyes were wide and dark, suddenly full of fear she couldn't hide. Against his intent, seeing that fear, he smiled at her and made his voice deliberately reassuring.

"I can ruin Traywick, and he will be made aware of it.

He's not going to chance that for a child who is not his own. He has too much to lose, and nothing to gain."

"What he has to gain is the satisfaction of causing pain. Revenge is a powerful motive. And I believe he's not...entirely stable. I think we all had a glimpse of that in the courtroom. Richard is the perfect way to make me suffer. He knows that, and he'll use it."

"Unless he's insane, Mary, this is a battle he won't undertake because, I assure you, he'll be made to realize that he can't win."

"You're so sure of yourself," she said, mocking him. "So certain you can have whatever you want. You were always so certain."

"The only thing I'm certain of is that I can remove your son from Marcus Traywick's control." Vail imbued his voice with patience and surety, fighting the quick anger her scathing comment had caused. She had a right to whatever bitterness she felt and the right to express it. He had acknowledged that in the long hours of last night. If he chose to make no explanation for what he had done, then by virtue of that choice, he could not defend himself against her rancor and lack of trust.

"I thought this was what you wanted from me," he reminded her. "To recover your son from Traywick. I thought that's why you came here."

"*My* son?" she repeated, scornfully emphasizing the singular pronoun he had used. "Don't misjudge your opponent, Nick. He's not afraid of you. With the help of the lord justice and your barrister, you may have won yesterday, but don't underestimate the extent of his enmity. For me and now for you. Of course, I want you to take Richard away from him. I know that you are the only person who can possibly accomplish that. But at the same time, because I know him, I must warn you to be very careful. As far as the courts are concerned, Richard is still *his* son. He always has been, and Traywick may legally do with him as he pleases.''

"What he'll be *pleased* to do, after I've explained his very limited options, will be to dispose of this matter as quickly and as painlessly as possible.''

Vail wished he were as confident of that as he had just indicated. Mary knew Traywick far better than he did. She was more aware of his possible reactions. However, his own uncertainty was not something he intended to burden her with now. Without resources, without his help, she had carried this particular burden—the heavy responsibility of securing the child's safety and well-being—through the past seven years. It seemed to him that it should be his turn now.

"A few days, Mary, and I promise you'll have the boy back.''

"Richard,'' she said. "His name is Richard.''

"I'm aware of his name.''

"But you don't use it. Why won't you call your son by his name, Your Grace?'' she asked challengingly. "Or don't you intend to acknowledge that he *is* your son? Your only son. The firstborn. Your heir.''

The silence was thick and strangely prolonged before Vail broke it. "I think at the moment we should concentrate on the child's present, rather than planning his future.'' He found that the fingers he had forced to relax had again, somehow, found the pen.

"I should warn you that it will be very difficult if you hope to deny him. Traywick won't be the only one who'll notice the resemblance,'' she said.

Her eyes were cold, and he knew that her accusation was only what his own coldness had led her to believe.

"I have no intention of denying I'm his father. I have acknowledged you as my wife—"

She interrupted him. "But you didn't know then that I had borne your child. I wonder if you would have been so willing to make that claim if you had known that the tie which binds us cannot be easily broken."

"Broken?"

"I assume you intend to divorce me or to renounce the marriage as false as soon as you've dealt with Traywick's charges. It's obvious that you never had any intent or desire to make our...relationship public. I assume you only acted now to prevent my transportation. I was told that was the most likely sentence for the charge he had brought against me. And it's not that I'm ungrateful," she added grudgingly.

"I don't want your gratitude, Mary. I've done little enough to merit it. We both are aware of how short I've fallen in honoring the vows we exchanged. But I have no intention of divorcing you. *Or* of denying the child."

"Richard," she said again, her eyes still cold.

Nick didn't tell her why he couldn't say the name. Perhaps it might appease some of her anger, ease the pain he'd afflicted. But to give the boy a name, to say it aloud, would make him too real. A son who looked enough like him that it was obvious even to casual observers. Perhaps if he named him, even in his mind, the boy would no longer be simply a stake in a game of chance he was engaged in. He would become flesh and blood, his own flesh and blood.

Believe me, he has suffered. Mary's words flicked like a whiplash into his consciousness, and then they were quickly rejected. Emotion had no place in what he had to do, in the dangerous game he must play. It would only weaken him, make him vulnerable to Traywick's moves. Nick knew he could not afford that vulnerability. None of them could afford it.

"I swear to you, Mary, that I'll bring your son to you," he said. She held his eyes a moment, perhaps trying to read his sincerity. He thought she was probably not even aware of the small negative movement of her head. She turned her eyes away from his face, and he watched her lips tighten, a barrier against whatever else she wanted to say to him.

She didn't believe him, of course. And why should she? he thought. Another promise. Why should Mary Winters ever again believe anything he said to her?

Suddenly, the same reaction he had experienced at her entry into this room surged again through his body. Whatever changes the years had wrought in them both, the passage of time had not changed how he felt about her. In his pride and his own bitterness, he had destroyed the girl she had once been. But the woman who had been forged in the fire of that experience was no less desirable to him. No less desired.

He wanted to touch her, to examine every inch of her skin. To run his fingers again over the flawless porcelain of her breasts. He wanted to care for her, to shelter and protect her, so that the thin, roughened fingers would again grow smooth and the strain would fade from the blue eyes and from the fragile, faintly shadowed skin around them. He wanted her.

He had never wanted another woman as he wanted Mary Winters. The woman he had betrayed and deserted to bear alone his child, the son he had never known, a son he had believed he would never have. And she had faced alone the agonizing decision to give the boy away. *To keep him safe.*

No longer your task, he vowed silently. *No longer your*

burden, but mine. He would not bother to make that promise aloud. She trusted nothing he said, and that was only just—the bitter price of his youthful pride.

So he said instead, his voice again controlled and ordinary, "Pierce will see you to your rooms. I hope you've been provided with everything you need. You have only to ask the staff, of course, if there is anything—"

"I've lived in gaol for the last three months, and in the years before that in a small, dark room in Marcus Traywick's house, existing on his charity. I don't need more servants or more *things* from you, Nick. I need my son. Your son. That's all I need from you. All I shall ever need."

She rose. She didn't look at him again before she crossed to the door where he knew Pierce would be waiting for her. She opened it and stepped out into the hall. He heard Pierce's soft greeting, and then she closed the door to his study, its closure isolating him from their friendship.

Nick sat a moment. Finally he put his hands flat against the top of his desk and, using their support, pushed himself to his feet. The sudden cramp in his thigh when he put weight on the leg evoked a small sign, a nearly silent acknowledgment of the familiarity of the pain.

He walked slowly to the windows behind the desk, limping more heavily than usual. He seldom bothered with the cane in private. Despite his long dependence on its support in public, it still annoyed him. A constant reminder that he was no longer the man he had once been, and never would be again. His strong fingers reached down and unconsciously massaged the aching muscle of his right thigh.

When he stood before the expanse of windows that looked out on the sweeping lawns and carefully maintained gardens of Vail, he saw nothing of the beauty that was beginning to be reborn there, as it was every spring. In his mind's eye, he saw instead the child he had been, given time and unlimited freedom to discover the endless wonders the property held for a boy. Despite his tutor's demands, his had been an almost idyllic childhood. The title he now held should never have been his, so he had not been groomed for its responsibilities.

He had not, however, he believed, failed in fulfilling them. He had had nothing else to distract him from carrying out those duties in the years since he tragically assumed the title. He *had* had nothing else, he acknowledged. And now, he thought, that had all changed. He had a wife. And a son.

A wife who cannot bear to be in the same room with me. A son whom I have never seen and who belongs legally to another man. So it seemed that still he had nothing. Nothing of importance. Nothing but the continued stupidity of his pride. And he knew that unless he was willing to deny its hold, the cold comfort of pride was very likely to be all he would ever have.

Chapter Five

"And why, Your Grace, in spite of what you offer, in spite of what you claim to be able to do if I refuse that offer, would you believe that your threats would make me willing to give you my son?"

Marcus Traywick's voice held amusement, Vail realized with surprise. Despite the consequences of refusing his demand, the parameters of which the Duke of Vail had just clearly outlined, there had been no fear in the merchant's voice. Despite the precarious financial position Marcus Traywick was now in, he was unafraid. And with that realization, suddenly Nick was.

Mary had been right. This man would far rather have power over her than the financial security he had just been offered to give up the boy. Beyond their one conversation, Vail had not discussed what he intended with Mary, nor had he told her of this meeting today. He had been provided with the information he'd requested from London far sooner than he anticipated. During those few days he had awaited it, he had not seen Mary. She lived in his home, but she had made it evident she wanted nothing to do with him. She wanted nothing from him but the safe return of her son.

"Because you and I both know that the child is *not* your son," Vail said. Nothing of what he had been thinking was revealed in his voice. It and his features were perfectly controlled, calmly portraying certainty in his superior bargaining position, backed by both his enormous influence in this society and his wealth.

"Prove it," Traywick taunted.

"I don't believe that should be difficult. I am told the boy bears…a certain resemblance."

"*She* told you that, I suppose."

"Her Grace," Vail corrected. There was an undeniable threat in the soft voice, but Traywick laughed.

"Her *Grace*, who carried the slops from my kitchen for seven years," he jeered.

"Her Grace, the Duchess of Vail. You should do well to remember the title," Nick said. "*And* with whom you are now dealing."

"That's supposed to make me afraid of you? Of what you can do to me? Is that it, my lord?" The improper title was a deliberate insult. "Such a great milord." Venom laced the coldly sarcastic voice. "Only," Traywick went on, "it seems you have forgotten this is England. There are laws designed to protect people like me from the abuses of people like you.

"In this case, I have the law on my side. I am the injured party," he said, and the spatulate fingers caressed the discolored scarring on his face. "Injured by that woman, that thief you have publicly named your wife. Children mock me now, and women turn away when I pass in the street." Traywick's nostrils flared with his fury. As in the courtroom, the burns seemed to pulse with color as his anger grew at his recitation of what Mary had done to him.

"I have come here to discuss the boy. Nothing else," Vail said. "Whatever happened—"

"What happened was that I was attacked by that woman for trying to protect my son," Traywick interjected. "The boy you seek is *my* son, recognized and acknowledged as my son from his birth, despite whatever resemblance you and Mary Winters may now claim to see. Perhaps you should have thought of this a long time ago—seven years ago, to be precise."

"How will you provide for the boy when I have ground your enterprises into dust?" Vail asked. The tone of his inquiry was neither caustic nor inimical, but simply bored. He flicked an imaginary speck of dust off the fine material of the black trousers he wore. When he looked back up at the merchant, he allowed one eyebrow to arch slightly to give emphasis to the question.

"I shall let him starve and be damned," Traywick said softly.

His mouth had moved into a smile, but no amusement lightened the mud-colored eyes. The merchant wanted him to know that he despised him, Nick recognized. And that he cared nothing for the boy. "And yourself?" Vail asked calmly. "Will you starve, too? Waste away in prison? Be transported for your debts?"

"If I am, I assure you I shall carry *my* son with me."

Nick fought the urge to respond, an almost biblical temptation to take up the challenge that had just been issued, to respond to that threat.

"What *do* you want in exchange for the boy?" he asked instead. There was almost disinterest in the question, the merest curiosity as to why this man would not give the Duke of Vail what he wanted.

"I regret to inform you that my son is not for sale."

"Then I shall see you ruined," Nick promised. His voice had not changed. There was no emotion in the vow. Traywick would, he was sure, feed off his anger. It would only fuel his determination if he believed that he had succeeded in angering him. Vail stood, and the merchant allowed him to cross the room before he stopped him at the door.

"She knows the price," Traywick said.

Nick turned to face him. The cold malevolence in the yellow-brown eyes had intensified. *He hates her,* Vail realized, *as much as Mary said, as much as she feared.*

"It hasn't changed," Traywick continued. "She has always known the price. I told her before, long before she pretended to be your wife. But somehow, that claim would, I must confess, add a certain...fillip to the business," he said. The thick lips curved again. "I can't tell you, milord, how much I should enjoy copulating with Her Grace, the Duchess of Vail. You be certain you tell Mary Winters what I said. As for you, my high-and-mighty Lord of Vail, get the hell out of my house."

Nausea surged upward into Nick's throat at the thought of this man with Mary, using her body as he had used that of his dying wife. Traywick was, he now knew, as mad as that story had suggested. However, Nick's sudden vision of darkening bruises marring the smooth, fair skin of Mary's body, the delicate perfection of which his own mouth had once been allowed to touch, to caress and to worship, was suddenly too powerful.

"I shall kill you," Nick said, his control broken. Intending to carry out the threat he had just made, Vail began to limp back across the space between them.

"If you do, then you may be certain that my instructions concerning the child will immediately be carried out. That is something I don't believe you would want to happen, given your sudden...interest in the boy." The words stopped Vail's advance as the merchant had known they would.

"Instructions?" Nick asked, struggling to master his

emotions, to find the icy indifference that had long been characteristic of his existence. Even he had grown to believe he was emotionless—until Mary Winters reentered his life, destroying the facade he had erected.

"Instructions that will be carried out if you attempt to harm me in any way, Your Grace. In *any* way," the merchant repeated. "I assure you that I have already made those arrangements. A good father should always arrange for the care of his son. So many refuse to take responsibility for the careless seeds they sow, so that others are left to make the important decisions regarding the future of their children." He smiled at Vail before he added, "The future of a small child can be so precarious. Don't you agree, my lord? So many things can happen to a defenseless child in this world. Things that are sometimes...difficult to prevent."

The merchant smiled at the powerful Duke of Vail, who was sophisticated enough to know exactly the kinds of things that did happen to children, the abuses to which their small, frail bodies were sometimes subjected. Traywick's eyes promised those and far worse, visions which Nick knew he would now see over and over again in his nightmares.

"You be sure to tell Mary Winters what I said, Your Grace," Traywick advised, his voice almost pleasant now. "Tell her I'll be waiting to hear from her."

Nick stood a moment longer, his instinctive response to murder checked by what he had read in the merchant's voice. That had not been an idle threat. This man, whose true madness now looked out of the transparent windows of his soul, was capable of doing exactly what he had threatened.

Without another word, the Duke of Vail turned and left the room, defeated by images he had fought from the beginning. The images of a small boy, alone and without protection from a man Nick now knew to be mad.

The man he left behind no longer bothered to hide his elation. No matter the Duke of Vail's exalted position, Marcus Traywick knew now that he held the upper hand. Mary Winters had given him that advantage when she came to his house years ago, her body swelling with that noble bastard's by-blow.

He had thought when he and Mary made their bargain that he would be able to mold the boy into someone worthy to take over the empire he was building, but instead the child had been marked by his heritage. That same arrogant contempt with which Vail had looked at him today he had seen mirrored too often in the boy's considering gaze.

But contempt had not been the emotion revealed in those noble eyes when the duke left, the merchant thought in satisfaction. Vail had come here expecting to have everything his way, as the corrupt courts had allowed him to do in the matter of the woman. *But that was not to be the case,* Traywick thought. *Not here. Not in my house.*

The merchant cared nothing for the boy, of course. With Abigail's death, he had quickly realized he was free to marry again, to find some woman to bear his own seed, a son of his loins in whose eyes he would never see that noble contempt. But now... His fingers stole to his cheek, unconsciously smoothing over the disfigurement, reminding himself of what Mary Winters had cost him. What attractive and well-placed woman would be willing to wed him now, a monster fit only to frighten children?

He didn't want the boy, but he was determined that because those two did, they should not have him. He did not doubt Vail *could* do everything he had threatened; he did not, however, believe that he would now be willing to do so and endanger his son.

What the duke was more likely to do, considering his political power and his notoriously derring-do background, Traywick suddenly realized, was to snatch the child. Vail could take the boy and hide him until he had time to convince the courts to give in, as they had before, to his claims. He had that kind of power, the merchant admitted bitterly. That had already been amply demonstrated.

But two could play at that game, Traywick realized, suddenly amused at the idea of playing hide-and-seek with Vail. He had been very adept at the game as a child, remarkably skilled. The small smile that had played over the loose lips widened. That would solve so many problems and could so easily be accomplished.

Suddenly he knew exactly where and with whom he would hide the child. He wondered that he hadn't thought of this before. It was perfect. All the people whom he despised the most would be affected. Again the chilling laughter of the courtroom rang out. Such damnably perfect revenge.

The one-armed ex-soldier stood nervously before his employer. Bob Smithers was not accustomed to being called into the merchant's office. Usually he was given his orders at the back step, the words brusquely thrown at him as Traywick was leaving to attend to one or the other of his flourishing enterprises.

He hoped he had not displeased his demanding employer in some way. It was hard enough for an able-bodied man to find employment in these times, and for a man such as himself, this job was literally the difference between life and death. He was grateful to Mr. Traywick, and he worked hard to please him. He could only hope that he had not been summoned because he had not.

"I have an errand for you," the merchant said, glancing up from the spread of papers on his desk.

"An errand, sir?"

"A very important undertaking I'd not be willing to entrust to anyone else. And as always, Bob, you must discuss the business with no one. No one," he repeated sternly. "Do you understand?"

That was always a condition, the merchant being as secretive as an old woman about his affairs. Smithers nodded, anticipating being given some message to carry. He had done that many times before. Sometimes he had been sent all the way to London.

"I want you to take my son into Scotland," Traywick said. For some reason the merchant's mouth twitched, almost a smile.

"Scotland, Mr. Traywick?"

"To visit my late wife's family. To Lady Keith, my beloved Abigail's grandmother, the boy's great-grandmother. She has never seen the child, and I believe, since she sponsored Abigail's entry into society after her mother's death, that she would be pleased to entertain her son. This will probably be an extended stay, of course. The press of business, you understand, demands my attention, and I haven't had time to find another governess."

"But I thought that soon, sir, you'd have another—" Smithers began. The yellow eyes had turned hostile, and Smithers choked off the rest of that idle thought. It had been speculated after his wife's death that Mr. Traywick would marry again. It was believed that he had been attempting to move upward in society so long ago when he eloped with Abigail, whom he had met and secretly wooed in London.

There had been rumors that Traywick's wife had connections, and considering the surprising instructions he'd just been given, those apparently were true. Their marriage had not, however, accomplished what Traywick intended. Gossip said his wife's family had disowned her, cutting all ties to the couple, and since Smithers had never heard Mrs. Traywick's maiden name before, it seemed that, too, might be correct.

But it didn't pay to remind this man of his few failures. He could never admit that he had been wrong. And if you reminded him that he had, the ex-soldier knew, you paid the price, either from his caustic tongue or in his sudden decision that he could do without your services for a while. Smithers was very careful now not to cross Marcus Traywick.

"I'm sure his great-grandmother will be delighted to entertain the child," the merchant went on, at Smithers's suddenly tactful silence. "You have simply to deliver him to her door. I have written out the directions for you. Then you are to return via London, where you will fetch a parcel from my bankers. They'll be expecting you. A very important package, Bob, which you will, of course, guard with your life."

Smithers nodded, taking the instructions the merchant held out. "I'm to take the boy by the mail coach?" he asked hesitantly. Traywick had as yet given him no money.

The wide mouth pursed as the merchant considered. "On horseback, I believe. The child is small. You can easily carry him before you. And you must avoid the main thoroughfares. That will be less apt to call attention to your journey."

Easy enough to manage a child for a man with two arms, Smithers realized, but for him...

"Is that all, sir?" he asked, stuffing the directions into

the pocket of his moleskin vest, thinking that it would take him quite a bit of time to do both jobs, especially given the mode of transportation Traywick had specified for the journey north.

"There is a slight possibility..." Traywick seemed to hesitate, thinking carefully about his words. "A possibility only, you understand, that I may not be here at home when you return. In that case, you must bring the package to this address. You've been there before."

Again Traywick handed his employee a slip of paper on which he had written out careful instructions. Smithers's brows rose as he read them, but he was, of course, not in a position to refuse.

"A fair distance, sir. To Scotland and back, and then—"

"Bring the packet you pick up in London as soon as you can, but only if you return to find I am not at home here."

"When do you want me to leave?"

"Why, now, of course. I assume you have no other plans."

Smithers thought about expressing his concerns, but Traywick had already begun to unlock the metal box in which he kept the household funds. The same box, he remembered, that the merchant had accused Mary Winters of stealing from, although the ex-soldier knew well enough there was only one key, that on the gold chain that dangled across the merchant's ample stomach. And when he remembered what had happened to Mary, he knew he must manage to do whatever Traywick had asked. This wasn't a man who forgave incompetence or disobedience.

"No other plans, sir," he agreed finally.

"It seems in my quest for justice against the child's former governess," the merchant said, counting out a small stack of coins from the supply in the box as he talked, "I have acquired some rather ruthless and powerful enemies.

I am depending on you, Bob, to guard the boy's where-abouts with your life. One word to the wrong person, and my son may suffer in their quest for revenge against me. I'm sure you don't wish to be responsible for any harm befalling the child,'' he said, pushing the stack toward the ex-soldier. He looked up. "That should more than cover your expenses. Whatever is left, you may consider your wages." The strange eyes were regarding him with amusement.

He meant it as a bribe, Smithers realized. Payment to keep his mouth shut. Which, of course, he already planned to do. But the merchant had never done this before. He knew the enemy Traywick referred to. The story of Mary Winters's interrupted trial and of the Duke of Vail's role in her rescue was common gossip in the village. Everyone knew it didn't pay to interfere with the nobility. Traywick should have learned that by now, but whatever enmity was between his employer and Vail was, of course, no business of his. His only concern was pleasing the man who paid his wages.

"I understand," Smithers said. He scooped up the coins and pushed them into the same pocket where he'd crammed the papers. "Is the boy ready?" he asked.

"Richard has not yet been told he's to undertake a journey. Perhaps you would be so good as to help him pack."

Again Smithers nodded, knowing he'd been dismissed. A strange business, he thought, but then, Traywick was a strange man. He had always known that.

"And, Bob…" the merchant said. When Smithers turned back, that same amusement was in the wolfish eyes. "He's to take nothing but his clothes. Throw the wooden soldier into the fire before you leave."

"Into the fire, Mr. Traywick?"

"Let him watch. He's far too attached to it. I don't believe such a strong attachment is...entirely healthy."

The merchant closed and locked the lid of the strongbox and picked up his pen, beginning again to enter a long column of numbers in the leather-bound ledger that lay before him.

Smithers watched him a moment, wondering if he dared to protest. What could it matter if the boy had a well-loved toy? All children did.

"Is there something else?" Mr. Traywick asked, without looking up.

"Nothing, sir," Smithers said, fighting his urge to defend the child. Perhaps it would be better for the boy to be with his mother's people. Traywick was a hard man, and children needed a woman's softness. Perhaps the place where he was taking the child would be better for him, despite the difficulty of the journey they faced. Seeing the boy there safely was all he could do. A man had to look after himself, he reasoned. And after all, this was the boy's father. He had the right to do anything he wished—with his son *and* with his belongings.

When the Duke of Vail entered his study, he threw the ebony cane across his desk and, without its support, limped to stand again before the windows. In the miles he had traveled from the village where Traywick's house stood, he had found no solution. He was still standing there when his valet entered, almost an hour later.

Pierce had grown tired of waiting. He had known, of course, about the mission on which the duke had embarked this morning, as he had been informed of the careful financial transactions that had been put into place concerning the merchant's enterprises. What he had not been told, the

information he had impatiently been awaiting since the
duke's return, was the outcome of the encounter.

Pierce suspected that his distraction had been apparent
to the duchess during the time he spent with her. He had
been teaching Mary to play piquet, attempting to find some
way to pass the slow hours while the duke sought the means
to pressure the merchant into giving up the boy as he had
promised her. The time Pierce and Mary spent together in
the few days she had lived in this house had resulted in the
forging of something that felt like friendship, an incongru-
ous alliance that the duke's batman knew had probably
scandalized the staff.

Mary seemed unaware, or uncaring, that associating with
her husband's personal servant was inappropriate. Apparently she needed to be reassured that Vail was doing something about the problem of his son, and because of his
relationship with the duke, Pierce knew he was the only
one who could truthfully assure her that was the case. And
the hours he spent with Mary had made him far more understanding of the man he served.

Mary Winters, Pierce had decided very quickly, deserved
what Vail had always felt for her. There was no one who
knew Nick Stanton as this small, unassuming man did, and
the secrets he guarded would never be betrayed. There had
been times, however, in his brief acquaintance with Mary
when he had to fight the urge to explain his master's actions.

But Pierce had never betrayed Vail's trust. Their friendship had been tempered by the fires of battle and, no matter
their respective positions, it was too valuable to them both
to chance its destruction. This was what Vail wanted, and
whether or not Pierce agreed with the rightness of that decision, he would never go against the man who had made
it.

"Did the merchant agree to give up the child?" Pierce asked his employer. He had stopped in the doorway, studying the fair, bent head of the man standing before the wide windows. Despite the fact that he could not see Vail's face, he thought he could read defeat in the rigidity of his hands, which were gripping the top of the sash.

The mission today had not gone as the duke had anticipated, and Pierce wondered what had happened. The plan had been carefully devised, meticulously organized, and because Pierce was familiar with Vail's skill as a tactician, he knew there would have been no unguarded positions through which the enemy might escape. He couldn't imagine what had gone wrong.

The duke did not turn at the question, but the broad shoulders beneath the perfectly fitted black coat straightened and then moved upward slightly with the depth of the breath he took. His voice was perfectly calm, every emotion again seemingly controlled, when he answered.

"He did not," Vail said simply.

"Did he tell you why?" Pierce asked.

The duke turned, and Pierce knew that whatever occurred this morning had been a disaster. The cost of his encounter with the merchant was in the handsome face, the skin stretched too tightly over the fine bone structure beneath. In the clear gray eyes was something Pierce had seen there only once before, and had prayed never to see again.

"You and Mary were right," Vail said. "It seems he wants only revenge."

"On the duchess?" Pierce asked carefully. Although the deep voice had been very soft, there had been something frightening about the duke's tone.

"Primarily," Vail agreed. "He hates me, of course, but that enmity is almost an afterthought."

"But he can't hope to hurt the duchess," Pierce began,

and then realized suddenly how mistaken he was. "The boy?" he asked, his voice almost a whisper. Pierce didn't have Vail's control. His emotions were rawly exposed, in his voice and in his face. Both reflected the sheer horror of the thought he had just had.

"Don't try to imagine what he might do," Vail advised. His lips smiled at the man who was his only friend, but there was no trace of humor in the smile. And there was sickness in the gray eyes. "Believe me," the duke said quietly, "I have imagined it all. There is nothing to be gained by speculating on what a man like Marcus Traywick can devise to make an innocent child suffer."

"That's what he threatened?"

Vail nodded.

"What are you going to do?" Pierce asked finally.

Vail looked up. There was silence for a long heartbeat before the duke answered. "I'm going to continue to do what I have been doing in the hours since I left the home of that madman."

Not understanding the comment nor the total despair he had never heard before in this man's voice, even in the darkest hours they had shared together, Pierce shook his head, his eyes still on his master's face.

"I'm going to pray," Nick said, "that nothing happens to my son."

The duke began to cross the room toward the door through which Pierce had entered. It was clear that he considered the conversation at an end. Pierce thought of the woman who waited upstairs, trusting his own assurances that Vail would prevail against the merchant.

"My God, Colonel," Pierce protested, "you can't give up. Every man has his price. You said that. You know it's true. All you have to do is to discover Traywick's. You have the money. It means nothing to you. We both know that. Give him what he wants. Find out what it is and then offer it to him. Get the boy. My God, Colonel, he's your son.''

Vail turned. "I *know* his price," he said. The light had begun to fade from the tall windows. By some trick of the approaching twilight, in the dimness of the room the gray eyes were almost luminous, mirroring none of the terrible darkness of the choice Traywick had offered him. "He was quite open about what he wants in exchange for Richard."

"Then give it to him," Pierce ordered sharply. But it was not that simple, he knew. Whatever the merchant had demanded was enough to shake this man whose raw courage he admired above that of all other men he had ever known. And Sergeant Major John Pierce had known more than his share of brave men through the long years he had spent in the king's army.

Again, the well-shaped lips of the Duke of Vail moved into a smile. The growing shadows twisted the movement, turning it into something grotesque. Or perhaps that was whatever moved behind his eyes, the images that had haunted Vail's intelligence, that had profaned his memories, since the merchant made his proposal. Those memories, cherished beyond his hope of eternity, were all that had sustained Nick Stanton during the hell he passed through in the months after Waterloo.

"He wants Mary," Vail said simply. "Mary is to be Traywick's price for the boy. If I send my wife to his bed, to suffer the obscenities he inflicted upon his own, then, only then, will he give me my son."

Standing outside the door of Vail's study, Mary shivered under the impact of those words. She had never intended to listen. Nothing but entering the room and demanding to be told the outcome of Vail's meeting with Traywick had ever crossed her mind. She was not an eavesdropper, but as she approached the door of the room where she had met with him four nights ago, Vail's voice had been clear and penetrating, even through the solid oak between them.

"Mary is to be Traywick's price for the boy. If I send my wife to his bed, to suffer the obscenities he inflicted upon his own, he will give me my son."

There had been nothing else, although she had stood frozen through seemingly endless seconds, trying to assimilate what she had overheard. Of course, she thought with despair. Why had she not realized what Traywick would demand? It was what he had wanted from the first. What he had tried to take the night he tore her clothes from her body, when his cold fingers— Her mind jerked away from those memories, from the feel of his hands moving over her flesh. Involuntarily she shuddered, sickened by the remembrance.

"...Traywick's price..." Nick had said. She should have known. *She* had the power to free Richard. She hadn't needed Vail, she realized. She needed only the courage it would take to return to the merchant's house and to give herself into his control.

And, she thought fiercely, some plan that would ensure that Traywick would send the boy here, that he would give him into Nick's care if she did what he wished. Even if Vail never publicly acknowledged Richard as his heir, he would make sure the child was fed and clothed and sheltered and, more importantly, she realized, protected from Traywick. She could trust Nick that far. Far more than she could trust the merchant.

The handle of the door she stood before began to turn, awakening her to the danger of discovery. Mary slipped into the lengthening shadows of the hallway. When Nick emerged, however, he moved across the wide foyer without looking back toward the room he had left. From her place of concealment, Mary stood watching as Vail began to climb the graceful, curving stairs. Unable to tear her gaze away, she watched until the limping figure had disappeared from sight.

Nick had been so certain he could rescue Richard, and she had trusted his easy confidence. But he could not have known the caliber of the man for whom she had worked. She had known. She was the one who had erred in her judgment. She had appealed to Nick because that had been easier than the other option. And perhaps because...

Because, she acknowledged, honest with herself, at least, *the feelings she had had for Nick Stanton were not, as she had once believed, dead and forever buried beneath the weight of his desertion.* Despite what he had done, he still possessed the power to stir her senses, to quicken her breathing, and to cause the hot rush of desire to flood her body.

But she was no longer the girl who had given herself to him, who had trusted him enough to do that. She was now a woman, and, more importantly, she was Richard's mother. Vail had tried, but, as Traywick's words had reminded her, somewhere inside she had always known his price.

Chapter Six

Long after she dismissed Claire, Mary sat by the glow of the small, banked fire, in the loneliness of the enormous bedroom. She had tried for hours to devise some plan that would allow her to accede to the merchant's demand and at the same time be assured that Richard would be safely conveyed to Vail.

All of that would have to be accomplished without the duke's knowledge and without the help of Pierce, her one friend, who would never let her go to Traywick. Nor would Nick, of course. His pride would prevent that, if nothing else. *My wife.* His words reverberated in her memory more strongly than she knew they should. *My wife.* There had been something in his tone...

The soft knock was unexpected. It was nearly midnight. It must be Pierce, she realized. Perhaps he had come to tell her about the meeting. She pulled her shawl more closely about her shoulders, and despite the fact that she was wearing only her night rail, she hurried on bare feet across the chamber to throw open the door.

The man who stood in the shadows outside her room was not Pierce. Nick was not dressed as he had been when she watched him climb the stairs earlier tonight. He wore only a soft linen shirt, open at the throat, and the doeskin britches and tasseled Hessians in which he had made his journey today. The fair hair fell, softly curling, over his forehead, just as it had that long-ago afternoon when her fingers had disordered it.

The youthful handsomeness of those days had given way to a man's strength, which somehow made the classic features more attractive. The natural confidence of his birthright had even then been intensified by his experiences on the Peninsula, his assurance in his own masculinity so appealing to the girl she had been. And now, even given what she knew he had been told this afternoon, there was no defeat in the calm gray eyes.

"May I come in?" he asked.

Mary stepped aside, not trusting her voice. She was unprepared for his nearness. She had not had a chance to reinforce her defenses, as she had before, when he summoned her to his study. Nick Stanton was in her bedroom, the last place she had ever thought she might have to face him.

He walked across the room to stand a moment looking down into the fire. She realized that, even without the cane, the hesitation in his stride was no more now than it had been so long ago when she had watched him cross the clearing to come to her.

"Close the door," he ordered softly, when he turned to face her.

She could not have said why she hesitated. She knew his only intention was that their conversation remain private. He had not come here to seduce her. The idea that this man might desire her was almost as unimaginable. The Duke of Vail might have any woman in England—however young, beautiful and well connected. He would no longer want Mary Winters, of course. Her lips tightened with that bitter acknowledgment, but she turned to the door, automatically obeying him, as she had always obeyed.

"Come and sit down," he said. "I need to talk to you."

She shook her head. "I think that whatever you have to tell me..." she began, and then the useless protest faded. What did it matter? If she were nearer, she could read his eyes in the low light of the fire. She knew what Traywick had said, but she needed to know why Nick had come tonight. To suggest that she comply with the merchant's request? Even as she thought it, she knew, as she had before, that that could not be true. His pride alone would not allow that. So she crossed the room and sat down. The gray eyes watched her, but nothing of what he was thinking was revealed in their shadowed depths.

"I met with Traywick this morning," Vail began. "It seems that you were right in your assessment of the merchant's motives," he admitted.

"He wants revenge," she said.

"I threatened him with financial ruin. I assure you a rational man would have been frightened by what I proposed."

"Rational," she repeated, shaking her head. "I told you he isn't rational, not entirely...sane."

Nick said nothing, but something had changed since the last time she had made that claim. There was no longer disbelief in his eyes. *Because he, too, now knows what Traywick wants,* she thought. Not the assurance that Vail would not harm his businesses nor even the wealth that could be his if he agreed to give the duke the boy. Now Vail also knew that Traywick wanted only to inflict pain. As he had always wanted.

"What will you do?" she asked. She had already decided what must be done, but he could never be allowed to suspect what she planned. Vail must continue to believe she was willing to leave it all in his hands.

"There must be something he wants, Mary," Nick said. "Some other leverage I can use. You know him better than anyone."

"You're asking me what to offer Traywick?"

"There must be some position or office, entrée somewhere, some possession. I shall offer him money, of course, but if there's something more..." For the first time, the quiet voice faltered.

Since she overheard the conversation downstairs, there had been within her the urge, small and vindictive, to remind him of his empty promise. Nick had vowed he'd bring her Richard, and he had failed. But at the pain revealed in that suddenly hesitant voice, she no longer wanted to taunt him with that failure. It was not Nick's fault that he couldn't give Traywick what he wanted. Despite all that had happened between them, she knew he would never willingly surrender her body, which had trembled beneath the force of his own passion, into the merchant's control.

"Steal him," she said suddenly, fighting those memories. They alone might have the power to make her hesitate to do what she knew that she must. It was a power she had not realized they possessed, not until she had again come face-to-face with the man who had created them. "Take Richard away from him," she begged. "Traywick doesn't want *things*. You have nothing he wants, Nick. Nothing to offer him. You and Pierce could overpower him. Or you could hire someone. Then we could hide Richard—"

"Mary," he broke in. It was a denial, and suddenly she was angry.

"You've fought for things that surely had less meaning to you than this. He's your *son,* Nick. Our son."

"Don't you think I would have taken the boy today and

sent Traywick to hell if it were that easy? Don't you still know me well enough, Mary, to realize that if it were possible, the child would even now be here?"

"Why isn't it possible?" she asked, not understanding. "Why can't you take him?"

Nick said nothing, but his features hardened as she watched. There had been something else, she realized. Something Traywick had said besides what she had overheard. Something that had made Nick know that he couldn't afford to try to rescue Richard by force.

Her eyes fell, trying to imagine what it might have been. Nick Stanton had never been afraid of the devil himself. He certainly wouldn't be afraid of anything Marcus Traywick could do to him. She had not been aware he'd moved, but Nick's hand was under her chin, lifting her face to force her to look up into his eyes.

"Trust me, Mary," he said softly. "Only a little longer. I swear to you I'll get him back."

His fingers were warm, and their callused strength was too familiar. The strong, competent hands of the fine horseman he had always been. She remembered them so well. The memory of his hands moving over her body, their warmth then not comforting, but seducing, enticing reactions that even now— Abruptly she turned her head away, breaking the contact that had flared between them.

"You still ride," she whispered. It seemed a non sequitur, but it gave voice to her sudden inner realization that nothing really had changed. This was still Nick. He was still the man she had loved, despite the title he had acquired, despite his betrayal and the long years' absence.

"Of course," he said. From his questioning tone, it was clear her comment had surprised him. "Because of this?" he asked, his fingers touching his right thigh. "You think that because of this—"

"No," she denied quickly. "No, it wasn't that."

Thankfully, he hadn't realized what she was thinking, although her reaction had, of course, been too revealing. She had never forgotten the feel of his hand, but she couldn't confess that.

So she smiled at him and said instead, "That was always to you the merest scratch." He had belittled both the reckless bravery for which he had been cited in the dispatches from Spain and the resulting injury to his leg.

He held her eyes, and there was something in his that she had never seen there before. And then he allowed his hand to fall to his side. "The merest scratch," he agreed.

He turned and limped to the door. Again she watched him. She had not been aware, until she realized how little time was left, of how much she wanted to watch him. To be with him. She had forgotten what it felt like to be a woman, to be with the man you loved. Those feelings were still powerful, almost too compelling, in spite of all that lay between them. But that was not an option. There was something else she had to do, something that only she could accomplish, so the emotions he had aroused must again be buried.

"Do you suppose there's a mare in your stables gentle enough for someone who hasn't ridden in a very long time?" she asked, praying he would not think it a strange request. When Nick turned back to face her, there was a small, puzzled crease between his brows.

"I never knew you rode," he said.

"I suppose there are many things we didn't have time to learn about one another."

"And you'd like to ride again?"

"I thought it would give me some way to make the hours pass."

"Pierce can ride with you," he offered.

"Not at first," she argued, smiling at him again. "I'll only ride here, on the grounds. I was never very good, and I'd be embarrassed to have Pierce watch me. Do you think you can find me a mare who will be very forgiving of her rider's incompetence?"

"I'll tell the head groom," he said.

"Tomorrow?" she prompted, knowing she was on very dangerous ground. Nick was no fool. He would suspect something if she weren't careful. "The days are so long," she added. "I only thought if I had something else to think about, something else to do..."

"Of course," Vail agreed, but the gray eyes searched her face. Deliberately she forced her lips again into the semblance of a smile.

"Thank you," she said.

"Trust me, Mary. I swear I won't let you down again."

She nodded, wondering if this would be the last time she would see him. Vail opened the door and stepped out into the dark hall, but Mary Winters would sit a long time before the dying fire, remembering.

It had been a mistake to come here, Vail acknowledged, leaning against the door he had just closed. Emotion and not logic had sent him. He had had no logical reason to ask Mary to suggest a solution. There *was* no solution to Traywick's ultimatum, to the choice he had been given.

He owed them both protection, and he had failed them before. So his son had grown up believing another man to be his father, and the girl who had once joyfully given herself to him could not bear the touch of his hand. And he was no closer to effecting the child's rescue than he had been when he first learned of his existence.

He now believed that the boy was no longer at the merchant's home. Traywick would never have been so confident today, had that been the case. As soon as he returned from his meeting he had issued orders that the merchant's house be watched, but Vail knew that, because he had underestimated his opponent, he had taken that precaution far too late.

Traywick had had ample time since the trial to spirit the child away. He would have known that Mary would make her appeal to her husband, and, given his own arrogance in the courtroom, the merchant would have been prepared for the duke to act. *He* was the one who had been wrong, Nick admitted. He had been so certain his threats and enticements would win the merchant's cooperation, and now he knew he had been a fool.

A fool about so many things, he thought bitterly. The things we fear most are not those which come to pass, his father had once told him. But when he finally realized the truth of that, it had been too late to make amends to Mary for what he had done. By then her father was dead and Mary had disappeared. Despite the endless efforts he had made—made too late, of course—he had never found her.

His fingers tonight against the softness of Mary's cheek had reminded him of all he had lost, the flare of desire running through his body strong and undeniable. She was his wife, and she recoiled from his touch. All she wanted from him was her son, and he could not even give her that. Nor could he explain to her why he could not. So he had gone to her bedroom and made empty promises that would echo in his heart through the long, dark hours.

Vail stood a moment in the silent hallway, torturing himself with memory, letting the short, forbidden hours they had spent together come alive again within his consciousness. Then, knowing the futility of allowing himself to remember, he returned to the long loneliness from which, tonight, those memories had finally driven him.

* * *

Despite Vail's promise, Mary had been surprised when Claire brought the riding habit to her room the following morning.

"I expect it must have belonged to His Grace's mother," the girl had said, shaking out the folds of the fine woolen skirt. The habit had been put away more than ten years ago, at the duchess's death. It had been wrapped in muslin, protected from moths with dried lavender, and that subtle aroma perfumed the chamber as the maid brushed out the fabric. "Mr. Thompson sent it to me this morning to bring to you."

Although there had been no riding attire among the wardrobe Vail had provided for her, Mary was surprised he would let her wear something that had been his mother's. Claire helped her dress in the black habit, its jacket fitted with a double row of gold buttons and a standing velvet collar. The folds of the white linen stock were secured with a gold-and-onyx stickpin.

There was no need for alterations. The habit fit as if it had been tailored expressly for her. When Mary finally stood before the cheval glass, the slim, elegant woman reflected there had been almost a stranger. And when she left her room and went down to meet Pierce, she had still been thinking about Nick's mother, about his family, none of whom she had never known, of course, and who had been so cruelly torn from his life.

The mare the groom brought out for her approval proved to be as gentle as Pierce promised, and Mary was a more accomplished horsewoman than she had admitted. Her own mother had been an excellent rider and taught her to ride as a child. Mary was thankful to find that those skills had not been entirely lost.

During the next few days, she found that having patience

was far more difficult than regaining her confidence on horseback. As her proficiency increased, she had to fight the urge to direct the mare away from the estate and toward the tall brick house and her son. She had at last realized the only thing that would prevent Nick Stanton from trying to take his son by force. Traywick had not threatened Nick. He had threatened retaliation on the child if Vail undertook any action against him, and so Nick's hands were tied. It was all up to her. She was, as he had told Vail, Traywick's price.

She wasn't even sure of the exact distance to Penhurst or how long the journey would take. And she dared not ask, for fear of arousing suspicions. She knew also that when she finally left Vail, her absence must not be noticed before she had time to arrive at her destination.

Once there, she had decided, she would demand Traywick send Richard, under the care of Bob Smithers, back to Vail's estate. She knew the ex-soldier would faithfully carry out any task the merchant ordered, and she also was sure the boy would be safe when he arrived here. Vail would see to that. Traywick would never again get his hands on the boy. Mary never allowed herself to think what would happen at the merchant's house after the departure of Smithers and her son. Because, of course, what lay beyond was unthinkable.

It was not until three days had passed that Mary was given the opportunity she had been praying for. Pierce informed her one morning that he would be unable to come up for their usual afternoon card game because he was to accompany the duke on a journey that would take them away from the estate for the day. With both Pierce and Nick away, she realized, this was the best chance she would ever have.

It was childishly simple to get rid of the groom who had been ordered to accompany her on her morning excursions around the grounds. With each passing day, he had grown more confident in her skills, and when Mary asked him to go back to the stables to fetch a riding crop because she thought she might try a quick gallop, he smilingly agreed.

As soon as he disappeared, Mary guided the mare through the grove of trees that separated the paddocks from the long, winding road that gave access to the duke's house. Once she reached the main road, she hoped she would recognize from her journey here which direction she must take.

When she broke through the stand of trees, she touched her heel to the mare. She couldn't allow herself to think about what lay at the end of this journey. Or about Nick. There was only one thing she could afford to think about now. Only Richard.

She had ridden less than a mile along the main thoroughfare when she heard the sound of a wagon approaching behind her. She threw a quick glance over her shoulder, fearing that her flight had already been discovered, but the driver was no one she recognized. He tipped his cap in greeting, preparing to direct his team around horse and rider.

"Could you tell me, please," Mary called to him, "how far it is to Penhurst?"

"Happens I can," he said, pulling his plodding cart horses to a halt beside the mare. "Going there myself. I've an order of felt to deliver to the hatter. It be a little less than forty miles."

An idea seemed to leap into Mary's mind. It was a plan that should give her the time she needed and had feared she would not have. It seemed she was becoming more and more skilled at deception, she thought bitterly.

"Would you take me with you?" she asked.

"In my cart, do you mean?"

"Please," she said, trying to think of some reasonable explanation for that request. "I need to get home," she offered. "To my father's house. He's very ill, you see, and I was on my way to him, but my mare's gone lame."

"That's a far distance for a woman alone. Have you no groom?" His eyes appraised the fine material of the habit she wore.

"I'm the governess at the Hall," Mary said, gesturing vaguely in the direction from which she had come and praying he was not familiar with the great houses in the district. At least not familiar enough to know that Vail would have no need of a governess. "Could you please take me with you?" she begged, trying to think of something that might tip the scales in her favor.

Suddenly she remembered the stickpin Claire had arranged to hold the folds of her stock. She stripped off her riding gloves to unfasten the pin, holding it out to him on her palm. "For your trouble," she offered.

His eyes examined the small piece of jewelry as she held her breath. When he looked back up into her face, Mary knew that he didn't believe her, but she also knew that it didn't matter. He could sell the pin for more than a year's wages. Why should he care if she was lying?

"Aye, I'll take you," the man said. He set the brake on the wagon and climbed down to help her dismount. "You want to take your mare with you? I can tie her to the back of the cart," he said when she was standing on the road beside him.

"No, thank you," Mary said quickly. Molly's return to the paddocks, of course, had been the most important element of this entire scheme. "If I can make her go home, they'll attend to whatever's gone wrong with her leg."

With the flat of her hand, she hit Molly's broad rump. The placid mare twisted sideways, surprised at the unaccustomed blow, but she didn't run. In desperation, Mary hit her again, harder this time. "Go home, Molly," she ordered. "Go home."

The mare moved away from her, but after only a few feet she turned back to looked questioningly at Mary. The driver picked up a clod of dirt and flung it with casual accuracy at the mare. Startled, Molly sidled a few feet, a touch of white showing at the corner of her wide, dark eye. When he threw another one, she trotted, reins trailing, some distance down the road toward Vail, displaying no evidence whatsoever of the lameness her rider had claimed.

"She'll go home," the driver said confidently. "As soon as we're out of sight, she'll head back. Aren't you afraid that when she shows up at the stables without you, folks there might believe something's wrong?" he asked shrewdly.

"Perhaps," Mary said, thinking about the poor groom she had tricked. And Pierce, who had so carefully chosen the dependable Molly for her. About Nick. "But I really must get to my father," she added, holding out the gold pin she had promised him. He held her eyes a moment, his again expressing his disbelief. Finally greed won out, and he took the pin, putting it away carefully, and then he offered his hand to help her into the wagon.

The Duke of Vail returned from his errand far earlier that afternoon than he had expected. He found his usually orderly household in an uproar, and with good reason, of course, given the disappearance of the duchess during her morning ride. It fell to Thompson to stammer out the story.

The majordomo had managed only a few sentences before the duke strode out of the room, on his way to the stables and the unfortunate groom who had been assigned to follow the duchess.

Vail had never in his life struck a servant. He had been taught from childhood that that was an action beneath contempt, but he found himself fighting the urge to plant his right fist, once justifiably famous in Jackson's practice ring, in the middle of the groom's blanched and sweating features. He managed to listen, however, to the man's explanation without giving way to his rage. When the brief narrative had ended, Vail addressed his questions concerning the breadth of the search that had been undertaken to the head groom, and not, of course, to the man who stood trembling before him.

"Every man, Your Grace, every foot of the grounds, and even on the main road. It's as if she's vanished. Or—" the head groom paused, fearing to suggest the dark suspicion that had crept into his head during the long, fruitless hours of the search he'd organized "—as if someone's taken her."

"Taken her?" Pierce repeated unbelievingly.

"Abducted her," the head groom said, thinking again, as he had as the hours passed and the sun climbed higher in the sky, of all the tales about children stolen by passing bands of gypsies. The main road was well traveled. There was really no way to know whom the duchess might have encountered if she had ventured there.

The suggestion did not cause the same fearful images to move within Vail's racing mind. Instead, Mary's own words the last time he'd talked to her echoed there. *Steal him,* she had urged. *Take Richard…* Was it possible that in her desperation to get the boy back she had tried to do exactly that? *Trust me,* he had urged, but he had never given her reason to believe that she might. Nick had known there was something strange about her request for a mare, about her desire to ride again after so many years. So he had given his careful instructions to the grooms, which apparently Mary had easily circumvented.

"Traywick," Vail said very softly, sure now where Mary had gone.

"You think Traywick's taken the duchess?" Pierce asked.

"She's gone to get the boy," Vail said.

Because he planned to join in the search, he had already issued the order for his own horse to be saddled before he confronted the groom who was responsible for leaving his mistress alone. He knew, given the hours since Mary's disappearance, that there was no time to waste. It might already be too late.

"You *told* her what he said?" Pierce asked, trying to understand what had happened.

"She intends to take the boy. There's no way she could know what the merchant proposed."

"But if that madman catches her..." Pierce paused, thinking about what Traywick might do if he found Mary trying to rescue her son.

"Exactly," Vail said. He swung up onto the gelding the stable boy had brought. "I'm going cross-country. It will be quicker. Gather what men you can and follow."

"You'll want your pistols," Pierce suggested.

Vail checked the horse, and the gelding circled, fresh and eager to be off. Vail had made the kind of run he intended today once before. Then he had abused his horse to reach London before dawn because he was determined to see Mary Winters before he left to join the forces massing near Brussels. Now he delayed a moment, considering what Pierce had suggested. Finally he shook his head, still exercising control over his restive mount. "That might make it too easy to give in to the temptation to kill the bastard," he said, smiling down at his batman.

"We'll follow you!" Pierce shouted, but he wasn't sure Vail had heard him. The duke had already given the gelding his head, his body stretched low over the reaching neck.

Pierce watched a moment longer, until horse and rider had disappeared into the grove of trees, and then he turned and began to issue the necessary orders to the men who would go with him, once again following Vail into battle.

Chapter Seven

Mary stood a moment before the merchant's house, thinking that, despite all that had happened, it seemed unchanged since she had left three months before. Its ugliness was more apparent to her, perhaps, after the graceful architecture of the mansion in which she had spent the past week. The only attraction this dwelling held was the fact that her son was inside. Surely Traywick would allow her to see the boy before—

Again Mary denied the remembrance of that part of her mission, trying to blame the sudden trembling of her legs on fatigue. It had taken far longer than she dreamed it would to reach Penhurst in the carter's wagon because he had failed to tell her he had several other deliveries to make as well. She knew there was no time now to spare.

She knocked on the front door, attempting to bolster her courage as she waited. She caught a small movement of the parlor draperies out of the corner of her eye, but they were twitched back into place before she could determine who had looked out. Richard? she found herself hoping. Only a glimpse, she prayed. Just to know he's well.

The door opened as she raised her hand to knock again. The owner of the house stood before her. She knew then it had been Traywick peering out of the window, trying to identify his visitor. Praying it wasn't Vail, she thought in satisfaction. Somehow she was comforted at the realization that, although Traywick might deny being moved by Nick's threats, in truth he had not been unaffected by the thought of the duke's power.

"Why, Mary," Traywick said, subtle mockery in his eyes, "what an unexpected pleasure. I must confess, I wasn't sure that your...paramour would give you my message." His thick lips pursed as he fought an open display of his amusement. "But apparently he has now decided that, as I told him, this is really the way to accomplish what he wants. Indeed, the only way," he added.

"Richard?" she asked, instead of answering that ridiculous assessment of why she was here. Nick had not sent her, of course, and she blocked the thought of his reaction to what she was doing from her mind.

"Please come in, Mary. There is no need for you to stand on ceremony. Such old friends."

Traywick stepped away from the door, gesturing into the dim interior of the house as if she were a long-awaited guest. And remembering why she was here, remembering what had happened between them before, and his desire for revenge, she knew that was true.

"Where's my son, Mr. Traywick? I want to see Richard."

His head tilted, as if he were questioning her demanding tone. There was a pause before he answered, but his voice was as pleasantly urbane as before. "I'm afraid you've just missed him. Smithers has taken the boy for a ride in the new pony trap."

"Pony trap?" Mary repeated the lie sharply. Did he think her so naive as to believe that fairy tale? She had long urged that Richard should be taught to ride and to drive. The merchant had decried such skills as useless to any but a worthless member of the nobility, which his son would never be. Numbers and figures, he had insisted, and the stamina to work long and hard. Those were the only skills the boy would need to succeed his father.

"You always implored he have something besides lessons to occupy his days. The thought that the boy now has his own pony must be a great comfort to you," he suggested, allowing the smile he had fought from the beginning of their encounter to spread.

"I want to see him," Mary said.

"But of course you must. Richard has missed you very much. He didn't really understand the reasons for your absence. I'm sure he'll be delighted to see you again. You're welcome to wait for him inside," Traywick suggested again, his gesture toward the dark entry hall repeated. "Please. Do come inside, Mary."

There was nothing to be gained by standing on the threshold arguing with him, Mary realized. She had come here to give in to Traywick's demands, and she supposed it was possible her son was with Smithers. The man's missing arm had always held a certain morbid fascination for the child, especially after her gift of the toy soldier.

Reluctantly, she stepped inside, automatically walking toward the small parlor where she had spent so many nights waiting for the merchant's return. Waiting to serve him, to see to his comfort, she remembered. She recognized the bitter irony that although she was now the Duchess of Vail, she was still engaged in those tasks—still in service to Marcus Traywick. Bile rose into her throat, but she forced it down. She walked to the fireplace and then turned back to face the man who had stopped in the doorway of the room.

"I want you to instruct Bob Smithers to take Richard to Vail's estate," she said, "to put him into the duke's hands.

I want those orders issued in my presence. I want to hear exactly what you say to him.''

The yellow-brown eyes considered her, their contemplation almost feral, despite his slight smile. ''Of course,'' the merchant agreed. ''Whatever you wish, my dear.''

The tone was wrong, even given the fact that he knew he was going to get what he wanted. Her body was the price Traywick had demanded for her son's release, and she had come here prepared to pay it. But something was wrong. She could read deception in his eyes and in his voice.

''Where is he?'' she asked. Richard wasn't here, she realized suddenly. The silent house *felt* empty. She had no sense of her son's presence within these walls. Somehow she was certain they held only Traywick and herself, the woman he hated and yet, for some reason, still desired.

''I told you—'' he began, but she shook her head.

''That's a lie. I want the truth. I have come here to give you what you told Vail you wanted in exchange for my son. You at least owe me the truth.''

''The truth,'' he repeated, smiling, apparently amused by her demands. ''I'm afraid the truth is, Mary, that you are not quite so clever as you imagine.''

She forced her eyes to remain fixed on his, her features calm, but her breathing faltered with her sudden fear.

''A man as proud as Vail would never have allowed you to come here,'' Traywick said, ''so it is obvious you are here without his permission. And since he never intended to agree to my very reasonable suggestion, I now find myself wondering why he would even tell you about it.''

Mary hesitated before she answered, but Traywick was right. He had read Nick's character very accurately. He would never have told her of the merchant's demand.

''I overheard. He was telling...a friend, and I overheard

them talking. You're right, of course. Vail would never have let me come here if he had known what I intended.''

"And I suppose that as soon as he discovers you're gone, I may expect the duke and his henchmen to show up, armed to the teeth and prepared to rescue you from your martyrdom.''

"This was what you said you wanted in exchange for the child. I agree to your terms. Vail has nothing to do with it. Send Richard to him. We have plenty of time to complete our...transaction before the duke even becomes aware I'm here.''

"How did you arrange that?''

"Vail was to be away from the estate all day. During my morning ride I sent my horse back and paid a carter to bring me here. When the mare returns to the stables, they'll assume I've been thrown. The search should occupy several hours, even after Vail's return, because he has no reason to suspect what I planned, no reason to believe I would ever come here.''

Traywick's gaze had moved over her body as she talked, deliberately appraising it and making no effort to hide that appraisal. "At least he dresses you well," he said finally. "Far more becomingly than when you lived here with me, always taking such care to hide your body.''

"When will Richard be back?'' she asked, ignoring his attempt to unnerve her. She had to make him send the boy to Vail. It must be now, before she fulfilled her part of this despicable bargain. She couldn't trust him to do it later.

"Not for some time, I'm afraid. You seem in a hurry, Mary. Somehow I never imagined you would be this passionate.'' Again his lips curved upward. "Vail's such a proud man," Traywick said. "Arrogant, really. He won't take you back, you know. No matter what explanation you make for coming to me, he won't ever want you again.''

Mary said nothing because she knew that was true, of course. But what did it matter? There was nothing between them now. Nothing left of the lovers they had been so long ago.

"I, on the other hand," Traywick continued, "am quite willing to give you a home. Despite what has passed between us."

"I don't want a home. Not with you. Not any longer. I've come only to give you what you demanded. Send Richard to Vail, and then..."

"Ensuring the boy's safety seems to be such a concern for you both."

"Let him go," she said. "You care nothing for Richard. He's not your son. You can have other sons now." Suddenly there was entreaty in her voice, and she hated it, hated begging Traywick for anything. Only Richard was important, she reminded herself. Nothing else mattered. Not what happened to her. And not Nick, not what he would think about what she was doing. Not even the memories.

"Did you really think it would be that easy, Mary?"

Her eyes widened at the change in his tone. His voice no longer contained the false friendliness. And nothing of the anticipation that had been in his eyes as they examined her body.

"Did you really think, after what you did, that you could come here today and make demands of me?"

"I came to give you what you said you wanted."

"You have nothing to *give* me, Mary. I want nothing you're willing to *give*."

"But you said—"

"We have unfinished business," Traywick interjected, moving out of the doorway and coming toward her. His nearness was as menacing as the quiet promise in his voice. "In the course of that, I *will* have what you came here to bargain with. I will have your body. But I'll take it, Mary. I'll take you. That's the pleasure. Poor dutiful Abigail was always too willing. I had to work so hard to make her unwilling," he said smiling. "I don't want another sacrifice. I *want* you to fight me, and I want to be looking into your eyes when you realize your struggles will do no good.

"There's a moment, Mary, a sweet, brief moment when the spirit is broken by what the flesh has been forced to endure. You can read it in the eyes. I've looked forward to seeing that surrender in your proud eyes for a long time. And then, *only then*, Mary Winters, will I give you the boy."

"No," Mary said, feeling panic surge upward. Why had she not known he intended to cheat her? "Order Smithers to take Richard to Vail, or I'll leave."

"How do you think to accomplish that? No one is here to hear your protests. No one is coming to rescue you. You arranged that yourself. And I assure you that this time, my dear, I am better prepared for any resistance you might try to make. You really don't have a choice."

Mary hesitated a moment, weighing what he had said. There was only one thing that was important, one outcome that must be achieved. Suddenly, she moved, running past the merchant before he could stop her. Again he reacted quickly for a man of his girth, but, perhaps because he had mistaken her destination, she was able to accomplish what she had intended. While he was trying to prevent her exit by the front door, Mary ran instead toward the back of the house, to the small nursery beside the room where she had lived when she pretended to be her own son's governess.

Her mother's instinct had not been wrong. None of the child's belongings were where they had always been, no article of clothing hung on the low row of pegs, no small, worn boots were lined up under it. Even the box and the beloved wooden soldier were gone.

"Where is he?" She turned to demand an answer from the merchant when she heard him enter the room behind her. She had been such a fool to come here, she realized, a foolish child to think she could bargain with a man like Marcus Traywick.

"Somewhere safe, I assure you. You need not worry about the boy, Mary. *Unless,* of course, your husband interferes with me."

"He'll kill you," she promised softly.

He laughed. "Do you think so? I can assure you, my dear, that's the *last* thing Vail will do. I told him what will happen to the boy if he harms me. Like you, he doesn't want anything unpleasant to befall the child. Blood ties, I suppose."

"What did you tell him?" She remembered the look in Nick's eyes the night he had come to her room.

"Why don't you ask him? Later. After we've completed our...transaction." He repeated her word, mocking her. "Yourself in exchange for your son. And *then,* afterward, I'll send the boy anywhere you wish. Do we have a bargain, Mary?"

She had never truly realized the evil he was capable of. Vail had known. What Traywick said to Nick had made him know that he could never risk an attempt to take Richard by force, as she had begged him to do. Vail's hands were tied, despite his promises. Only she could get Richard back. And allowing Traywick to have his revenge against her was the price—a price she had come here prepared to pay.

"A bargain, Mary?" Traywick prompted. "I don't want Richard. As you pointed out, he now stands in the way of my own sons' inheritance. Why should I want Vail's bastard to be my heir? Do what you came here to do, and you may have the boy. With my blessing, I assure you.''

"If I do," she asked, "how will I know you'll keep your word?"

"You, of all people, have reason to know I'm a man of my word. A businessman must honor the terms of his contracts. You have had ample reason through the years to know that I will. I give you my word, Mary Winters, that when we are through, I will tell you where you may find your son. You have my promise, my solemn oath.''

In spite of everything that had happened between them, for six long years Traywick *had* honored the terms of their original bargain. Surely he would hold to this one. After all, it would be made on his terms, all the advantage his. And, as he had reminded her, she really didn't have a choice.

She looked up, fighting her despair, to find him smiling at her. Unable to push the words of surrender past the cold, hard knot of sickness that crowded her throat, finally she nodded.

The merchant had pulled the draperies over the windows of his bedroom, but he had lit no candles in the resulting dimness. The filtered light gave his scarred face a diabolical cast, sometimes hidden in the shadows and at other times too clearly illuminated.

"Disrobe first, Mary," he ordered, still smiling. "I always like to see exactly what I'm buying."

She obeyed as he watched, closing her mind to his presence. She slipped out of the habit that had belonged to Nick's mother and then her undergarments, carefully folding the items of clothing, as if she were alone. She laid them neatly over the back of the chair beside the bed, just as she might have done in the small room at the back of this house where she had once lived.

When she finally looked up, it was to find the merchant's eyes tracing slowly over the contours of her body. She fought her instinctual impulse to hide from their invasion.

He nodded, his thick lips unsmiling now. "I told him exactly what I would do to you. But he didn't tell you, of course, that I thought topping the Duchess of Vail would somehow be a more exquisite pleasure than taking my son's governess. And it seems it will be far more exquisite than even I had anticipated."

As he talked, his hands began the process of removing his own clothing, shedding the garments with a casual efficiency that belied his claim to eagerness. His nakedness was shocking to her, his torso thick and his limbs, in comparison to its bulk, almost grotesquely thin. She had seen only one man's body, and the perfection of Nick's had been nothing like this middle-aged disproportion.

She held her eyes on his face, forcing calmness, until he began to walk across the shadowed room. It was only when he stood before her that she gave in to her sickness and allowed her eyes to close, attempting to shut out the reality of what was about to happen, allowing only the image of Richard's dear face to invade her mind. Nothing else.

"Open your eyes," Traywick commanded. "Look at me." Because she had no choice, Mary obeyed, gazing into the muddied pools of hatred and insanity that Vail had already faced. Traywick reached out to cup his fingers around her breast, squeezing painfully, hard enough to bruise.

Mary had believed she was prepared, but she knew from the first touch of Traywick's hand on her body that she had been wrong. Something of her disgust must have shown, although she had been determined to school her features, to guard her inner horror, so that at least he would not have that satisfaction, of seeing her soul's surrender reflected in her eyes.

He caught her fingers with his other hand and brought them to the rough, mottled discoloration of the burn on his cheek. "Touch me," he ordered, pressing their flattened tips against his face. "How do you like touching this?" he asked. "How do you like feeling the results of what you did to me?"

When she made no response, he pulled her unresisting fingers downward, over his throat and onto the coarse mat of dark hair that centered his chest. His skin was too white, and the unpleasant miasma of perspiration that surrounded his unwashed body was strong. She forced down nausea as his big hand guided hers downward, over the protrusion of his belly, the flesh there loose and moist under her palm and trailing fingers.

She had fought him before, and had believed then, despite the charges he brought against her, that she had won. But this time struggling would give him the victory, satisfying his compulsion to see her surrender, to know that he had caused her pain. He himself had told her that. And so, even as he guided her hand downward over the rounded protrusion of his stomach to touch the still-flaccid masculinity below it, she forced herself not to resist.

"Show me how you touch him, Mary, how you caress him. Touch me as you touch that magnificent nobility," he jeered softly. "The sweet, innocent vicar's daughter, who gave herself to be Vail's whore. Did your father enjoy finding out what a slut you are, Mary? What did you say to him? How did you explain to him all those years ago that you had Vail's bastard growing here inside you?"

He touched the small convexity of her stomach with his left hand, but his right hand still controlled her fingers, forcing them to move against his body. "Did you say, 'He

used me, Father'? Or did you whisper, 'He loves me. He'll
marry me'? What did you say, sweet, innocent Mary Winters, to explain what you had done?''

As he talked, he continued to guide her fingers, captive
under his hand, up and down over his sex. There was no
response. No leap of flesh. No movement at all under the
repeated caresses.

Mary's eyes lifted to his, and without her conscious vo-
lition, there was within hers the knowledge that by her very
lack of resistance, she was again defeating him. He slashed
a backhanded blow, as sudden as the strike of a viper,
across her face with his left hand, the same hand that had
just gently touched her stomach. The force was taken on
her cheek and the corner of her mouth, the flesh cutting
against her teeth.

Shocked, she could not keep the reflection of that unexpected pain from her eyes. He had not released the hand
he held against his body, and although she instinctively
tried to pull it away, he grasped it firmly. Unbelievably,
she felt the response to her agony, his body stiffening suddenly under her fingers.

He smiled at her, and then, using the hand with which
he had just hit her, he gripped her breast again, drawing
her nearer to him by the pull of his hard fingers over its
softness. This time she fought not to respond to her discomfort, not to give him any further satisfaction. She had
offered herself to him, had agreed to his price, but something within her still resisted letting him have that almost
spiritual victory. He might have her body, she thought, her
eyes held on his through sheer force of will, but not her
soul. And her soul, she realized, was what he really wanted.

Suddenly the merchant released her breast. He put his
left hand around her throat, the grip of his spread fingers
tight enough to cause a small reactive panic. He was hold-

ing her so tightly she had to fight to draw breath into her brutally compressed windpipe. He began to back up, pulling her with him, easily controlling her by his grip on her throat.

When they stood beside the bed, Mary was almost faint with the lack of oxygen and the constriction of the blood flow to her head. Traywick forced her down on her back on top of the smooth coverlet. He positioned his big body above hers, moving her thighs apart by pushing his knee between them. He seemed to loom above her in the shadowed stillness like the embodiment of every nightmare she had ever had about him.

Still she fought the mental battle, fought to keep any reflection of fear and sickness out of her eyes. While he maintained his hold on her throat, he began to move his other hand against her body, pinching the most tender places, twisting delicate flesh between his hard fingers, deliberately bruising her, hurting her as he had hurt his wife. Seeming to relish the knowledge that, despite her determined lack of reaction, he was causing her pain.

Mary tried not to respond, not to let any soft gasp occasioned by his success escape between her bitten lips. She could not, however, prevent the involuntary tears. She saw satisfaction in the yellow eyes, and his hands shifted again, as he prepared now to try to enter her.

Nick, she thought, a last despairing prayer, grieving for what she had lost. What she was doing was so wrong, so against those vows that had always bound her. She had thought their power broken by the cold disinterest in the gray eyes. But no matter what Nick Stanton had intended when he uttered those promises so long ago, she had meant them, every syllable written indelibly on her heart. And now, instead of giving herself to Nick, who was her husband...

The sounds that exploded from the front of the house were unmistakable—sharp cracks of splintering wood, shattering under repeated, echoing blows. Something solid and heavy was being pounded again and again against the front door of this house. Traywick stopped all movement at the first sound, paralyzed, listening as intently as she to what was happening. As shocked by its unexpectedness.

"Mary?" The shout came on the heels of the noise the door made when it fell inward. "Answer me, damn it. Where are you?"

The words broke the breathless stillness into which the couple on the bed had frozen. *Nick,* Mary realized. *It was Nick.* Her responses were a jumble of confusion. Relief, of course—and fear, fear of his reaction to finding her here, of his knowledge of why she had come.

"Vail?" Traywick asked her in disbelief, his distended eyes demanding an explanation for this interruption she had promised him could not occur. Before Mary could formulate a reply, he lurched across her body, his long arm reaching toward the small table that stood beside the bed. He jerked open the drawer and fumbled inside.

When the merchant's big hand reappeared, it held the small pocket pistol he kept in the drawer, always loaded and ready for any thief foolish enough to believe that he might try to steal Marcus Traywick's hard-earned wealth with impunity. And that weapon was pointed now at the door leading into this room.

When Mary realized what he held, she stretched out her arms, both hands reaching, trying desperately to grasp the gun, but she was pinned securely beneath his weight. She struggled a moment before she accepted the futility of her effort. "Nick!" she screamed in warning, but it was too late. Her gaze flew to the open doorway just as Nick appeared within the darkened rectangle.

Despite the fact her eyes had seen and her brain identified what the merchant held, the noise of the shot, fired so close to her head, took her by surprise. Nick's movement into the room seemed to be checked at the sound; apparently he had been as shocked as she. The smell of burned powder was acrid, and she saw the smoke from the muzzle of the pistol drift aimlessly across the space between them. And then Nick's forward motion into the room continued.

When he reached Traywick, he didn't hesitate. His face contorted with rage, Nick put one hand into the merchant's thick hair and the other around his neck and jerked him off the bed. Despite Traywick's bulk, Nick threw him against the wall. The merchant stumbled into the table, knocking it over. Vail's fist thudded once into the fleshy face, the compact, muscled power of his entire body behind the driving blow. A trickle of blood appeared under the nostrils of Traywick's suddenly distorted nose, and he huddled against the wall, both hands lifted protectively before his face.

Nick stood a moment, fists raised in the classic fighter's stance, his body swaying slightly. Mary had watched, unmoving, the seconds-long exhibition of her husband's wrath, the exchange too one-sided to be called a fight. When the gray eyes turned away in distaste from the merchant's cowering nakedness, she was still lying motionless in the middle of Traywick's bed. Nick's gaze moved slowly over her exposed body, seeming to pause and examine each mark the merchant's hands had made on the smooth white skin.

When they came back to meet hers, Mary couldn't be sure of the emotion that was in their dark depths. Not the fury that had been there before. And not, surprisingly, the disgust she had expected.

Finally Nick moved again. He took a step nearer the bed, standing over her body now and not that of his defeated enemy. His hand moved, and she flinched away from it, believing that he intended to strike her.

"Mary," he said softly, his tone slightly chiding, as one might correct and comfort a terrified child. She saw his lips tighten, and then, holding her eyes, he completed the movement he had begun. He grasped the fabric of the coverlet she was lying on and pulled it across to cover her nudity.

"Nick..." she whispered, her voice trembling away into silence. There was nothing she could say to him. No explanation she could make for what she was doing here. There *was* no explanation for what she had done. Not even if she had done it for Richard.

"It's over," he said. "He won't hurt you anymore."

Her eyes glazed with tears, and through their mist she watched him turn back toward the chair where she had laid her clothing. He began to walk toward it, but there was something wrong. He caught the back of the chair, and held on, leaning against its support as if he had been forced by the length of that small journey to stop and rest. She sat up suddenly in the disordered bed, clutching the coverlet against her breasts, watching him. Something was wrong, but she didn't yet understand what.

Nick picked up her chemise, which was lying on top of the small pile. He turned back to the bed, his lips flat and white with the pressure he was exerting. He took a careful step, and then another. He stopped beside the bed, looking down into her eyes. Slowly he held the chemise out and, never looking at it, holding instead his eyes, she took the garment from him with her free hand.

He seemed suddenly to be leaning toward her, and he even put his hand down on the mattress beside her, but the elbow bent. Then his knees gave way, and he sat down on the floor, his shoulder leaning against the bed on which she lay. Mary scrambled off and dropped to her knees beside him, her right hand still holding the coverlet, which she had pulled from the bed, around her body.

Even in the shadowed dimness, she could see the hole the ball had made in Nick's coat, high on his chest. And the dark stain of blood beginning to seep out around it. Her hand trembled as she pulled the lapel of his jacket away from the wound, finding the white shirt and striped waistcoat already soaked with the crimson flood that seemed now almost to be pumping out.

"You shot him," she whispered, her gaze swinging from Nick back to the merchant. Traywick's mouth opened and then closed, but he said nothing, apparently as stunned as she by the realization of what he had done. "You've shot Vail." She whispered the accusation again.

The yellow eyes were full of fear when they met hers. For the first time since she had known him, Marcus Traywick's confidence in his destiny was destroyed. One did not kill a peer in England and get away with it. He knew that as well as Mary. There was no story he could concoct this time that would explain away what had occurred.

"I didn't mean..." he began, and then he stopped, his eyes again moving back to the man he had shot. "You'll tell them, Mary. It was an accident. The gun went off by itself. I never intended to fire."

"They'll hang you," Mary said softly, but the words echoed in the chamber like a curse. "And I'll bring *his* son to watch."

Then, the spell of horror broken, she turned back to her husband. She knew she had to stanch the flow of blood. She could hear Nick breathing, struggling to draw the necessary air into laboring lungs. She slipped her fingers into the knot of his cravat to loosen it, and then, realizing it would make an ideal bandage, she pulled the cloth from around his neck. She folded the linen into a thick pad, which she pressed against the bloody hole in his shirt.

Nick's eyes were still open, focused on her face. They seemed to be trying to communicate with her, but gradually whatever message had been in them began to fade away. *He's dying,* Mary thought, watching his lids slip downward to cover the gray eyes.

As she attempted to stanch the flow of blood, she was no longer even aware that Marcus Traywick was in the same room, nor was she aware when he began struggling into his shirt and trousers, pulling them and finally his boots on with shaking fingers. *They'll hang you,* Mary Winters had said, and Traywick knew it was true. Despite the threats he had made against the boy, he truly believed that Vail had come here prepared to kill him. The gun he held had seemed to go off by itself. His brain had not consciously ordered the pressure of his finger on the hair trigger. His panic had done that.

But it would not be enough for the courts, not given Vail's position. *They'll hang you,* she had told him. And he knew that they would. He had only one chance. To get out of England, where Vail's power and position would demand that his death be swiftly avenged.

Quickly and noiselessly, Marcus Traywick disappeared down the dark hallway that led to the back of the house. By the time Pierce and the men he had brought with him from Vail arrived, there was no one else in the tall brick house, no one but the Duke of Vail and Mary Winters, still kneeling beside her husband, pressing the cravat hard against the hole Traywick's bullet had blown in his chest.

Chapter Eight

Pierce's small, competent hands replaced Mary's, even as he questioned her about what had happened. When he had heard the story, the batman issued the orders that sent some of the men he'd brought after Marcus Traywick and another to find the village surgeon—orders none of them thought to question, as they did not question Pierce's right to take command in this exigency.

"Colonel," Pierce said softly when they were alone, only the three of them now. It seemed very quiet in the small room after the noise the milling men had made. Mary watched as the duke's eyelids lifted slowly in response to that familiar voice. "Hold on," Pierce ordered. "The surgeon's on his way. Just hold on."

The focus of the gray eyes shifted to Mary's face, and Vail's hand rose to touch the darkening bruise where Traywick had hit her, the small smear of blood vivid against the corner of her mouth, such a contrast to the paleness shock had given her skin.

"So sorry, Mary," Nick whispered. "I'm so sorry I failed you."

He sounded defeated, and like Pierce, Mary found herself wanting to compel him to hold on, to demand that he not give up. She caught the fingers of the hand he had raised, and pressed them against her cheek, but they rested limp and unmoving in her grasp.

"Don't," she said. "This is *not* your fault, Nick. None of this is your fault. I came here because I thought it was the only way to recover Richard, but I was wrong."

What had occurred was the result of *her* error, her misjudgment. She had wanted to free Richard from Traywick's control, but not at the cost of Nick's life. She should have known he would come to find her. Once again she had gone against all she believed, all her father had taught her. By offering herself to Traywick, she had again tried to break laws that should be inviolate, in order to achieve something she desired. And again, she feared, she would have to pay a price that was far too terrible for her sin.

"Richard?" Nick whispered. The word was little more than a breath, but she knew what he had said. It was the first time she had heard his son's name on his lips. And perhaps the last. She banished that despairing realization and smiled at him before she answered.

"He's not here. Traywick sent him away. I think he's hidden him." She touched his cheek lightly, her thumb caressing.

"So sorry," Vail whispered, and the gray eyes began to close. The watchers were aware that the last of his strength had been exhausted. He was slipping away from them even as they watched.

"Colonel," Pierce said again, but there was no response in the still, composed features. "Damn it," he breathed softly, pushing the rapidly reddening cloth more firmly against the wound. "Colonel," he demanded. Still there was no response.

"Is he...?" Mary began. But despite what they both knew, she couldn't put the fear into words. All the long years lost between them, and now, finally, when she was with him again...

"Talk to him," the valet ordered. "Talk to him about the boy, about anything. Make him understand that he doesn't have your permission to go. Tell him that the boy needs him. That *you* need him. Tell him, Mary, and make him understand that he mustn't let go."

She met Pierce's eyes, wondering, and then, seeing her own terrible fear reflected in them, she obeyed. "Nick," she whispered. She still held the strong, callused fingers in hers, but there was no reaction in them, or in the graying features. "Nick," she said again, making her voice stronger. "We have to find Richard. We have to discover where Traywick has taken him. I need you, Nick, to do that. We both need you. Please don't leave us again."

There was no bitterness in that plea, and this time, no recrimination. Whatever had happened in the past, whatever the reasons for what he had done, she knew that she would do anything to keep him alive. "Promise me, Nick," she said, willing him to respond. "Your word. Give me your word that you'll find our son. I want your oath. You owe me that. And you owe Richard."

His eyelids moved, struggling against shock and blood loss. But when he had succeeded in opening them, his eyes were unfocused, and she was afraid that he might no longer be able to see her, his vision obscured by the enclosing mists. At least he had responded. At least—

"Talk to him," Pierce ordered again. "Tell him about the boy."

She glanced at the batman's face. A fine film of perspiration covered his upper lip and his forehead. He was as frightened as she, she realized, that same ice-cold stream of fear running like poison through his veins. No one, however, knew Nick Stanton better than Pierce, and so, although she wasn't sure of his reasoning, Mary again obeyed, turning back to Nick, whose face was waxen in the dimness.

"He's so like you," she said softly, remembering—for the first time in so long allowing herself to remember—her son. "Like you in so many ways. I would look at him...and suddenly I would see you. In his eyes. His coloring." Her voice hesitated, the memories of the little boy she loved rushing into her mind in an overwhelming flood of emotion.

She made herself go on. "But...it was all the other things that were so hard. He moves like you. The same confidence, that surety of motion. Your strength of purpose. There were times that he'd look up at me, Nick, and I'd see you. As you were the first time I saw you. In my father's church, I think. Or that last day in the clearing. Or later, in the chapel," she whispered, and her throat was thick with suppressed emotion.

From the corner of her eye, she saw Pierce turn toward her, and again she made herself go on. "Despite the number of times that happened, it would always catch me off guard. Unprepared, somehow, to see you so clearly reflected in your son."

The gray eyes had found her face as she talked. Nick's gaze had fastened on the movement of her lips, as if it were necessary now for him to see the words form, as well as to hear them. But there was no doubt he was listening.

It seemed that she talked for an eternity, watching Pierce's hands, pressed hard against the wound, trying to keep the lifeblood from seeping out as they waited. She would never remember all that she had told him. About the wooden soldier, she knew. She described the uniform, blue and gilt, and the child's pleasure in it. She even told him about her sudden apprehension after she gave it to him that the boy would, like his father, want a military career.

She recounted all the quiet details of her days with Richard, the small pleasures drifting together in a pattern of peace and serenity. Then, remembering, she told him how she had begged the merchant to let her teach the boy to ride, and the reasons for his refusal. Nick's hand had tightened over hers, the movement very slight, but enough that she looked down into his eyes, called back from her recollections to the terrible fears of the present.

"Pierce," he said. The single syllable was very low, and it seemed out of context.

"No," the batman said, understanding what she had not. "That's a father's place. There are more lessons to be learned from a horse than good hands and a firm seat," Pierce said. "You know that right enough. Courage and honesty and heart—that's what he'll learn from his first horse. If it's the right horse, right for the boy. And that's *your* job, Colonel. *Your* place. No one else's."

Mary had turned at Pierce's comments, and she watched a tear track downward over the brown, lined skin of the valet's cheek. Blinking to clear the sting of moisture in her own eyes, she looked down again at Nick's face.

There was an infinitesimal movement of his head in response to what Pierce had said. A denial, Mary recognized. Or a surrender. *He isn't going to make it,* she thought. It was taking too long for the surgeon to come. Too long. The gray eyes began to close, and she knew with certainty that if they did, they would never be able to bring him back. They would have failed, she and Pierce, and Marcus Traywick would have won.

"No," she said, her voice too loud in the quiet, timeless vacuum the three of them shared. "No," she demanded again. "Not this time, Nick. Not again. Don't you dare desert us again."

"You were wrong before," Pierce said, adding his voice

to her argument, "and *they* paid for your error, Mary and your son. There's no room here for mistakes. And no room for cowards. You can't be a coward. Not this time. Not again."

The words were harsh, and surprised by their cruelty, Mary's eyes lifted to Pierce's face, shadowed as Traywick's had been with the growing darkness. "Pierce..." She whispered the protest, but the valet didn't look at her. His dark eyes were locked on the man whose blood had already soaked through the thick pad he held.

"This is not as bad as it was before," Pierce said, ignoring her, still talking to the man he loved better than he had ever loved anyone else on earth. Still denying him the release that would be so easy for him to accept. "We fooled them then, Colonel. Together we proved them wrong. And this time there's far more to live for. This time the boy needs you. You can't let that madman have your son. You're the only one who has any chance of getting him back. If you give up now..."

Pierce let the sentence trail off. Vail knew what the merchant had threatened. There was no need to remind him of what could happen to a defenseless child. The duke's gaze had moved to Pierce's face, and the gray eyes held on the tear-streaked features a long time. Finally Vail nodded, a minute downward movement of his head, but there was no doubt in the mind of either watcher what it meant.

And in Pierce's heart, at least, there was again hope. If will alone could keep a man alive, he knew, then Vail would live. He had given his word, and this was a man who did not make vows and promises lightly. Once made, Pierce knew, they would be kept. As, God willing, this one would be.

Vail's eyelids fell, and Mary's throat closed with fear.

"Pierce?" she questioned, that sudden terror in her strained whisper.

"It's all right," the valet comforted. "He needs his strength now. There's nothing else we can do for him. But if he can, Mary, I promise you, if he can…" Pierce's voice faded.

The woman beside him nodded, but she didn't release the cold, limp fingers she held until after the surgeon arrived and, kneeling beside her, took Pierce's place.

Mary could not bear the thought of Nick lying in the same bed where Traywick had brutalized Abigail, and no one questioned her decision. At her direction, they had carried the duke to the small bedroom at the back of the house where she had slept alone for almost seven years.

The surgeon's instruction before he left had been enough to shake them all. "Send for me tomorrow if he survives the night," he had said.

Mary and Pierce had watched as he probed for the ball, but Vail had never moved. Of course, his deep unconsciousness was a blessing, given the difficulty in finding and removing the bullet. Desperate then to stop the bleeding, the surgeon had applied a heated instrument to the wound, attempting to seal off the blood vessels.

The fingers of both hands pressed tightly over white lips, Mary had retched at the terrible sound, and at the resulting stench of burning flesh. Thankfully, Nick had not responded even to that agonizing procedure, sunk too far in shock, all his resources concentrated on maintaining the slim thread of life that bound him to this world.

Pierce had walked with the surgeon to the front of the house, but Mary could not bear to leave Nick. She remained in the chair they had placed beside the narrow, cotlike frame of her bed. His skin was so pale it was almost translucent. She could see, even in the candlelight, the small blue tracery of veins within the closed and sunken lids.

When the batman returned, he went to the fireplace where a low fire had been laid against the night's chill. Mary watched as he removed the stopper from a small glass vial and then upended the container over the blaze. The liquid that he poured out sizzled faintly as it struck the glowing logs, too reminiscent of the sound when the surgeon had cauterized the wound.

"What is it?" Mary asked, as the valet shook the bottle to send the last drops down into the open flame.

"Laudanum. The surgeon left it."

"Why did you pour it out?" Mary asked, shocked that he would deny Nick whatever medication the doctor had thought he needed.

"It's what they gave him before. All they had to give. Too much and for too long," Pierce said, pushing the stopper back into the empty bottle.

"In Spain?" she asked, puzzled by his tone.

"I didn't know him then." Pierce was still looking down, but she could see enough of his profile, highlighted by the fire, to be aware that the corner of his mouth had moved upward into a slight smile. "Only by reputation," he amended softly. "Only from the stories his men told about him."

Finally he turned to look at her, and then he walked across the room to stand beside the bed. He put the empty vial on the night table.

"Whatever happened before, you shouldn't have poured it out," Mary said. "When he wakes up, he'll need something for the pain."

"They gave him too much," he said again, as if that explained it all. "Not for the pain. Not *only* for the pain."

After a moment, Pierce put the tips of his fingers, their

touch as gentle as a woman's, against the thick bandages that wrapped across the duke's chest and over his right shoulder. No trace of red marred the stark white. The surgeon's desperate gamble had apparently stopped the relentless loss of blood. Although he had verified that the dangerous procedure was their only chance of closing the wound, he had also warned them quite frankly that it would probably kill his patient.

"But he'll die anyway, if this bleeding continues," he had said, standing beside the bed with the glowing instrument in his hand. The valet had glanced at Mary, hoping she would make the decision. It was her place. She was Vail's wife. But the blue eyes had been too wide, stunned with the sudden violence and filled with horror, instead of their usual calm serenity. So he had nodded, giving the surgeon permission and accepting this burden, too, as he had accepted that of caring for Nick Stanton so many years before.

It seemed to Pierce that the odor of burning flesh still pervaded the room, that same hot stench of death that had hung over the battlefield for days after Waterloo. Vail had survived in conditions far worse than these, Pierce told himself. And he had given them his word. *He'll do it if he can,* Pierce thought again, holding on to all that he knew about the man who lay too still, lost in that deep, unnatural sleep that is so short a distance from death itself.

"Pierce?" Mary questioned.

"Never give him opium, Mary. They knew nothing else to do for him. He finally broke his body's cravings, denied the drug's hold, but it was the only battle I was ever afraid he might lose. He can never have it again. Whatever Vail has to endure, he must do it without the drug. Do you understand?"

"Yes," she whispered. "Will you tell me, Pierce, what happened to him in Spain?"

"I've told you more than he'd ever want me to. The rest must come from him. Make him tell you the truth, Mary."

Pierce had never looked at her. He stood instead looking down at the man whose secrets he had just betrayed—secrets that had nothing to do with the war in Iberia.

Finally Mary's gaze followed his to study the alabaster paleness of the Duke of Vail's handsome features. She had thought her own life hard during those long years, and she had never even wondered what his had been. She had never considered anything but the broken promise—Nick had not come to claim her and his son. With Pierce's words, she began to wonder for the first time if there might have been a valid reason for that failure, a real explanation for why Nick Stanton had not come to find her the summer he came home from Waterloo.

Make him tell you the truth, Pierce had said, and she could only pray now that she would be given that chance.

The long days and nights slipped into a routine, a pattern of duties that she and Pierce shared but never discussed. It seemed they both understood their roles intuitively. She was the one who wrung out the cool cloths and then pressed them to Nick's burning forehead, trying to fight the climbing fever. The one who patiently coaxed him to swallow the water she spooned between his cracked lips, sometimes drop by slow drop. And it was to her that the surgeon had given his brusque instructions for cleaning the suppuration that crusted the angry red slash his hurried surgery and the subsequent cauterization had left on the bronze chest.

For all the other unpleasant tasks required in the care of an unconscious invalid, she was banished from the room, leaving Vail to Pierce's more than competent and remark-

ably gentle ministrations. They both knew this was what
the man they cared for would prefer. Even in this extremity,
they had unconsciously considered his wishes.

Mary had put Richard's situation from her mind, knowing that Nick's condition was a more immediate crisis.
Thankfully, she truly believed her son was not now with
the merchant, but had been sent away, perhaps with Bob
Smithers, who would be kind. *Somewhere safe,* Traywick
had said, and despite the character of the man who had
given her that assurance, she repeated it to herself a hundred times a day.

Pierce had promised her that everything that could be
done to find Traywick had already been set into motion.
All the vast resources of the Duke of Vail were being used
to hunt his enemy and ultimately to find his son, even while
the duke himself was engaged in this life-and-death struggle.

Mary had been surprised to learn that Pierce had not
called in the constables to bring formal charges of attempted murder against the merchant.

"Vail wouldn't want any more scandal, and I thought it
might be best, given what Traywick threatened...." He had
hesitated, the shrewd brown eyes assessing her face.

"I know what he said," she assured him. "Traywick
himself told me that he'd used threats against Richard to
protect himself from Vail."

"What I can't understand is why he shot the colonel.
That's the thing that makes no sense to me. Until then,
Traywick had the law on his side, and with his threats he
had insured that Vail would never dare harm him for fear
of whatever he'd arranged for the boy. Why would he risk
all that?"

"I don't think he intended to," Mary said, remembering
the merchant's words. "He reacted. He was afraid of Nick,

of his reputation, perhaps. Or afraid of what he'd do to him when he found…''

Despite the fact that Pierce was aware of the situation in which she had placed herself, Mary found it impossible to put that confession into words.

"*I* thought Nick would kill Traywick," she said instead, "no matter what he had threatened. Traywick must certainly have believed the same thing. He had taken the gun out of the drawer, he had it in his hand, and when Nick came in, he reacted. He pulled the trigger."

"He's a fool," Pierce said bitterly.

"He's a madman," she corrected. "A madman who is the only one who knows where Richard is."

"We'll find him, Mary. I swear to you. There are a hundred people looking for him. And if he believes Vail dead, he'll have no reason to carry out his threats against the boy. That gives us time to find out where he's hiding."

"And when you do?" she asked.

"He'll tell me where the boy is." Pierce's gaze fell to the still figure on the narrow cot. "When I get through with him that bloody bastard will be only too glad to tell me anything I ask," he promised.

The night had been endless, and Nick's fever and restlessness had increased as the slow hours crept past midnight. At some point, Mary had left the chair where she had maintained her long vigil to sit on the floor beside the bed and hold his hand. She had realized during the past week she cared for him that Nick was calmer if she touched him, if her fingers smoothed over the hot, dry heat of his skin, or if she simply talked to him.

But, exhausted by the long hours, she slipped finally into her own restless sleep. She still sat on the floor beside the bed, her head pillowed on her arm, which was propped along the edge of the narrow mattress. The soft night sounds in what had once been her room were all familiar, and their familiarity had been comforting, lulling her into sleep, despite her determination to watch over her desperately ill husband.

She awoke to the feel of a hand touching her hair. Because she had endured Traywick's hated caresses, she jerked out of sleep, panicked by the unexpected contact of what she had believed was his hand. She raised her head, pulling her hair away before she realized that the fingers that had been moving through her tangled curls were Nick's. The long strands were still spread out over the white bandage. One or two tendrils were caught in the perspiration that gleamed on the portion of his chest that was not covered by the dressing.

His eyes were open and looking into hers. At her recoil, he had lowered the hand that was stroking her hair. She could think of nothing to say. Nick was awake. Alive and conscious. In spite of the prayers she had whispered through this endless week, that was unexpected. Undeserved. She had truly believed Nick would die because she had tried to break her marriage vows, because she truly feared that she deserved to have to bear that punishment.

Instead, his fever had finally broken, she realized, looking down at the strands of her hair clinging to the dampness of his body, caught against the moisture on his skin like a lover's after a night of passion.

"Mary?" he said. Her name was a question. As if he couldn't believe she was really here.

"Yes," she whispered. She had not cried when Nick was shot. Or even as she watched the surgeon's seemingly merciless attempts to save his life. But now that it seemed he might live, the sudden flood of tears was too strong to deny. She felt the first trace downward, hot as it slipped over her cheek. Nick's eyes followed the path it took, watching even as it fell off her chin and onto his hand, which lay on the bed between them.

His gaze came back to her face. It was almost like the endless moment after Traywick's shot. She knew that Nick was trying to tell her something, but there was too much of the past between them. Too many unanswered questions. *Make him tell you the truth,* Pierce had said, but this was not the time, of course. This was the time to simply glory in the fact that he was alive. And after seven long years of unanswered questions, what difference could a few more days of waiting for that explanation make?

"Why are you crying?" he asked, his tone puzzled.

She smiled at the question. He probably didn't remember what had happened. Or even why she was here beside him. Fever robbed not only the body of strength, but also the mind.

"Because I'm glad you've finally decided to wake up," she answered truthfully.

"Where are we?"

"In Traywick's house. In my old room."

His head made a small, negative movement against the pillow.

"I don't..." He closed his eyes, allowing the sentence he had begun to fade away.

"I know," she whispered. "It's all right. You'll remember it all later."

She should tell Pierce. He deserved to know that Nick was awake, conscious and asking questions. He would recognize, as she did, what a promising sign this was that he would recover.

She pushed upward, her hand against the frame of the bed. Her knees were stiff from the hours she had spent sitting on the floor, so she stood a moment, waiting for the blood to circulate again through her legs.

His fingers fastened weakly around her wrist. "Don't go," he said.

She took his hand in both of hers and held it a moment, enjoying the feel of its long bones and the familiar calluses. "It's all right," she said. "I have to tell Pierce you're awake. He's been so worried."

"You'll come back."

"I promise," she whispered. She bent her head, obeying impulse and not logic, to put her lips against his fingers. And then she placed his hand gently back against the mattress.

Vail turned his head as Mary moved away from the bed, the gray eyes following until she had disappeared into the shadowed doorway. He was still watching when Pierce entered the room through that same door a few minutes later. And watching still, waiting for her promised return, when, exhausted by the small exertion of their conversation, he fell asleep again, Pierce's hard fingers this time enclosing the long, elegant horseman's hand.

Make him tell you the truth, Pierce had said. But she hadn't asked. Not yet, she had thought, carefully spooning the warm, nourishing broth into his mouth. Not yet, her heart had echoed, as she sat beside his bed through the long afternoons and watched him sleep—a natural sleep this time. Healing.

It was not until late in the evening of the third day after he regained consciousness that they exchanged more than a few, perfunctory words. Mary had been carefully cleaning the wound, and she knew the procedure was painful, although Nick had said nothing throughout the prolonged ordeal.

The gray eyes remained on her face as she worked, her hands trembling over the task for the first time. Too conscious that he felt what she was doing, too conscious that he was watching her.

"I'm sorry," she whispered when she had finished.

"For what?" he asked, dismissing her concern.

"For hurting you."

He shook his head.

"The doctor left laudanum," she went on, steeling herself against the sudden question in his eyes. "But Pierce poured it into the fire," she finished, watching his face.

Nick said nothing for a long heartbeat. And then he turned his head, his gaze no longer meeting hers, but focused on the merchant's fine plastered ceiling, over his head.

"Obviously he told you why," he said. His tone was more bitter than Pierce's had been when she had forced him to explain.

"Yes."

The silence stretched so long this time that she thought he intended to say nothing else. She had already begun to gather up the things she had used to tend the wound before he spoke again.

"Pierce told me about the opium eaters he had seen in India. About what happens to them. I didn't even understand that my body needed the drug. Surely nothing the doctors had given me could be harmful, I thought. It helped the pain, I told myself. And it helped me sleep. That's why I took it. Not for...the reasons Pierce said. But then I realized, as he pointed out, that I had gradually been increasing the dosage, and that finally... Pierce convinced me that whatever the cost, breaking my dependence on the drug had to be done."

"He told me that he was afraid..."

"I'd fail," Nick finished, when she paused. His lips moved into a smile, but there was no amusement in whatever he was remembering. "He should have been," he admitted softly. "He damn well should have been afraid I'd fail." His eyes came back to her face. "Have you ever seen an opium eater, Mary?"

"No," she whispered, shaking her head.

"You probably have, you know. They don't use the term in England, but the effects of the drug are inevitably the same. There are hundreds of us, sent back from the battlefields. Even now, the surgeons will deny the addictive power of laudanum, and they administer it freely. To ease suffering," he added, and the bitterness was again in his voice.

Mary waited through the long silence this time, hands clasped tightly together in her lap, knowing that eventually he would go on.

"Sometimes in London," he said, his voice as quiet as before, "looking out the window of my coach as it passes through the streets, I'll see a man huddled in a doorway, trying to find shelter from the rain. From the cold. And there will be something about him that will tell me... A look in his eyes, a missing arm, a crutch. Something. And I'll know what he is. As he would know me. I'll remember how it felt. The endless craving, so strong my very skin screamed for release. Only once more, I'll think. Even now—after all these years. Only once more."

"What do you do?" she asked softly.

"I pray for the strength not to go back and find out if he has any of the drug. For the strength not to beg him to share it with me. I drive on, never knowing if I'll be able to do that the next time."

"Pierce said—"

"Pierce had no right to tell you this."

"He was afraid the doctor would give the laudanum to me the next time. And I wouldn't understand. He was afraid I might give it to you."

"He had no right," Vail repeated.

"I needed to be told," she said. *Make him tell you the truth.*

Nick didn't look at her again, and he said nothing else, although she waited a long time. Finally she took up the basin and the stained bandages and carried them from the room.

Chapter Nine

When Pierce entered with the duke's supper, he realized very quickly that Vail was angry. He had seen his master's temper often enough in the past, but he had seldom been its target. Now, Vail's displeasure with him was clear in the winter landscape of the gray eyes and in the rigid set of his lips.

Pierce set the tray he carried on the table and sat down in the chair beside the bed. It was better to get it over with than to let it fester. He had broken Vail's trust, but for good cause. And the colonel had never been unreasonable. Eventually he'd admit the necessity of what had been done.

"You had no right," Vail said finally. His tone was calm enough, but Pierce had known him too long to be fooled by the deadly softness, a product of the control he was exerting.

"I thought you had enough to deal with, without chancing that. And she's your wife. She had a right to know."

The coldness in the duke's eyes was not mitigated by the explanation. "And the rest?" Vail asked.

Pierce shook his head. "I didn't tell her. Although it seems to me that she has a right to know that, too."

"I swear, Pierce, I'll dismiss you," Vail vowed.

"Before or after I tend your bodily functions, Your Grace?" Pierce asked, his own anger clear in the sarcastic pronunciation of the title he seldom used and in the less-than-subtle reminder of the services rendered during the past week. Apparently the remembrance of all the reasons he had to be grateful for his batman's devotion stopped further recriminations, but Vail's face was still hard-set. And the silence was as bitter.

"You tried to find Mary Winters for years," Pierce said finally, his tone reasoning. "What did you intend to do if you had?"

"To see she was safe. That she wanted for nothing."

"But *not* to make her your wife?" Pierce asked.

"At the time, I believe, there was some doubt as to that possibility," Vail said bitingly.

"And now?"

"She can't bear my touch. She flinches away if my hand brushes hers."

"She's nursed you like a baby. You're smarter than this, Colonel. Tell her. Explain it all, and begin again. You've been given a chance you never dreamed you'd have. You have a wife and a son, a fine boy you've never known. Will you throw that away again for the sake of your pride?"

"Is that what you think, Pierce? That it's only my pride between us?"

"What the bloody hell should I think? You tell me what *except* your damned pride is holding you back from telling that woman how you feel about her."

Again, there was silence. Finally the gray eyes looked away from Pierce's, to focus again on the ceiling.

"I called you a coward," Pierce said. "When he shot you. I thought you were dying, and I was trying to keep you alive."

At something in the tone, Vail turned back to meet the brown eyes.

"I had intended to make my apology for that," Pierce said, "but I don't believe now that I owe you one." He stood up and left the duke alone in the quiet dimness of Mary Winters's small bedroom.

Vail was still awake, still staring upward into the midnight darkness when Mary came in hours later. At the soft noise of her entrance, he turned his head toward the door, expecting that Pierce had relented and returned to sit with him through the long night.

Mary wore her rail, the same woolen shawl pulled around her shoulders that she had worn that night when he went to her bedroom. As she stood in the open doorway, the moonlight was behind her, outlining the shape of her slender body through the thin garment as clearly as if she wore nothing at all. And his heart paused, its familiar rhythm stopped by wonder and by memory.

Then she crossed the darkened room to look down on him. Did she come every night to check on him as he slept? He rejected that pleasant fantasy, remembering the way she had recoiled from his touch. She had not come here because she wanted to be with him. Something had happened. Something had provided a reason for her presence here tonight.

"What's wrong?" Nick asked. "Has there been news about the boy?"

"Richard," Mary corrected.

She put her hand lightly against his forehead. Her touch was impersonal, but still he reacted. Even weakened by illness, his body's response to her nearness was as strong as it had been in his youth—almost shocking in its intensity, mocking the old doubts. Ironically, despite the flood of heat that had flared through his body, she was apparently satisfied that he had no fever. She removed her hand, but instead of leaving, she surprised him by sitting down in the chair beside the bed.

"There's been no word," she said, "about Richard or about Traywick, but Pierce says everything that can be done is being done. He seems to be spending a great deal of your money to do it."

"We'll find him." Another meaningless promise, Nick thought bitterly, even as he said the words. A promise he had no way of carrying out. All he was capable of doing was lying here, entrusting the search for his son to others.

"Why are you still awake?" she asked.

"There are only so many hours of the day I can sleep," he said truthfully.

"And you didn't eat," she said, touching the tray Pierce had left on the table. "You have to at least try. Do you think, if I helped you, you could manage a few bites?"

"Thank you, Mary, but no. It's all right."

He didn't tell her that Pierce had been too angry to stay and feed him. His batman probably felt he deserved to do without supper, and he truly wasn't hungry. Too much had been said that he didn't want to hear. He knew Pierce well enough to be sure their confrontation tonight would not be the end of it. The ex-sergeant was not one to mince words, and they both knew the threat to dismiss him was an empty one.

Vail couldn't imagine his life without Pierce's friendship. He was the only person who told him the truth, and in the dark, lonely hours between the time of his batman's departure and Mary's unexpected arrival at his bedside, Vail had been forced to acknowledge that Pierce had told him the truth this time. He was a coward. At least where his wife was concerned.

"I needed to talk to you," Mary said, her voice floating to him out of the darkness. "When no one else is here. I wanted to tell you something that...I thought you should know. About Traywick. About the day you were shot."

"It doesn't matter," Nick said. It didn't matter to the way he felt about her, the way he had always felt. Pierce had been right about that. But he wasn't sure he could bear to listen to what she intended to confess, not even for her sake. Mary had done what Traywick demanded. She had done it to free his son from that madman, because he himself had not been able to, despite his promises.

"I think it does, Nick. I believe that it matters very much. I know that..." She drew a breath before she continued, deep enough to be audible in the quietness of the surrounding night. "I know that when you entered the room and found us together, you must have believed..." She paused again, because what he must have thought was too hard to articulate. "I want you to understand that I *would* have done anything to get Richard from Traywick." That made it sound as if she were offering excuses for what she had done, but explaining her actions was not really why she had come to him tonight.

"I'm not trying to justify what I did. But I wanted to tell you... When I heard your voice that afternoon, I knew I was wrong. I understood for the first time how wrong. And then...I was so afraid you were going to die because I had been wrong. Because of what I had tried to do. I thought I would have to pay for that sin, just as my father's death had been the price of the other."

"Mary..." He interrupted the painful narrative because he could not bear the guilt in her voice. He had been responsible for what happened between them in the clearing. His responsibility, and not hers. And he had always understood the motivations that sent her to Traywick's house.

She had borne alone the burden of assuring Richard's safety too long to relinquish it to the stranger he had become. A stranger who had once before betrayed her. Why should she have trusted him to do what he promised, to rescue the boy?

"But nothing happened that day, Nick," she said softly.

The impact of those words was far greater than even he could have imagined. He had accepted that she had given herself to Traywick, because he understood why she had, and because he loved her enough to accept. But with those words, somewhere deep inside, somewhere dark and hidden, an agonizing pressure eased. His eyes stung suddenly with tears that he prayed the darkness would hide.

"Not because I was unwilling," Mary whispered. She had come here to tell him the truth, and that was true. "But because he couldn't. He said he wanted me, but then... There was no response unless he was hurting me. That's the only way he can take a woman—to hurt her. That's why he mistreated Abigail. And when I—"

"Don't," he ordered softly, the images her words had created painting the darkness between them.

"He couldn't take me," she said, and there was something in her voice that he recognized as satisfaction. And triumph. She had defeated her enemy. "In the end, he wasn't man enough to do what he said he wanted to do."

Vail closed his eyes, the vivid memories of the small clearing where his son had been conceived in his head. His body straining above hers, his response to her so powerful. The instantaneous, unthinking reaction of his body to the touch of her hands and her mouth, to what she had offered.

He wasn't man enough to take me, she had said. And in her voice had been ridicule.

"Thank you for telling me," Vail said softly, because there was nothing else to say.

"I've never broken the vows we made, Nick. I swear to you that I never will. Whatever sins I may be guilty of in the future, I promise you that will not be one of them. Not even for Richard."

Those long-ago promises had been as binding to him through the years, but he couldn't tell her that now. Not with the images of Marcus Traywick's impotence so strong in his head.

"Go to bed, Mary," he whispered finally.

"Will you be able to sleep?" she asked.

"Better without you here," he answered truthfully, but even when she had gone, the sweet scent of her body lingered in the still darkness of the small room, and he couldn't sleep. Instead, he listened to the soft, feminine mockery that had been in her voice, echoing endlessly in his head.

The days slipped by as they waited for some word about the merchant's whereabouts. With the careful nursing Pierce and Mary provided, Vail began to regain his strength.

Despite their enforced proximity, despite her assurance that nothing had happened with Traywick, Mary knew that the distance between them had not lessened. She had been forced by Pierce's revelation to consider the possibility that there might have been some valid reason for what she viewed as Nick's desertion, so her own long-nurtured resentment had eased.

If her husband had given her any indication that he wanted a more normal relationship between them, she knew she would have responded. This was Nick, and she had discovered that what she had felt for him was not, not by any means, dead and buried in the past.

Vail, it seemed, had once more become the cold, distant

stranger who appeared that day at her trial, like some powerful deus ex machina, to rescue her. She could only guess that his renewed coldness had been occasioned by what had almost happened between her and Traywick. She didn't blame him. She, too, was sickened by what she had come to this house to do.

Occasionally, however, she would glance up to find Nick watching her, and then, before she could identify it, whatever emotion had been briefly revealed in the depths of his eyes would quickly be replaced again with polite disinterest.

One morning, almost two weeks after they had entered Traywick's house, another of the seemingly endless stream of messengers arrived. She took the news in to Pierce, who had undertaken the active command of the forces engaged in the search since Vail was injured. The batman was shaving his master, who was sitting in the chair where Mary had spent so many long hours. She stood a moment in the open doorway, watching them, before interrupting their masculine ritual.

"There's a messenger," she said finally. Two pair of eyes turned toward her in surprise.

"Would you finish this?" Pierce asked as he crossed the room to answer the summons she'd brought. He held out the razor he'd been using. "It's harder if the soap's allowed to dry."

She hesitated, because she knew that would be uncomfortable for them both. But she was uncertain how to refuse Pierce's request without making it obvious that she was conscious now of Nick as a man and no longer simply as an invalid in need of her care.

"Of course," she said finally. She had no choice. She took the razor the valet offered, and then watched Pierce hurry from the room, leaving her alone with her husband, something that had happened less and less frequently as Vail moved beyond the need for constant nursing. When she turned back to Nick, the gray eyes were lowered to study his hands, which were clasped together in his lap.

"It's all right," he said, as if he had read her mind. "Pierce can finish when he returns."

She raised her chin, determined not to offer any further revelation of the unnerving effect his nearness had on her. "I don't mind trying," she said, walking toward him. "Pierce makes shaving you look so easy, but I suspect it might not be." She cupped his chin lightly with the fingers of the hand that held the razor, turning his face so that the unshaven side was toward her and the light. "Don't worry. I promise to be careful. I really don't think you can afford to lose any more blood."

She put the thumb of her left hand against his cheekbone, holding the skin taut as she had watched Pierce do. She pulled the edge of the razor downward, removing the film of soap and, she hoped, despite her inexperience, the fair golden whiskers, as well.

Mary was very conscious of his nearness. She could smell the light sandalwood fragrance of the soap Pierce had used to soften the beard. And underlying that, she could also smell the unmistakable scent of Nick's body—clean and yet totally masculine. As the touch of his callused fingers had been, that fragrance, too, was still familiar.

Determinedly she ignored the sensations fluttering under her heart and, changing the position of her thumb slightly, she made another careful stroke with the blade. She was so close she could see the texture of his skin, fine-grained and beginning to regain the healthy color it had lost. She could even see a few strands of silver scattered in the golden hair at his temple. She had never noticed them before, because they blended so well, gilding the dark blond with shimmers of light.

She was almost afraid to breathe, because she feared the subtle, pleasant aroma of his body would cause her hands to tremble. Two more strokes, she told herself, and then she could escape. She would use as an excuse her curiosity about the messenger's news, although Vail knew as well as she that the arrival of such a courier was almost a daily occurrence. Pierce received constant reports about the search, despite its apparent lack of progress.

"Almost through," she said, wiping the blade against the rag Pierce had placed over the duke's shoulder. Her voice was thready, breathless with emotion, far too revealing of the effect this was having.

She looked up, straight into Nick's eyes, and this time they made no attempt to evade hers. Despite the passage of time, it seemed suddenly that they were back in the sheltered clearing, the soft sounds of twilight gathering around them. Alone. Together.

Almost against her will, her hands slowly lifted to frame his face. Her left thumb touched the center of his mouth, and her eyes left his to follow its movement along the outline of his lips. She swallowed, her heart beginning to pound.

She had wanted so much to touch him. This was why she had agreed to Pierce's suggestion. She could have pled ineptitude, inexperience, but instead she had agreed, because she wanted to be this close to him. Because she wanted his mouth over hers again. Where it belonged. Where it had always belonged.

"Nick," she whispered, her hands exerting a gentle upward pressure on his face, drawing him nearer for the kiss she was already imagining. He was her husband, and no matter the past, this was right.

She put her lips against his. Despite the years, there was no awkwardness. It seemed that this, too, was something she had never forgotten. The memory of how her mouth fit over his. The small, automatic tilt of her head to align them. His lips parted, and his tongue invaded, demanding, seeking, and her body responded, with the quick flood of moisture and the aching pressure between her legs. She wanted him. She had always wanted him. And the endless years of denial had only sharpened the sweet, hot edge of that longing.

Nick's hands found her waist, and he pulled her down into his lap, but he didn't release her mouth. The kiss continued, all doubts and questions forgotten in the strength of this single answer. Nothing here had changed. She was his wife, and he wanted her. She could feel the undeniable evidence of that desire, the hard arousal of his body straining upward under the softness of her hips. There was no doubt that he wanted to make love to her.

Memories moved in fleeting patterns through her mind, shifting as the sun through the leaves had shifted that day, dappling their joined bodies with light and shadow. His fingers caressing, gliding with surety and grace over soft, feminine contours. His warm lips following where his hands explored, moving against all the hidden, suddenly erotic places, evoking a heat within her that matched the passion of his. Until she had begged him to complete what she had begun.

She had been unschooled, unlettered in these arts, until he undertook her instruction. With infinite patience, he shattered her world, and then rebuilt it again, with himself at the center. Re-creating her, touch by touch, kiss by soft kiss, invasion by demanding invasion, he had shown her these mysteries. And she had never forgotten.

His hand cupped under her breast, curving with familiar

tle pressure, she felt again the agony of Traywick's broad, spatulate fingers, gripping there to control her, to cause pain, rather than the sensuous pleasure of Nick's lovemaking.

Into her head, chasing away the shadowed wonder of the clearing, came other memories. The merchant's grotesque, flaccid nakedness. The loose, hot wetness of his lips. The casual brutality of his nightmare hands moving over her body, and the bruises they had left on her skin, marks that were only now fading to yellowed smudges against the blue-veined whiteness of her breasts.

She lifted her head suddenly, mouth open and gasping slightly for air that seemed too thin, too rare. She put her hands on Nick's shoulders and pushed away from him, out of his lap and away from his hands. Nick's hands, she remembered. Not Traywick's. She had nothing to fear from Nick. He had never hurt her. And he never would.

Those other memories did not belong here, between them. They had no place. She wanted to explain it to him, but it made no sense that, held in his arms, she should have been afraid. It made no sense, even to her. Another punishment for what she had done, for what she had tried to do? Would the memory of Traywick's assault always be in her head when Nick touched her?

"Mary?" he said softly.

His eyes were watching her, questioning also, she realized as she stood trembling beside his chair, still breathing too rapidly, still inexplicably afraid. Without offering any explanation for what had happened, Mary put the blade Pierce had given her down on the blanket he had spread over the duke's legs and fled the room.

Vail had not slept that night, remembering what had been in Mary's eyes. Fear, he had finally decided. Memory of what Traywick had done to her? Or memory of his own betrayal? He could still see her pupils, wide and dark, the rim of blue narrowed and almost lost. But he had not mistaken what was in them before. Her mouth had lowered to his, and everything that had once been between them was in her kiss. Trust and forgiveness. Desire. Love. But when she raised her head, breaking the contact, in the midnight blue had been something he had never seen there before. He might not be sure of the emotion that had prompted her withdrawal, but there was no doubt that it was he she had fled.

His pride, Pierce had confidently assured him, was all that stood in the way of reconciliation with Mary. And when her lips lowered to meet his, sweetly offering herself to him again, almost he had believed that might be true. But Pierce couldn't understand all the things that lay between them. That tangled web of old fears. And now the new ones, created by Traywick's insanity.

What good would it do to make the painful explanation of those terrible months after Waterloo, if the woman he loved could not bear his touch? Would she desire him more because of his open admission that only his cowardice had led to that long-ago betrayal? And he heard again the unthinking mockery in her voice when she told him of Traywick's failure.

With the arrival of dawn, Vail had finally thrown off the covers and carefully risen, protecting the damaged muscles of his chest from his movements as well as he could while he drew on his trousers. This was not the first night he had secretly risen from this narrow cot. Pierce hovered over him like a hen with one chick, but Vail knew time was running out. When word came that some trace of the merchant's trail had been discovered—as he prayed God it would soon—he would have to be ready to act, despite the frustratingly persistent weakness.

Pain was a familiar companion, one that could be ignored. It was the other, the debilitating effect of fever and blood loss, that concerned him now. And so, despite Pierce's admonitions, he sought every opportunity to rebuild his strength and to test his slow success. He had not so far ventured beyond the confines of this small room, but there was something he needed to do, something he had wanted to do now for several days.

He took a couple of unsupported steps until his fingers closed gratefully over the tall back of the chair that still stood beside the bed. Continuing to use pieces of furniture, he navigated the short distance out of the room and into the narrow hall. The door of the nursery had been left open, so Pierce could hear him if he called in the night, he imagined. Nick smiled at the thought of that overprotectiveness, but he understood the love that was its source.

As if drawn by a magnet, his hand occasionally against the wall for support, he continued to move into the room where his son had lived. There was enough light seeping in from the high, curtained windows to allow him to examine its meager contents. A schoolboy's desk and slate. A cot pushed against one wall, the still form of its occupant almost hidden in the shadows.

There was nothing else. No item of clothing hung now on the low row of pegs. There were no small boots lined up beneath. No miniature riding crop. None of the disordered collections that small boys invariably treasure. And no toys.

The nursery at Vail had teemed with toys and riding gear, with birds' nests, stones with intriguing shapes and textures, strangely colored feathers that had floated down from some exotic wayfarer of the sky. Even the multihued leaves of autumn—all the plundered flora and fauna of the English countryside, the beloved kingdom of childhood through which he and his brother had roamed at will.

His own hoard had included what he, at five, was sure was a tiger's tooth, until Charles, with the mocking superiority of older brothers, called him a dolt and informed him there were no tigers in Britain. Nick's mouth moved slightly, almost a smile, remembering the hot flush of embarrassment at having his ignorance pointed out. And remembering also the simple pleasures of his boyhood.

There were none of those things here. There was nothing reminiscent of his own explorations and endless adventures. His son's room was as barren as a prison, devoid of the simple joys that all children have a right to. Instead, like the merchant's house itself, this room was as dead and cold as the gray ash that lay beneath the empty grate.

As he turned, preparing to make his way back to his own room before he woke Pierce and was forced to endure another lecture, something caught his eye. A shaft of dawn sun threaded the space where the curtains almost met, and a touch of gold glinted suddenly against the dark hearth.

Nick gripped the narrow mantel with his left hand and eased his body down, lips set tight against the pull on the half-healed wound and the familiar ache in the muscles of his thigh. He must have made some sound, a small sigh of effort or some almost unconscious acknowledgment of that discomfort, because behind him he heard the sleeper stir. By that time, Vail had managed to lower himself far enough to touch with the tips of his fingers the object that had attracted his attention.

It was a fragment of wood that had fallen through the grate. Despite the charred and blistered condition, there was enough of the blue and gilt paint left to identify what he held—part of the wooden soldier's leg, blackened with heat. He rubbed at the soot with his thumb, and the painstakingly applied double stripe of gold up the outside seam of the trousers sparkled suddenly in the growing light.

Mary's description of this had whispered out of an enclosing mist. Her words had almost been lost in the circling darkness of shock, but because it was Mary's voice, he had forced his wandering mind to listen. The child's only toy, she had said, a painted wooden soldier.

All that was left was this charred remnant. Vail did not understand the significance of the toy's destruction, but because he understood so much now about the evil of the man whose house they occupied, his throat closed with fear, and his heart ached for the son he had never known. He had deliberately fought any paternal pull since he learned of the child's existence, knowing that those feelings would only weaken him, but standing now in this joyless room, he was profoundly disturbed by the thought of the boy's loss.

"What is it?" Mary asked from the shadows across the room. "What are you doing here?"

Mary had been the occupant of the cot, Vail realized. Not Pierce. It had been Mary who slept next door to the room where they had taken him. She had been the one who listened through the night for his call.

He was surprised by the impact of that realization. *She's nursed you like a baby,* Pierce had said. Because she still cared for him, despite what he had done? His hand closed around the fragment he had found, and using the support of the mantel, he pulled himself upright. His head swam slightly with that effort, and he leaned a moment against the wooden lintel, trying to think what he could say to Mary that could possibly explain his presence here.

"I didn't know you slept here," he admitted. "I came because I wanted to see..." He paused, knowing that be-

cause of his pride his son had been deprived of the childhood he himself had known. If not for that, and for the
decision that his pride had led him to make seven years
ago, he might have had the shaping of the boy's life in his
own hands, instead of fragments.

"To see where he lived," Mary said. She had not been
mistaken. Nick had not changed.

"There's nothing here, Mary. Nothing children treasure—leaves, rocks, feathers. A tiger's tooth," he whispered, remembering. "There's nothing."

"Because that wasn't allowed—to bring something from
the outdoors into the house. Traywick was not...fond of
nature," she said simply. It was an understatement, of
course. He had practically forbidden her to take Richard
outside. And so she had tried to fill his days with other
things. Stories told or read aloud, and simple children's
songs after lessons. The warm ritual of afternoon tea. To
make the child's constricted life pleasant had been an
unending effort in which Abigail was a willing conspirator.
But Nick was right, of course. She, too, had had the same
country childhood he remembered. For their son there had
been no meadow romps, no childhood games with neigh-
boring children, no woodland excursions.

"But he wasn't unhappy, I promise you," she said, almost defensively. Her eyes fell to the coverlet that she had
lovingly tucked around Richard so many nights. "I did the
best I could, Nick, to see that he knew joy. He loved the
soldier. Whenever I watched him play with it, I alway
thought of you," she confessed. "And wished he coul
know his father."

So many refuse to take responsibility for the careless
seeds they sow... Traywick's words had haunted him. Careless seeds.

"I wish..." Nick said, and then again his throat closed

hard and tight, with all the things he wished for. "Dear God, Mary, I wish I had done so many things differently."

"If wishes were horses," Mary said softly. She smiled at him, as she had smiled at Richard when she had to answer that same desperate longing for something he knew he couldn't have.

Nick watched as a single tear tracked downward across her cheek, her blue eyes suddenly brimming with moisture that was visible even in the shadows.

Then beggars would ride. She was right, he thought. He was a beggar. Despite all he possessed, his life had come down to this. A lonely, hungry beggar, desperately wanting something infinitely precious that he had never had.

Chapter Ten

All over England Pierce's agents searched without success for any trace of the merchant. It was as if Traywick had vanished the day he shot Vail. Almost another week passed before they had the news they had been waiting for.

Vail was standing by the window of the merchant's parlor, looking out into the front garden, when the messenger arrived. He watched the exchange of information, and then listened with both dread and anticipation to the sound of Pierce's boot heels as the batman hurried down the hall.

"There's news," Pierce said simply, stopping in the doorway. The hushed excitement in his voice was enough to let the duke know that he believed whatever he had come to tell them was important.

"What is it?" Nick asked. He watched Mary put her needlework down in her lap, obviously attempting to remain calm. He could imagine that her anticipation was far greater than his. Finally, some word, and he prayed it was what they had been waiting for.

"On Monday a man picked up a packet for Traywick from his London bank. Our informant remembered the courier quite clearly, because he had only one arm. A countryman, he said, judging by his clothing."

"Bob Smithers," Mary said. And then she asked the important question. "Was Richard with him? Did anyone see Richard?"

"There was no sign of the boy. Not then and not later."

"Later?" she asked, still hoping that this was leading somewhere.

"Smithers was also seen here in the village yesterday."

"But he didn't come to the house," Mary said, trying to understand. "If he was on an errand for Traywick, why wouldn't he report to him? Why didn't he come to this house?"

"Because by now gossip has surely spread the word about our occupation of it. And probably the word that Traywick has fled."

"Do you know what was in the packet Smithers picked up in London?" she asked.

"We have no firm information about that, either," Pierce admitted.

"Surely the bankers—" she began, and Pierce interrupted.

"They've pled their client's confidentiality," Pierce explained. "But it doesn't matter. A clerk at the bank, who was more than willing to be bribed, believes that what Traywick sent Smithers to pick up was money, the result of financial dealings he knows Traywick had ordered the bank to carry out several weeks ago."

"Liquidating unencumbered assets because I had threatened to foreclose on his debts?" Vail guessed.

Pierce again nodded his agreement. "It seems likely."

"But how can knowing any of this possibly help us find Richard?" Mary asked.

"Apparently as soon as Smithers heard the village gossip, he left." Pierce paused, his sense of the dramatic strong, but Vail waited, unmoving, because he knew that eventually they would be told. They had waited this long. And for all his efforts on their behalf, Pierce deserved his moment of glory.

"Traveling east," Pierce said, his voice rich with triumph, "toward the coast. I've already sent riders to track him, although if he chooses to avoid the main roads—"

Mary interrupted him. "The coast?"

"Good God," Vail said softly, realizing all the implications, apparently before the others. "To meet Traywick there. Traywick's leaving the country," he said. "That bastard is leaving England. And if he does—" He stopped, because of the sudden fear in the blue eyes that lifted to his.

"Wait," Mary said into the sudden silence. "Maybe you're wrong. There's another explanation. Traywick owns a house on the coast. Somewhere to the south of Deal, I think."

"There was nothing about coastal property in the information I received," Vail said.

"But he's sent Smithers there in the past. To carry messages for him. I've heard him give the orders, Nick. Whether or not it's his property, I can't be sure, but he uses it as if it is, and he has for years."

"If that's true, then it's possible he's been waiting for Smithers there," Pierce said, thinking of the search he'd set into motion. No wonder no one had seen him. "He's just been sitting there, waiting for his money to come to him, as snug as a bug in a rug."

"Can you give us any more direction, Mary?" Nick asked.

She shook her head. "All I know is that the house is on the sea." She looked up suddenly. "And it has a name. I remember because I thought it was such a strange name for a house. It's called Owls' Maze."

"Owls' Maze," Pierce repeated. "Why would anyone name a house—"

"Owlers?" Vail suggested, his mind racing over the possibilities. "Smugglers are called owlers on that coast, because they use the bird's calls as signals. If that's the case, it's no wonder the property isn't listed in Traywick's name."

"You think he's engaged in smuggling?" Pierce asked.

"It's possible. But the important thing now—"

"Is getting there," Pierce finished. "We shouldn't have any trouble finding the house. Someone will recognize that name." He turned away from the door to begin the arrangements for their journey.

I should have killed the bastard when I had the chance, Nick thought bitterly, *when my hand was fastened around his thick neck.* Instead, he had let him go, trying to protect the boy, and now there was a distinct possibility that as soon as Smithers arrived with the money he'd been waiting for, Traywick would simply disappear into Europe.

Vail again blocked the images that had haunted him since the merchant made his threat. He couldn't let Mary know he was afraid, but he had also found that he couldn't make another empty promise about finding the boy. Because, for the first time, with the knowledge that Traywick was sitting poised and waiting on the edge of the Channel, Nick was no longer sure that they would.

Despite his recent injury, despite the promise of worsening weather, which they all knew would make the day's travel a nightmare, Vail was adamant. They would not leave him behind. That was not even a possibility. *And not open to discussion*, he said to Pierce, the gray eyes hard as stone, but still Pierce argued with him the whole time the arrangements were being made. Until finally Mary put her hand on his arm.

"You're not doing him any good," she said. "Help him dress instead. You know he'll never give in."

The batman's eyes met hers, and in them she could read his frustration and even his fear, but she knew that *she* would not consent to be left behind, worrying and wondering about their success. Vail's determination to travel with them to the coast was somehow comforting. She had not been wrong about that, at least. Whatever problems might lie between the two of them, he was as determined as she to find his son.

For the duke's sake, Pierce had planned their travel in easy stages, despite the acknowledged need for haste. Vail, however, quickly countermanded most of his valet's instructions. There would be no armed outriders, only the three of them, traveling in an unmarked coach. The trip would be made as swiftly, and as unobtrusively, as possible, to prevent any chance that Traywick might somehow have warning of their approach.

The hired coach and four thundered along well-maintained thoroughfares, at least until the rains turned the road into little more than bog. A fresh team was harnessed at each posting inn, but conditions worsened as the day progressed, slowing their progress. It was almost dark before they reached the coast, the scent of salt sharp, despite the rain.

Mary's legs grew stiff with the infrequent opportunities to descend from the coach, but, of course, she did not complain about their speed. Nick's orders were sure and precise, and the driver pushed the coach through the lengthening, rain-drenched shadows of late afternoon and into the misty, sea-fragranced twilight, stopping only long enough for the hostlers to change teams, without any consideration of his passengers' discomfort.

As the journey progressed, however, Nick's set lips and his unobtrusive attempts to protect his body from the rough motion of the struggling coach convinced Mary that he was suffering far more from the effects of the trip than she. She wanted to urge him to lean against her and let her body cushion the toll the pace he had ordered was taking, but he had given her no indication that he would welcome her concern.

After hours of sitting beside him in the forced intimacy of the closed carriage, she was too tired to sort out the feelings that had bombarded her heart and her head during the last weeks. Too tired to exert control over her instinctive desire to care for the man she had acknowledged, to herself, at least, that she still loved, and too fearful that they might not find Traywick and Richard at the end of this journey. She needed Nick, and she thought that he needed her, that they needed to comfort each other, if there was nothing else.

Pierce sat in the opposite seat, but it had grown increasingly difficult to see his face with the rain and falling night. Perhaps he would not be able to see them, she thought, and then she realized that she no longer cared if he could. If Nick rebuffed her, then at least she would have tried—one less thing to regret when this was finished. So she moved against him, easing her tired body next to the solid warmth of his. She did not dare look up at him, but she was aware of the small movement of his head, turning toward her in the dark interior of the carriage.

Nick's weight shifted slightly, and for a heart-stopping moment she thought he was preparing to move away from her. Instead, his arm came around her shoulder, and he drew her closer. His lips gently touched against her hair.

He said nothing, but words were not important. Not any longer. She didn't need explanations. She needed Nick. To hold her.

Her hand slipped bravely into his. Thankfully, she felt the long fingers of his left hand encircle hers. She closed her eyes and leaned back, resting her head against his shoulder. And through the last difficult miles they were once more together.

Just as Pierce had predicted, they had had no trouble finding the house Mary had told them about. The old man they questioned on the outskirts of Deal had recognized the name at once.

"Aye," he'd said, taking off his cap as Pierce called to him out the window of the coach, "I know the Maze. A bad place, especially for strangers. A right unwelcoming house, if you take my meaning." But the directions he provided had been accurate, and within half an hour they had arrived at their destination. The coachman pulled up the exhausted team at the foot of the bluff the structure crowned to give them their first view.

Unwelcoming it certainly was. The brooding hulk, silhouetted against the evening sky, seemed deserted. It loomed above them in the darkness, more menacing somehow in the rain, with a narrow, muddy track winding up to it, the footing almost certainly too treacherous for the tired horses.

"If this is the place," Pierce said, "then it seems we're too late. It looks uninhabited, and as if it has been for some time."

"By design, I should think. If Traywick's hiding here, he couldn't afford to let anyone suspect," Nick suggested.

"Pray God, he *is* here," Mary said softly. That was exactly what she had been doing during this seemingly endless day's journey. Praying that Traywick had not already escaped to the Continent. Praying that Richard would be here and be safe.

Nick's hand tightened over hers. As if by a miracle, the long-guarded barriers between them, which had seemed insurmountable only days before, finally began to crumble.

"Shall I knock, Colonel?" Pierce asked when they were at last standing before the front door. The house appeared as deserted as it had from below. There were no lights and no sounds in the gathering darkness.

"No," Vail said. "As little warning as possible. He'll know we're here soon enough."

He picked up a rock, hefted it to feel the comfortable, solid weight in his hand, and then he slammed it against one of the thick, old-fashioned panes of the window. The glass shattered inward, making far less noise, with the rain and the wind, than Mary had expected it would. Nick reached inside and released the latch, pushing the window upward. He stepped back, and turned to look at his batman.

"Pierce," he said, smiling invitingly. "I think the honor must be yours."

"Me, Your Grace? You want me to climb into a man's house like a thief in the night?" the batman said innocently, but then he quickly placed his hands over the sill and pushed upward, drawing his slight body through the opening and disappearing inside with the skill and grace of an acrobat performing at a country fair. It was a matter of seconds before he had the front door open and Vail and Mary stepped inside.

The smells that greeted them were all unpleasant. There was an underlying odor of stale cooking and mildew. As they stood in the open doorway, the dank, malodorous air inside the house seemed to swirl by them, attempting to join the salt-touched freshness of the rain-washed night beyond.

"Do you think we might be lucky enough to locate a lamp?" Vail asked.

Despite the clouds and the rain, there was enough moonlight from the open doorway to allow Pierce to find a flint and to light the candles in the tarnished silver candelabra, which he found ready on the entry hall table. The illumination they provided was no more flattering to the dwelling than the murky dimness of the storm had been. Each room they traversed was depressingly the same: water-stained paper peeling from the walls, rugs so dark with dirt and mold that their patterns were no longer distinguishable, massive furniture shrouded under mildewed holland covers. And no sign of recent occupation.

"There's no one here, and apparently no one's been here for a long time," Mary said despairingly when their exploration had reached the back of the house. The wide windows here looked down on the overgrown back garden, on the narrow path that ran along the top of the cliff, and beyond that on the sea. In the cloud-filtered moonlight, whitecapped waves churned against a narrow ribbon of shingle beach dotted with standing rocks, gleaming black with moisture from the spray and the rain.

"Upstairs?" Pierce suggested. He glanced at Vail, but the duke was still looking downward toward the sea.

"I think," he said, "that we might have better luck below."

Pierce was surprised to see that the duke was smiling. "On the beach, do you mean?" he asked.

"Owls' Maze. Remember? I'd wager the most interesting part of this building lies under our feet."

"In the cellars?" Mary asked.

"And below them. It's an old smugglers' trick. To cut

tunnels that lead from some isolated spot along the coast to whatever building they're using to hide their activities. That would be easy enough to do in the chalk. Their goods are then stored in the passages, both entrances carefully concealed from the king's revenue officers, until they can be taken out of the house.''

"To bring in contraband? That's why Traywick has this place?'' Pierce said.

"He's a merchant, and by all accounts he's been a remarkably successful one during the last fifteen years, despite the uncertainty of the postwar economy,'' Vail confirmed.

"He did it all illegally,'' Mary said. She was not even surprised by the revelation. She now knew that Traywick was, of course, exactly the kind of man who would circumvent the law and think nothing of it, if it turned a profit.

"Smuggling has long been a way of life along this coast, those who engage in it more frequently admired than despised. The war simply made what they'd been doing for centuries more profitable.''

"But the Saxon coast was garrisoned,'' Pierce said. "Are you saying Traywick was able to carry on the trade under the very noses of the army?''

"The forces stationed here were looking out for an invasion of Napoléon's navy, not for smugglers. That wasn't their job.''

"But if you're right, how do we get down into the tunnels?'' Mary asked.

"We find the entrance inside the house—and it won't be easy. Don't underestimate the ingenuity of whoever built this place.''

It was Vail, of course, who discovered what they were looking for, cleverly hidden in a panel of the wainscoting in the dining room. He opened the concealed door, and it moved readily, the perpetually damp wood creaking only slightly in protest. Pierce held the candelabra into the opening.

Steps had been cut in the rock foundation on which the house had been built, steps that led downward to disappear abruptly into blackness beyond the reach of the feeble light cast by the candles. Even this far from the sea, the stone walls on either side of the narrow stairs were wet with glistening condensation, glowing eerily in the flickering light. But the air in the passage seemed cleaner, somehow, than that which they had been breathing inside the house.

"I'll go," Pierce said. "The two of you can wait here until I've seen what's down there."

"Not bloody likely," Vail said softly. He took the candelabra from his batman's hand before Pierce could protest and started carefully down the narrow steps, his free hand on the sweat-slick wall. There was a metal holder near the top of the stairs, obviously intended to contain a torch that could be used to light the descent, but it was empty now.

Pierce glanced at Mary before he stepped down onto the first of the winding stone-cut stairs, once again following Vail. Mary knew that they expected her to remain here, safe at the top of the stairs, but she had no intention of being left behind. She hadn't from the beginning. She wasn't sure what to do about the door to the passage, so she left it open, and followed what were by now only the sounds of Pierce's descent before her. She stepped bravely down into the cloying blackness, lit by the thin, wavering light of the candles Vail carried far ahead.

The stairs wound downward as the air grew colder. Eventually they led to a room, large and level, like the floor of a cave. The worked walls made it obvious, however, that this had been man-made, cut by hand into the chalk. There was a table littered with dirty dishes and a narrow cot pushed against one wall. A few boxes were stacked on the other side of the room, the condition of the wood from which they were fashioned making it obvious they had not been sitting in these conditions for very long.

Vail walked over to examine them. He set the candles down on the top of one stack and, picking up a crowbar that was lying nearby, pried a board off the box on the top of the adjoining pile. The candlelight shimmered off the thick green glass of the bottles the crate held.

"Brandy?" Pierce asked.

"Spirits, at least."

"There's no embargo on French spirits now."

"But there are still duties. Bringing it in illegally and avoiding those would mean much higher profits."

"Look at this," Mary said softly, moving into the light.

"What are you doing down here?" Vail asked.

She stood at the bottom of the stone steps, shivering slightly in the cold.

"Finding this," she said. She held up the torch that had been missing from the holder at the top of the stairs. She had found it lying in the shadows beside the bottom step. Even in the dimness, the thin trail of white smoke that drifted upward from the top was clearly visible. As they watched, it was caught by the current of colder air they had felt since they entered the room. It wafted slowly past Pierce and Vail. to disappear beyond the light cast by the candles.

"Someone was down here, only moments before we arrived," she said.

It was obvious from the torch that she was right. Vail picked up the candelabra again, following the direction the smoke had taken. It led him to a rock wall, gleaming with moisture in the flickering light of the candles. It seemed they had reached the limits of the underground room.

Mary was surprised when, instead of exploring in another direction, Vail held the light higher and began to examine the wall slowly, almost inch by inch. When the flames suddenly bent toward what appeared to be a natural seam line running through the rock, Vail moved closer, using the limited illumination to track the crack upward and then, in the other direction, down to the floor. Finally, he handed the candelabra to Pierce, and began pressing his hands along the seam, obviously feeling for something. Apparently he found what he was looking for. As if by magic, the wall shifted before him, swinging inward. A narrow chalk tunnel lay beyond the opening, slanting downward toward the sea.

Vail turned back to face them, putting his finger across his lips in warning. Then he took the light from Pierce and again led the way through the tunnel he had discovered.

It was a more harrowing descent than the narrow, winding stairs had been. The angle at which the floor slanted made walking difficult, and the passage they followed would level out unexpectedly or would abruptly fork in front of them, forcing the duke to choose between two seemingly identical branches. There were markings on the wall, and once or twice Vail stopped, holding up the candelabra he carried to examine them. But the symbols made no sense—they were obviously some type of code—and eventually he ignored them. Owls' Maze, Nick thought, had been aptly named.

He wondered how far from the house they were now and how high the tide was at this point on the coast. They had been traveling laterally for quite a time. From the slant of the tunnels, he knew they had also descended deeply enough into the bowels of the cliff that a high tide might be dangerous, sweeping in to fill the narrow tunnel if, as he believed, the passage eventually led to the sea.

It seemed he could hear the sea more clearly, and the air

was thick with moisture, making each breath an effort. The wound in his chest had begun to burn, and the deep ache in his leg was as much a product of the cold dampness as the strain the steps and the slope of the tunnel had put on it. But he believed Mary had been right in her conjecture. Someone had descended through this labyrinth only minutes before they entered it. If their speculation that this was Traywick's lair was correct, it seemed there was still a chance they might stop him before he left England.

Nick had come to another branching, and he stopped a moment to catch his breath, unconsciously massaging the aching muscle of his thigh. The noise that suddenly surrounded them was muffled, but it rumbled through the chalk walls on either side, vibrating even through the ground on which they stood.

Not the sea, Nick knew, but *something* he had heard before. He should recognize the sound, tantalizing in its familiarity, but it was out of context here, so his identification was too slow. It was not until a stream of rushing water lapped against his boot that he made the connection.

It was the sound made by raising a drawbridge or the portcullis of a fort or a castle. Something equally heavy, operated by gears and pulleys, was being pulled upward. Something just as cumbersome, perhaps even more difficult to raise, he had finally realized, because of the pressure of the water dammed up behind it.

"What the hell is that?" Pierce whispered behind him.

Vail turned, and the light he held highlighted the strained faces of his companions. It flickered briefly over the moisture caught in Mary's hair, drops flashing in its darkness like diamonds. Her eyes were on his face, and he hoped none of his sudden terror was reflected there.

"Sluice gate. Someone's opening a sluice."

"But why?" she asked.

"To flood the tunnels."

"From the sea?" Pierce asked.

"It's coming from the wrong direction. It must be backwater, a marsh or river they've dammed. Get Mary out of here, Pierce. Take the candles and go. Back the way we came."

"Dear God, Colonel, I can't remember the way we came."

"Then just upward. You have to get above the level where the water is coming in. And keep climbing. Just climb, damn it. Go on."

"What about you?" Pierce asked. Vail had thrust the candelabra into his batman's hands, but at the question, he pulled a single candle from it.

"I can't make the climb back, not quickly enough, anyway. I'm going on to the sea." That was not the reason, he acknowledged, to himself, at least. His leg would probably slow them down, but not enough that they couldn't get above the incoming water. He could not give up the thought, however, that Traywick was ahead of them—or the desperate hope that there might still be a chance to stop him from leaving England.

"We're going with you," Pierce said, his face white in the shadowed darkness.

"But you can't swim," Vail reminded him gently, smiling at him again, just as he had when he invited him to crawl into the window he'd broken. "And neither can Mary. You go up, and I'll go down. There's certain to be a path from the top of the cliff down to the beach. You can find it once you get her out, and join me there."

"Swim," Mary repeated. "Surely you don't think you can—"

The water swirled around their feet, and the low rumble

continued, joined now by another sound. The faraway rush of a great volume of water coming toward them.

"Now," Vail said softly, but there was no question it was a command. The tone was not one the batman had often heard from the man he served, but Sergeant Major John Pierce had been a soldier too long to ignore an order from his superior, most especially in the heat of battle. He grasped Mary's arm and pulled her, still protesting, back up the way they had come, leaving Vail alone in the tunnel.

Chapter Eleven

Vail began to run—not, he acknowledged ruefully, with the unthinkingly smooth and graceful stride of his boyhood. But the motion of his forward progress, awkward because of the damaged leg and the steep slope of the passage, was much faster, at least, than the careful descent they had made before. He prayed that by now Pierce had gotten Mary above the level of the waters' entrance into the tunnels, and he prayed, also, with grim determination, that he would reach the beach in time to stop Traywick.

The water rose far more quickly than he had imagined it would. Too soon, it was more than knee-high, pushing against the back of his tired legs as he slogged onward. He fell once, his crippled leg suddenly giving way under him, throwing him forward down the slope as the brackish water rushed over his head. He pulled himself up to lean against the chalk wall, gasping for air, his eyes and nose stinging from their immersion in the brine.

The worst part of that accident, however, was the loss of the candle. He was trapped now in a tunnel that seemed blacker than night in hell. Even as he rested, leaning against the wall, drawing precious air into his aching lungs, the water continued to rise, swirling now almost around his waist. He wondered if he could find the strength to take the next step, and then suddenly he realized what a fool he was. He bent his knees, sinking almost gratefully into the foaming cascade, which surged with growing power through the narrow channel. He stretched his arms in front of him, streamlining his exhausted body, and let the strong current take him exactly where he had wanted to go all along—downward, to the sea.

His arms and shoulders bore the brunt of the unexpected twists and turns, more abrupt branchings, which the water rushed him through, and which in the darkness he had had no way to avoid. But still it was better riding the crest of the small flood—better until, after what seemed another eternity, his head scraped hard against the top of the tunnel. He turned his face to the side for a last quick inhalation, knowing the passage was now completely flooded. Then he began to swim with the last of his strength, forcing the movement of arms that felt almost detached from his body and far too heavy to lift.

Finally, when it seemed that he must open his mouth and breathe, even if it was only to welcome the certain death that surrounded him, his body popped like a cork to the top of the stream that had carried him. He lifted his head and took a deep, gasping breath, cold air rushing into his starving lungs like a miracle.

Eyes stinging, he strained to see into the blackness before him. He was in a room, another man-made chamber cut into the chalk, he realized. But this one opened onto the beach. Between the dark sides of its opening, he caught a glimpse of the ocean and the night sky, stretching across the narrow horizon that lay before him. The current, which had carried him through the tunnel, flattened out after it swept through the fissure, becoming a fanlike channel that rushed outward into the incoming tide. The next time he managed to raise his head above the level of the water, he saw the boat, struggling slowly across the churning surface of the sea.

There was no sail, and the rower was frantically plying the oars, fighting against the force of the tide, which was attempting to push the vessel back to the shore. The beach had almost disappeared, covered by the merging waters. The crest he had ridden out of the tunnel continued to carry him into the spume of the incoming waves. He could distinguish the scattered rocks from the black water by the white spray that shot upward around their bases. He turned his body, almost managing to avoid the boulder that had risen suddenly before him. The stone scraped against his back, but the pain was so much less than the others that he scarcely was aware of what had happened.

He pushed his arms down against the dark water of the next wave, lifting his head to get another look at the boat. A fishing vessel, he decided, large enough only for the two men it carried, silhouetted above the ocean and against the lesser darkness of the evening sky.

As he sank into the trough between waves, the small boat disappeared from sight, but he had registered several important impressions in the seconds he watched it. There was only one rower, his thick body hunched with the effort of pulling at the oars. The other man sat with his back toward the land. He was not rowing, but guiding the tiller. Because, of course, it was impossible to row with only one arm. Smithers. And Traywick.

The realization that he was this close seemed to explode within Vail's brain and then move through his exhausted body like an electric current. He would have said he had no reserves of strength, but the sight of the boat had energized him. Somehow his arms, which had only minutes ago seemed as heavy as stone, began to flail again through the waters.

He ignored the waves breaking over his head, breathing in the troughs between. He didn't bother to look up to pinpoint the boat again. He could only trust to the divine providence that had brought him this far that he was still headed in the right direction.

He swam, no longer conscious of exhaustion or pain. No longer conscious of directing his body to repeat the movements, he simply swam, hoping to catch the boat, with no idea what he planned to do if he did. All he knew was that Traywick was escaping, and with him would disappear any hope of finding his son.

He almost passed them in the darkness. Only at the merchant's startled shout did he look up. The dark side of the boat loomed above him, blocking any view of the sky. Somehow, he managed to throw his arm over it. His fingers locked on something, and then he began the nearly impossible process of pulling himself out of the water and over the side of the boat.

"Get away, you bastard!" Traywick screamed. The wind caught his words and flung them into the rainswept night.

Nick ignored him. He managed to clamber halfway into the boat, its wooden side rubbing painfully against the nearly healed wound in his chest as the boat rocked. With the next wave, water poured over the edge he was clinging to, threatening to swamp the vessel. Which, he decided grimly, might be better for his purposes than attempting to climb in. If he could dump Traywick out of the boat and into the water, he could drag him back to shore and make him talk.

"Get off!" Traywick screamed again, obviously terrified that Nick would accomplish what he had just thought of. The merchant threw one of the oars he had been using into the bottom of the boat. With the broad end of the other oar, he began to push against Vail's shoulder, attempting to dislodge the man who held on like a stubborn barnacle. The vessel rocked more strongly with the next wave, water again rushing in a flood over the side.

"Mr. Traywick!" Bob Smithers shouted, wrestling with the tiller. "Be still, sir, or you'll swamp her!"

"*He's* the one who'll swamp us!" Traywick shouted back, his scarred face contorted with rage, appearing almost inhuman in the driving rain and the brief snatches of cloud-dappled moonlight. "Help me get him off," he ordered.

The ex-soldier, long accustomed to obeying the commands of his employer, began to move forward, abandoning the tiller. The boat plunged violently with the shift of his weight, and he lost his balance, sitting down abruptly in the bottom.

"You clumsy fool!" Traywick screamed at him.

Undaunted by Smithers's failed attempt to stand in the pitching boat, and having apparently realized that his efforts to push Vail off were having no effect, the merchant stood up, legs spread wide, swaying like a drunkard to keep his balance. He raised the oar high over his head, preparing to bring it down on the back of the unprotected skull of the Duke of Vail.

"Look out!" Smithers screamed. For years he had served Traywick without question, pushing to the back of his mind the knowledge that not all the things the merchant was involved in were legal or moral. But he was not prepared to see murder done. Not on a defenseless man.

At the ex-soldier's warning, Nick looked up in time to see the descending blade of the oar, black and growing enormous in the split second he watched it. Instinctively he released one hand's frantic hold on the boat and threw up his forearm in an age-old protective gesture. The heavy wooden paddle struck Vail's arm, which seemed to go numb, paralyzed by the force of the blow. The agonizing shock was so great that the fingers of his other hand unclenched, losing their desperate hold, and Vail fell backward into the sea. Even as the oar descended, Smithers had thrown himself forward in a desperate attempt to prevent Traywick's strike. Aware of his movement, the merchant then swung the oar toward the ex-soldier, this time sideways, as if it were a scythe, catching him in the midriff and knocking him into the water on the other side of the boat.

Without a backward glance toward the two men he had thrown into the cold, dark waters of the Channel, Traywick grasped the other oar and set to work again, propelling the small craft through the darkness of the storm, rowing frantically like the madman he was for the sanctuary of France.

Pierce and Mary stumbled upward, hurrying through the maze of the tunnels like a pair of hapless mice chased by a London rat catcher. Mary's legs trembled from the steep upward angle of the climb, but despite the fact that it was clear that they had left the rising water behind, Pierce wouldn't let her stop to rest.

"The colonel said to the top," he gasped, again taking her arm to pull her onward. "And when he gives an order, it's for good cause, and he expects it to be carried out. If he thinks the water might rise this far…"

The words stopped as he ran out of breath, but there was no need to finish the thought. Vail had said they were to go to the top and then down to the beach, Mary remembered. And with the promise of what Nick had believed they might find there, she began to climb again, despite the ache in the muscles at the back of her calves.

After too many false turnings, they finally found the rock

door that led to the room that held the contraband. Once inside it, Pierce allowed her a brief rest. She leaned against the stacked boxes, panting with the exertion of the climb they had just made. Too quickly, Vail's batman touched her arm and pointed toward the stairs that twisted upward into the darkness.

Pierce took time to light the torch, leaving the candelabra behind. It smoked damply, but once they had begun the ascent of the narrow stone steps, the fumes drifted upward, away from them and toward the house. The light the torch provided was much better, illuminating enough of the passage that this time Mary could, if she wished, have seen her hand before her face.

By the time she had crawled back through the secret entrance in the dining room, Pierce was running to the front door through which they had entered the house. She could hear him, once he reached the outside, shouting to the coachman they had left standing below, in the rain, with the poor horses.

She doubted that he would be able to distinguish the words of Pierce's message, given the wind and the distance, but there could be no mistaking the sweeping gesture of his arm. She looked down in time to see the coachman secure the reins and begin toiling up the muddy road the three of them had climbed earlier. Pierce didn't wait. He rounded the house and began to run along the path that followed the rim of the cliffs, stopping occasionally to look downward. Finally, he scrambled over the edge and disappeared.

Mary ran after him, ignoring her aching legs and lungs. By the time she reached the spot where Pierce had descended, her skirts, drenched with the rain, were tangled around her ankles and calves. She stopped at the summit, gathering them in one hand and making a loose loop of the wet fabric to keep them out of her way.

When she looked over the side of the cliff, she could see Pierce, moving rapidly down a set of shallow steps that had been cut into the face of the chalk. Below and beyond his hurrying figure there was only the gray-green darkness of the sea, shrouded by rain. And in the midst of it, moving up and down with the swells, was a small boat, a dark smudge against the horizon, surrounded by the capping waves. Traywick, she thought in despair. Traywick.

There was something else in the water, she realized, wiping the rain from her eyes to get a better view. There was a man in the water. Nick? Dear heavenly Father, she prayed, please don't let it be Nick, foolishly swimming out that far in pursuit of the merchant. However, as she watched, it became obvious that the figure, little more than a blackened speck against the lighter waters, was not moving in the direction of the boat, but struggling to come back to the beach.

Knees trembling, Mary began the descent, no more careful of her footing down the treacherously wet steps than Pierce had been. Nick, she thought again, but when she paused, halfway down, holding her cupped hand above her eyes to block the rain, she couldn't see anything in the water but the boat, rapidly diminishing in size as it widened the distance between itself and the shore.

By the time Pierce reached the foot of the white cliff, the incoming waves were sweeping up over the bottom steps of the stairs that had been cut from the top of the cliff. He ran across the shingled beach, water splashing under his boots. Two men staggered out of the sea, holding to one another, water streaming from their clothing. Before

Pierce could reach them, one of them collapsed, falling to his knees into the shallows.

"Colonel!" Pierce yelled. "My God, Colonel, are you all right?"

His mind automatically made the identification of the other man, the man with only one arm, who stood gasping beside the fallen figure. Suddenly his body arched forward, his remaining hand resting on his bent knee, as he was shaken by a paroxysm of coughing. As Pierced watched, his body convulsed and a stream of seawater spewed out of his mouth into the foaming surf.

The other man was Vail, Pierce had realized as he got closer to the pair. The duke on his knees, his left hand hidden by the water. Apparently it was resting on the shingles, holding him upright. Pierce had already begun running toward him when Vail's elbow bent and he fell forward into the water. The batman knelt beside his master, helping him to sit up, supporting his shoulders with his arm.

"What happened?" he asked, looking up into Bob Smithers's face, which was pinched and white with the cold.

"Traywick hit him with the oar," he gasped. "Then he knocked me out of the boat when I tried to stop him. Knocked the wind out of me in the process. I'd have drowned out there if he hadn't held me up until I could get me breath."

Pierce's eyes cut to the sea, but the small vessel Vail had been trying to stop had disappeared into the darkness and the rain. He would send runners, Pierce thought. They could pick up the trail again in France. He'd see to it all. As soon as he'd assured himself that Vail was all right.

"Colonel," he said again, his eyes on the exhausted man he held.

"Go after him, Pierce. He's getting away."

"He's already gone. We were too late to stop him."

Vail's eyes closed against the pain of that. He had failed them again. Mary and the boy.

"Can you get up if I help you?" Pierce asked.

"Of course," Vail said, but, unthinkingly, he put his right hand down on the gravel to push his body up. He gasped aloud when he put pressure on the wrist Traywick had struck, and he was forced to fall back against the support of Pierce's arm until the agony faded.

"The bastard may 'a broke his arm when he hit him," Smithers explained, bending down to help.

Between them, they got Vail to his feet. Pierce put the duke's left arm over his own shoulder, and they began the slow journey to the foot of the cliff.

Vail looked up to see Mary running across the shallow water toward them. Her skirt was tied up over her chemise, and the material of the wet undergarment was plastered against her legs as she ran. Her long dark hair had come loose, and strands were clinging to her face and neck and whipping behind her as she ran. Her midnight-blue eyes were wide and dark, searching their faces for some clue as to what had happened.

So brave, Nick thought. As courageous as the men he had once led into battle. She had followed them downward into the nightmare trap of the tunnels, and then here, negotiating in the darkness the narrow steps cut into the cliffside. He wanted to open his arms and catch her to him, to hold her, to explain to her how hard he had tried.

But trying wasn't enough, of course. He had tried to find her before, during the long years his stubborn pride and his fear had cost them, and that effort had not been enough. Nor had his efforts tonight. Traywick was gone, and there was nothing he could do. He removed his arm from Pierce's shoulder and straightened his body.

"He got away, Mary," he said. "I couldn't stop him."

She had checked her rush at the realization that he was injured, fighting her urge to throw her arms around him.

"What's wrong?" she asked softly.

"It's his arm," Smithers said. "Traywick broke his arm, I think, for trying to hold to the boat. For trying to stop him."

Mary glanced toward the ex-soldier for the first time, as if she had just realized he was there. "Were you helping him, Bob?" she asked unbelievingly.

"Not to do murder," he assured her. "I don't do murder for no man."

"I'm so sorry," Vail whispered, his eyes still locked on Mary's pale face.

"We'll find him," she said comfortingly, turning back to him, trying to find a smile to give him, to reassure him that she understood. "We'll find Richard, I promise." Neither of them realized the irony. He was the one who had made those same empty promises through these past days. And now Mary was offering comfort for his loss.

"Why do you want to find Mr. Traywick's son?" Smithers asked.

"He's not Traywick's son," Mary said fiercely. The old lies would not serve, not now. It was even possible, she thought, that Smithers, who had been helping Traywick, might have some information about the boy's whereabouts. "He's *my* son. My son and Vail's," she said, looking back toward Nick.

"But…he's always been Mr. Traywick's son," Smithers argued. He clearly remembered the merchant's warning that his enemies would try to harm the boy if they found him. These two were, he knew, the enemies his employer feared.

"He's *never* been Traywick's son," Mary said, remembering all the horror the merchant had put them through.

"I only let him be raised as his son because..." The old guilts, or the old urge to protect her son, made her hesitate over the confession. "I gave him to Traywick and Abigail when he was born." She could see the doubt on the ex-soldier's face, and she knew that the reasons for what she had done were all too complicated to explain tonight. "He's my son. And Nick's."

"But..." Smithers began, wondering if it could possibly be true. He had always known that Traywick had lied about Mary Winters stealing the household money. Was it possible he had lied about the other?

"Look at him," Mary said softly.

Following the direction of her eyes, Smithers turned back to face the duke. Vail's fair hair, darkened from his immersion in the sea, fell over his forehead, and the gray eyes looked straight into those of the man whose life he had just saved.

Breathlessly Mary waited, while the ex-soldier examined Vail's features, which had—to her mind, at least—been so flawlessly mirrored in his son's.

"I've seen you before," Smithers said, still studying the duke's face.

It was not the response she had expected, and Mary almost broke in to urge him to consider the resemblance, but the ex-soldier went on, speaking again before she could interrupt.

"I don't ever forget a face, and somewhere I've seen yours," he said.

Vail shook his head, having no recollection of ever having met the man before.

"You called him 'Colonel,'" Smithers said to the batman.

"Stanton," Pierce said simply, knowing the name and the reputation were almost legendary. Vail would need no other introduction to a veteran. "With Wellington in the Peninsula, of course, and at Waterloo."

"Stanton," Smithers echoed.

Into his voice had come a tone that Pierce, at least, had no trouble recognizing—the same soft awe with which his own men had always spoken of Nick Stanton. He hadn't heard the sound of that reverence for years, but he had no trouble identifying it.

"I saw you that day," Smithers went on. "That day you went after that drummer boy who was downed. Never saw nothing like it for raw courage in my life, and I've seen lots of brave things done by good men. I even thought for a moment you was going to make it back, carry that boy to safety, despite the French barrage. And then... I swear, Colonel, when I saw that shell hit, I thought you was dead."

"So did I," Nick agreed softly, remembering it all too vividly. The force and even the heat of the shrapnel striking his own body and that of the child. The last shuddering breath the dying boy had taken in his arms. Their mingled blood, far too much blood, grotesquely staining the breeches of his uniform. And then, finding the memories still, after all these years, almost too painful to bear, he destroyed those images.

Vail smiled at the ex-soldier with the camaraderie that was automatic between those who had served, never affected by differences in rank or position. "Luckily," he began, and then realized, almost for the first time since he had regained consciousness in that crowded, makeshift hospital, the stench of death and the noises of dying men all around him, how true that was. "Luckily," he said again, softly this time, savoring the sound of it, "we were both wrong."

"They said you was a good officer. Not one of them as stands behind and lets his men take the brunt. You was front and center, they said, leading the charge. But in spite of that, I couldn't believe what you done that day. I never saw nothing like it. You, not only an officer but a prime nob, they all said, risking your life to save that poor boy. A boy who was nothing to you. Not even—''

''It happened a long time ago,'' Nick said, interrupting him. He had never lived in the past, recounting his exploits. He had no respect for those who did. Despite all he and Pierce had shared through the years, the battles they had fought in were never a topic of conversation between them.

''At Waterloo?'' Mary whispered. *I thought you were dead,* Smithers had said. Had Nick been wounded again, without her ever having known? Could that explain...?

Smithers turned toward her when she spoke, and then, apparently recalling what she had asked him to do, he looked back at the duke. ''He's your son?'' he asked simply, knowing now that if this man said it, it was true. ''Richard Traywick is your son?''

''Stanton,'' Nick said softly. ''His name is Richard Stanton.''

For some reason, at that quiet avowal, Mary's eyes filled with tears. She had not known, until he said the words, how much she longed to hear Nick make that claim. To finally hear him openly acknowledge his son.

''If you have any information about his whereabouts that might help us find—'' Nick began.

''I can take you to him,'' Smithers said.

Mary's breath caught at the simple words. ''To Richard? You know where he is?'' she asked.

''I should,'' he said, smiling at her. ''Since I'm the one that took him there. Traywick's orders, of course, but I'm the one who carried him. All the way, riding pillion. And it was no easy journey for either of us, I don't mind telling you.''

''All the way?'' Nick asked. For the first time since

Traywick had beaten him off the boat, he dared again to hope.

"Scotland. Took him right up to his granny's door," Smithers said. "Except now, I guess..." He hesitated, trying to get it all straight. Not Traywick's son, but Stanton's. A great improvement in situation for the lad, to his way of thinking, and he wasn't even considering the title this man now held.

"It's all right," Nick prodded. "Go on."

"They was wary of one another at first, but she'd already begun to warm up to him before I left," he said, remembering the proud old woman, and how quickly the child had won her over. "He's a taking lad, a fine, sturdy boy, Colonel Stanton. A son to make a man proud."

Vail nodded. He had had no part in the boy's raising and could take none of the credit for how the child had turned out, but still he was pleased with the soldier's assessment. "His mother's responsible for that. I'm afraid...I've had no part in his upbringing," Nick admitted.

"But you plan to now?" Smithers suggested, watching his face.

"I plan to now," Vail agreed. He cleared the emotion from his voice to ask the most important remaining question. "What other instructions did Traywick give you?"

Smithers's shoulders hunched upward, and he tried to remember exactly what he had been told. "To help the boy gather his things for the trip," he began, and then he remembered the painful episode of the wooden soldier. "He ordered me to burn the boy's toy," he admitted, ashamed, as he had been that day, of the fear that had made him obey.

"The wooden soldier," Vail said.

"It hurt him fierce," Smithers acknowledged, remembering the child's white face, the gray eyes, fringed by those long lashes, filling with moisture, "but he wouldn't cry. He wouldn't let himself. Like a soldier, he was, standing there watching me, straight and tall and trying not to let on how bad it hurt him.''

Again Vail denied the images the low words created. Like this man, he admired courage and heart above all things, and apparently, despite his failure to play the proper role in the boy's life, his son had acquired both.

"Traywick has a lot to answer for," he said simply. He might never have the opportunity to call due that particular debt, he knew, so he concentrated instead on his son's situation. "What instructions did you take from him into Scotland?"

"Written instructions, you mean, Colonel?"

"A letter to be delivered to someone? A message?" Vail asked. Was the threat Traywick had made that day real, the suggested danger to the child that had circumscribed their actions since? Was there someone in Scotland simply awaiting Traywick's order to harm his son?

"There was nothing else," Smithers said, shrugging. "Just to take the boy to the house he'd given me direction to and then pick up a package for him in London."

"Did he ever give you orders to harm the boy if he sent you word?" Pierce asked bluntly.

"Harm the boy?" Smithers repeated incredulously. And then, with a simple man's dignity, he said, "I should hope he knew better than that. I'd never harm a child. No one would hurt a child. That's...insane."

"Exactly," Vail agreed quietly. "Was there anyone else working for Traywick, anyone that you know about?"

"No one else was desperate enough, I suppose, to put up with him. But me..." The ex-soldier paused, and then he touched his empty sleeve with his hand, the gesture eloquent, as he was not. "I didn't have no other choice," he confessed. "No one wants a man with only one arm."

"A strong arm, which was used for a good cause tonight," Vail said. "Would you be willing to employ it further in my service?"

"Of course, sir. I'd be proud to say I served under you."

"An extended commitment, I hope," Vail offered, smiling.

"For as long as you'll have me, Colonel Stanton," Smithers vowed. He was embarrassed to feel his own eyes burning, but, like the boy he'd admired, he fought the moisture, hoping the darkness and the rain would hide it. "But what will you do about Traywick's claim that the boy is *his* son?"

"Fight it. In the courts, if necessary. Fight him, if he wishes. But...somehow I believe we've seen the last of Marcus Traywick," Vail said, looking out into the darkness where the boat had disappeared. "He wouldn't dare return now."

"He's a strange man, Colonel," Smithers warned, and then he finally remembered his new employer's present title. "Begging your pardon, Your Grace, but he's a bad man to have as your enemy."

"He won't come back to England," Pierce said confidently. "Why should he? To face prosecution for attempted murder and smuggling?"

"All the same..." Smithers said, shaking his head.

"Will you take us to the house where you carried the child?" Vail asked, and the soldier looked up into gray eyes—exactly like the boy's, he realized—and then he nodded.

"I'll take you. I have a score or two to settle with Traywick myself," he said, thinking that one of the murders the merchant had attempted tonight was his own. "I'll take you there as soon as you can be ready to leave."

Chapter Twelve

There was nothing they could do tonight, Pierce had argued once they made the harrowing climb back to the top of the cliff. They were exhausted, and they needed to send for a doctor to look to Vail's arm. Even the horses could go no farther, he had reminded the duke. They would reach Scotland much sooner if they found accommodations for the night nearby and made proper arrangements tomorrow for the journey.

He could sense the mental battle Vail fought, his head fighting against the inclinations of his heart. Like all good commanders, however, Nick knew when his forces had fought as long and as well as they could, but still he looked at Mary for permission before he gave in.

"Pierce is right, of course," Nick told her. "But it's up to you, Mary. It's your decision."

She knew that if she asked, he would again climb into the coach and set out. Despite his assurances that his arm was not broken, she, like Pierce, wanted another, more professional opinion. Nick's face was still marked by his recent illness, and shadowed smudges surrounded his clear gray eyes.

"Tomorrow," she said, denying the urgings of her own

heart. "Pierce *is* right," she acknowledged. "We need time to make arrangements. We'll reach him sooner if we do it this way."

Nick held her eyes a moment, and then he nodded.

They found an inn on the outskirts of Deal, and Pierce took care of the arrangements. The innkeeper's wife had already retired for the night and was obviously resentful of being awakened. Resentful, at least, until Pierce took a heavy leather pouch from his pocket and began to line guineas along the tap room bar, laying out a coin or two for each demand he made.

The woman's claim that the inn was already full came in response to his request for three of her best chambers, the fires there to be built up and warm, dry sheets put on the beds. Her protests continued to be repeated through the quiet suggestion that water should then be heated and sent up to those chambers to fill bathing tubs.

By the time Pierce began enumerating his exacting standards of care for the horses and a bed in the stables for the coachman, the line of gold coins stretched almost half a foot, and she was no longer protesting anything he asked. Her eyes had grown wider as Pierce continued his quiet instructions. Finally, she had begun to nod agreement as the golden line lengthened, seeming to catch every gleam of the late-night candles she had brought with her to answer their knock on the door.

When she and her husband had gone to rouse their staff, Pierce led the way into the inn's best parlor. In short order, a cold supper and a steaming pitcher of mulled wine were brought in by a sleepy-eyed serving girl.

"Remarkable," Mary said, complimenting the batman, as the girl laid out a profusion of dishes that had appeared as if by magic from the kitchen.

"Just money," Pierce said bluntly, "but a proper bivouac makes all the difference in how well tired troops perform," he added softly. He gestured toward the man across the room. Eyes closed and head back, Vail was sitting in one of the chairs before the fire Smithers was stoking with a shovel of sea coal. The duke held the elbow of his right arm with his left hand, unconsciously cradling the injury against his body. His clothing was beginning to steam slightly in the growing warmth of the room.

"Is he all right?" Mary whispered.

"He's still a soldier, Mary, for all the other titles he bears. He just needs to rest. We all need to rest."

"Thanks to you, we'll be able to do so with all the amenities," she said, smiling at him. "Thank you, Pierce, for everything. I know that what you've done, you've done because of Vail, but I want you to know that I'm grateful. Finally, it seems, we've found Richard."

"And after we retrieve the boy?" he asked, his tone still low enough that their conversation would not reach the ears of the man he served.

She studied his face a moment, seeing under the fine lines that surrounded his eyes the same circled exhaustion that had marked Vail's. Then, because she didn't know the answer to his question, she let her eyes fall before the penetrating dark gaze. "I think that will be up to him."

"He looked for you for years. He didn't know about the boy, of course, but he never stopped trying to find you."

"If that's true, if he really wanted to find me, why did he wait until it was too late?" she asked. "Until I was forced to go to Traywick? Why didn't he come to my father when he came home from Europe?"

Make him tell you the truth, he had told her before. And it was obvious that she didn't know about those terrible months after Waterloo, the same months when she had sought sanctuary for Vail's unborn child, whose existence the duke was unaware of.

"I know that his father's and his brother's deaths must have been—" she began, seeking to formulate some excuse for Vail's inexplicable behavior. All the heartless aristocratic villainy she had credited through the long years for his desertion of her was not true. The character of the man had not changed. And therefore, she had finally come to realize, there must have been a compelling reason for his betrayal.

Pierce shook his head, the movement small and quick, but obviously a denial of the explanation she had begun. "It's not that he didn't grieve for them. It was a harder blow than I believed he could bear. Especially..." Pierce glanced up, knowing that she hadn't really comprehended the importance of what Smithers had said. The news about her son must have driven the story of Vail's bravery on the battlefield that day from her mind. "It must have seemed to him when they died that there was nothing left. I was the one who brought him home to London, but I was almost a stranger. We came to that great empty house, none of his family left, and just the two of us who knew..."

"Knew what?" she asked when he paused.

"The truth," he said simply. "Make him tell you the truth, Mary. And then, perhaps, you'll understand. And be able to forgive him. For the boy's sake, if for nothing else," he added.

The brief silence after his words was interrupted by the arrival of the bonesetter Pierce had instructed the innkeeper to send for. Then, recognizing the wisdom of the batman's next suggestion, quietly made, as the man began his examination of the duke's arm, Mary went upstairs to the chamber that had been prepared for her.

Her portmanteau had already been brought up. Pierce's

blessed efficiency, she acknowledged. Again he was taking care of them all. As she laid her clothing out to dry before the fire and then stepped into the steaming water of the bath that had been brought up, Pierce's advice echoed again and again. *Make him tell you the truth.*

It was very late, and the inn that had been roused into activity by the exhausted travelers settled once more back into the peaceful stillness of rural night. Despite her tiredness, however, sleep eluded Mary. She sat for a while beside the cheerful blaze that had been laid in the chamber, allowing its heat to dry her long hair. She combed slowly through the tangles that the wind and the rain had woven through the dark strands as she thought about all that had happened.

Make him tell you the truth. It was time, she knew. Tomorrow they would begin the journey to Scotland, and at its end, Nick would meet his son. There was too much still unsettled between the two of them. There were too many ghosts. Too many unanswered questions. And there was only one person who could answer them. Pierce had told her all he intended to. The rest, she knew, must come from the man who slept in the room next door. Morning would be too late. Then they would be surrounded again by the friends who accompanied them. They would never be alone, not even within the sheltered confines of the coach.

In order to let go of the last small, bitter barrier of distrust, she needed to know why Nick had not come home to her seven years ago. Before she could give him the son he had once deserted, she must finally understand all the reasons for what he had done. And so, long after midnight, Mary Winters opened the door that separated her bedroom from her husband's.

* * *

Vail had also been unable to sleep. So many emotions, feelings he had been forced to deny because of the enormity of the task Traywick's threatened evil had presented him with, had tonight demanded release. Mary lay sleeping in the next room. All he must do, Pierce had told him weeks ago, was to find the courage to open that door and then all the others, the secret doors between them, which he himself had created and which were guarded now only by the old fear.

He had been sitting beside the fire, looking down into the heart of its flames, all the memories that had been re-awakened echoing through his head. There was no light in the chamber other than the diffuse red glow from the low blaze in the grate. There was some small sound, and he looked up to watch the door that led to Mary's chamber slowly open. The soft light of the lamp she had left burning there outlined her slender figure as she hesitated within the doorway.

"Mary?" he whispered, wondering if exhaustion or a renewal of fever might have created this apparition, or if he had simply conjured her up out of his need. She stepped into the room and closed the door behind her, seeming to disappear into the shadows there that the firelight failed to penetrate. Then she reappeared suddenly out of the darkness, walking toward him.

Her nightgown fell straight from its high waistline, gathered under the curve of her breasts. Her dark hair, lying over her shoulders, gleamed like silken ribbons, its color a contrast to her skin, almost the same alabaster of the thin fabric of her rail. The gown she wore did nothing to conceal the contours of her body, and his throat closed at the knowledge of how much he had always loved her.

He watched, unable to speak, as she came to kneel at his feet. She, too, said nothing for a long time. Finally she put her hand on his knee. He thought he could feel each individual finger, burning his skin through the soft material of his knit underdrawers, the only garment he wore. Nightshirts were an inconvenience he had discarded during the long years in Iberia, but now it seemed that his undress was too intimate, even between the lovers they had once been.

She raised her eyes to study his, and then she smiled at him. Her face, glazed by the soft firelight, was so beautiful, unchanged, he thought, exactly as when he had fallen in love with her. So many years ago. An eternity of loss.

"Tell me why," she pled softly. "Finally explain it all to me. Perhaps it's wrong, but...I need to know. I need to understand, Nick, why you never came for me."

He held her eyes a moment, and then, unable to resist the impulse, instead of answering what she had asked, he slipped his hand under the fall of dark hair to the back of her neck. His long fingers spread, moving upward to cup her head, threading through the mass of curls, touched now with light, exactly as they had been touched with sun that day in the clearing.

Slowly he lowered his mouth toward hers, giving her time to deny him, to turn away, but the blue eyes held, wide and trusting once again. Her lashes fluttered downward only as his lips brushed over the softness of hers.

He lifted his head, and his eyes focused briefly on the trembling mouth he had just kissed. Then they raised again to meet hers. He watched the slow rise of her eyelids, and in the exposed midnight blue was the same desire that had defeated his intent seven years ago.

He felt the breath she took, her body shuddering slightly with the depth of the inhalation. His eyes skimmed over her face, savoring again, finally allowed to savor, the perfection of its structure: fragile curve of bone; the sweep of long, dark lashes touching against the purity of her skin;

the wide, sensuous mouth, created to tremble beneath his. He did not see the small telltale differences time had etched there. In his eyes, she was still the girl he had loved. And in them alone, through the long years that lay ahead, always she would be the same.

She smiled at him, tremulously, her eyes luminous with unshed tears. She raised her hand and laid her palm against his cheek. And in that moment, she knew that the answers she had come to demand were no longer necessary. Whether there were reasons or not for what he had done so long ago, this was enough. Again she was his, as willing and as open to his desire as she had been the day she gave herself to him.

Her fingers glided downward, feeling the slight masculine roughness of his skin. Down to the strong, ridged column of his throat, and then lower, to touch the scar of the surgery he had endured after taking Traywick's bullet the day he came to find her. It had been her mistake, her fault he was hurt.

She followed the welt with her forefinger, the heel of her hand sliding over the muscle that underlay the bare, hair-roughened skin of his chest. She glanced up to find that his eyes were focused on her fingers as she deliberately trailed them across the small brown nub of his nipple and then pulled them downward again. Her forefinger traced the narrow channel made by his breastbone, which centered the swell of corded stomach muscles on either side.

When her fingertip reached the narrowed ribbon of coarser hair that led under the waist of the garment he wore, he caught her hand, holding it too tightly. Startled, she looked up into his eyes.

"What is it?" she whispered. "What's wrong?"

He said nothing for a long time, holding the hand he had captured in the callused horseman's fingers she had always loved. She wanted them now, wanted their warmth and their strength moving over her body. Never forgotten. Never forgotten.

He stood up suddenly, and for an instant she was afraid he intended to leave. She had come here to demand answers and had discovered instead that the only answer that truly mattered was this. Did he still want her?

He pulled her to her feet, his hand never releasing her fingers, which had suddenly begun to tremble—first in fear of his rejection, and then, as he led her toward the wide bed, in wordless anticipation.

Like a courtier, he seated her on the edge of the mattress that had seemed to stretch, wide and empty, before them. She waited, but instead of joining her, he stood a moment beside the bed, almost a stranger in the shadowed play of firelight. And then, even as she watched, his features changed, their alignment shifting slightly, hardening. A muscle jerked beside his set mouth, and finally even that was still.

He released her fingers, the hand that had held hers moving slowly downward to touch the drawstring that secured the thin knit drawers on his narrow hips. She watched, mesmerized. His right hand came up to join the effort, the wrist wrapped tightly with the bonesetter's white bandage.

She had not even remembered to ask about his arm, she realized suddenly. But obviously it hadn't been broken, because he was using both hands now to push the undergarment off his body, over the slim hips and down muscled thighs. The knit drawers fell down over his feet, to puddle against the wooden floor.

She had watched their fall, and then, slowly, her eyes moved upward. Even in the soft light of the dying fire, what they found was shocking. His lower body was a mass of scars. Unlike the one she had traced on his chest, these were old, whitened with the passage of time, but the injuries they represented, she quickly recognized, had been no less terrible. The worst slashed a deep, puckered ridge across the muscle of his right thigh, but there were others, far too numerous to count. They marked both legs and the area of his groin. They even marked...

She looked up at that realization and found he was watching her reaction, his features rigid with tension.

"Oh, Nick," she said softly, the instant compassion in response to what was in his eyes, rather than to the damaged body he had revealed. She had seen him in the clearing before, young and unmarked, his strong arousal clearly revealed during their lovemaking. These injuries had not occurred in Spain. Waterloo, she realized. This was the injury Smithers had described. Saving a child, a drummer boy. He had been wounded that summer, and she had never known.

"I never knew," she whispered. "My father never told me you'd been hurt. Why wasn't I told? Why didn't I know?"

"No one knew. No one was ever intended to know...given the nature of the injuries."

"But how...?"

"The surgeons had told Wellington they could do nothing for me. I don't know what his message to my family said, but...it was enough that Charles and my father decided to make the crossing despite the storm, and their yacht capsized in the Channel."

"Nick, I'm so sorry," she said—too little consolation for that loss.

"My father may have been carrying the ring you'd brought. But I swear, Mary, he hadn't written to tell me. I didn't know. Perhaps he waited because..." He paused, remembering it all, despite the years he had spent trying to forget.

The doctors had been unwilling at first to make any commitment that he would live, and then, when it finally seemed that he might, they had refused to venture an opinion as to whether he'd ever recover sexual function. And through those first days, all he'd been able to think about was Mary. With bitterness, at first, for his own loss. And guilt. In making love to her before he left England, he had finally realized, he had bound her to a man who might never be capable again of being her husband. And the memories of her sweet, unpracticed responses to his love-making that day had haunted him.

"Because of this," he continued, glancing down at the familiar disfigured landscape of his body, "I thought I'd never again be able to make love to you. Never father a child. I never even thought about the possibility that already... You hadn't contacted my father—at least, I didn't know that you had, but I knew that enough time had passed that if..." He paused, shaking his head.

"The truth is, I suppose, I never really thought beyond this. I hoped you'd forget. Forget me. Forget what had happened. No one would ever have to know about the register, about the marriage. You were so young and so beautiful. I wanted you to go on with your life. I truly wanted you to find someone who could be the man you deserved." Finally, the bitter confession faded.

"Surely you must have known there could never be anyone else. Surely, Nick, you must have known."

"I was...consumed, I suppose, with what had happened. Too blindly selfish. Too young, perhaps. Afraid."

"And no one knew?"

"Pierce," he said, remembering the sergeant's kindness. "He'd been brought in to the same field hospital where I'd been carried. Some minor wound. There were too few orderlies. The surgeons were overworked, and for some reason Pierce decided to look after me. He overheard when Wellington came with the news about Charles and my father, and he knew about the other, of course, because it was he who…cared for me." The endless humiliation of those days was suddenly in his face, reflected in the gray eyes, but he forced himself to go on. "If it hadn't been for Pierce taking care of me, Mary—"

She broke in. "I would have come to you, Nick. Surely you must have known that. Even then, you must have known."

His eyes searched her face again. It was true, he knew. She would have taken care of him, but that had never been what he wanted for her. "I think that might have been the one thing I couldn't bear. Afraid that I'd never again be able to touch you. Afraid that I had tied you to a man who, like Traywick—"

"Oh, Nick, my darling, don't," she protested, finally understanding so much that had made no sense before. He had loved her, as much as she had believed. She had not been wrong about that. Even as young as she was, as inexperienced, she had not been mistaken about the depth of what he felt for her.

"Even when I could travel, and Pierce brought me home, I didn't want anyone to know what had happened. I consulted several London physicians, who were as vague as the surgeons had been. No one could tell me anything with any certainty, except," he said bitterly, remembering again the endless frustration, "that time would finally provide the answers I sought. And time, I know now, was a luxury you didn't have."

"But eventually…" she began, and then she hesitated.

"Eventually," he confirmed, and his mouth relaxed fractionally as the color stole into her cheeks. "I can't ever remember seeing you blush," he said softly. "You were always so poised, so sure of your path."

"Until that day in the clearing."

He held out his hand, and without being certain of what he intended, she stood up, trustingly placing her palm over his, and his strong fingers closed around hers.

"I've thought, since I found out about Richard..." He looked down at their joined hands, his thumb moving slowly across her knuckles.

"What did you think?" she asked. His eyes came back to her face, and he smiled at her.

"You told me he was my only son. It's possible, Mary, that he may always be...our only son. I may not be able to father any more children. I've even thought about the possibility that, despite all the grief that resulted, if we had not made love that day, we might never have had a child."

"Out of my sin," she whispered, remembering the long years of guilt and regret. For her father's death. For her endless, seemingly unanswered prayers that summer, waiting for Nick's return. For the choice she had made to safeguard Richard's well-being.

"Perhaps out of the wrong we did..." he said.

"Came some right," she whispered.

"We have Richard. I may never be able to give you another child."

"But..." she began, and then the question, which was not truly a question, faded. Without her being conscious of it, her gaze fell, as she sought reassurance that what he had feared then was not true. The glance at his body was evidence enough, blatant proof of his masculinity, that despite the scars, there was no impairment.

"Can I make love to you?" he finished for her, his eyes on her face and his mouth relaxed, finally released from the tension that had held him. "I certainly intend to try, my darling," he promised softly. "If you still want me."

"I don't believe, even in the years when I thought you'd betrayed us, that there was a single instant when I *didn't* want you," she said truthfully. "I wonder if you can ever understand all the long, aching loneliness of those years."

He said nothing, but then, he had already made the confession of his aloneness, which had haunted the endless nights they had been apart. "There's no reason to be alone tonight," he said. "Or ever again. But that's your decision, Mary," he offered, as he had on the beach. "Your right to decide what happens now."

There was no hesitation in her response, but her fingers were trembling again as they found the ribbon that fastened the throat of her gown. She untied the narrow satin, allowing the neckline to loosen until the gown slipped off her shoulders. She was aware suddenly that he was watching her, and as the soft lawn fell downward, she caught it with one hand, holding the fabric almost protectively over her breasts.

"It's all right," he said comfortingly.

She didn't know how he could understand that she needed that reassurance. She had shown him her body before. Provocatively, almost proudly, delighting, as he had, in the small, upward tilt of her breasts. Knowing then that he would find her beautiful.

All she could remember now were the minute silvered lines etched by the months she had suckled his son, her breasts so achingly heavy with milk. The same soft marks marred the smooth skin of her stomach, and they had not been there before. She remembered suddenly how much his body had changed and how little that mattered to her. So she released the cloth she held, and let the gown fall.

Her body was highlighted by the golden firelight. It flickered over slender curves and intriguingly darkened the shadowed, secret places only he had known. So beautiful, he thought. So perfect. More perfect than before, because she was a woman now, and no longer a girl. Because she had already belonged to him, and there would be no discomfort this time. Because the slenderness of her body had once guarded his child, sleeping safely beneath her heart.

With the wonder of that realization, Nick's eyes traced downward to the small convexity of her belly. The marks of that pregnancy were there, tiny imperfections where her body had grown, skin stretching to accommodate the body of his son. He might never see her like that, he thought. Unconsciously he reached to caress her slender waist. His fingers spread as he tried to imagine what the warm velvet of her skin might feel like with pregnancy. Taut, filled, hard and tight, with the growing body of his child.

Mary watched his hand, wondering what he was thinking as he touched her. She had never forgotten this gentleness, the slow, sensuous grace of his fingers. Such a contrast to— But that memory had no place between them, and deliberately she put aside the thought, rejecting the images that had accompanied it, and closed her eyes, willing her entire concentration on the feel of Nick's hand moving over her body.

It turned, the long fingers slanting downward, and her bones became liquid, hot, molten, wanting to melt into his touch. Instinctively she leaned toward him, anticipating. Wanting. The sweet, dark wetness of her desire, so ready for his entrance. So long. It had been so long.

"I wish I had seen you," he said, his voice low, as intimate as the soft firelight.

When she had carried Richard, she realized. When she had carried his son.

"I would have held you while he was born," he whispered.

His hand slipped farther downward, the tips of his fingers moving into the soft, dark curls. She closed her eyes, the memories tangling together in her head. Soft infant mouth over her breast. Nick's was there instead, his breath feathering over her nipple, its warmth intensifying the aching fullness between her legs. His lips touched and then released. His tongue circled over the hardening nub, and her breath caught, a small sobbing gasp of response.

His hand shifted again, still downward, and her bones softened again, lowering into his caress. So sweet. Unconsciously, she let her head fall back, her face drifting upward as she released the breath she had drawn in a long, shuddering sigh. She had wanted this so long, even when she was not aware of what she wanted.

His tongue circled again, slowly. And back. And then his lips settled over the peak he had created, and with the small pressure of their caress, the flood of moisture released, scalding an aching passage through her body. His fingers hesitated, and she knew he had been aware of her reaction. There was no embarrassment in that realization. She wanted him. Every particle of her being, every cell of her body, called to him. Every nerve was prepared for his invasion. Wanting. Wanting.

He bent his knees and, slipping his arms under her body, he laid her on the bed that she had almost forgotten stretched behind her. She opened her eyes to find him still standing beside it, looking down on her.

The gray eyes were very dark, and the past was in them. Despite the scars his body bore, his face was the same, still as beautiful as before, but strengthened now, tempered by loss and pain and the long years' deprivation. She smiled at him—with permission and perhaps even forgiveness—and in the fire-touched darkness he moved over and then into her waiting body. And the doors that had been guarded so long were thrown open to the light.

Chapter Thirteen

When the soft light of morning stole into the inn's best chamber, it did not disturb the occupants of the high bed. Mary Winters slept—the dark banner of her curls spread across the pillow they shared, her cheek cushioned at last against her husband's shoulder, and her slim fingers lost in the golden hair that covered Nick's chest. One slender leg lay across his body, unintentionally hiding most of the brutal scars he had shown her last night.

Eventually she had forgotten even to think about the long-guarded secret he had at last revealed. Forgotten to think about the past and the loneliness of the empty years that lay between them. Forgotten, finally, to think about anything at all.

Under the soul-shattering movements of his hands and his lips and his body, she had remembered only that this was Nick, and she was his. That was the only thing that had ever truly mattered in her existence—except for the son he had given her.

He had made love to her through the shadowed hours of the night. First with demanding urgency, exorcising with the hard strength of an almost mindless passion all the fears that had once stood between them. And then slowly, deliberately, carrying her with him through the heart of the storm he created, wave after wave of sensation roiling sweet and hot through her body, as the sea rushes to cover the waiting shore.

They had drifted to sleep, intimate whispers silenced at last by the knowledge that all questions had finally been answered. Nothing mattered now but this—their bodies again joined. Again one.

And then, sometime in the silent predawn darkness, he had moved over her once more. There was so little light in the room that when she opened her eyes, she could see nothing but his face, its perfection highlighted by the surrounding darkness like the profile on a cameo, cut by a master's hand. The gray eyes had been luminous, and he had never closed them, watching as he slowly pushed into her body and then began the ancient retreat and invasion of this battle. On this soldier's field, he had always known, there could be no victor but the heart.

Her eyes held his until the exquisite torture of sensation became too much to bear. Her mouth opened slightly as her breathing increased, slow pulse by slow pulse. As self-control spiraled away into the darkness, her eyelids drifted downward, hiding what was happening within her body, too intimate even for his eyes.

Her body arched, straining upward to meet the powerful downward thrusts of his hips. Inside, somewhere as deep and as dark as the night that surrounded them, the small quake of reaction began, growing and expanding again like the silk balloons they had filled that summer at Vauxhall. She arched, control lost, and the sound of his name was a gasp, torn unthinkingly from her lips. And then again.

She was aware when he joined her there, the thick, hot stream of his seed enclosed again in her body, and even in the wordless, mindless ecstasy of this fulfillment, she hoped. A child. Another child.

Then that thought, too, drifted away, out of her head, as the force that had taken her eased, her body shivering in the quick chill that follows the heat of lovemaking. Nick raised his upper body slightly, pushing away from her onto his forearms, his eyes again examining her face. A shimmer of perspiration gleamed on the delicate features, her upper lip and throat dewed with moisture. His and hers. The fluids of their bodies mixed here, too. Joined. One again.

"I love you, Mary Winters," he whispered. "I have always loved you."

"I know," she said. There was no longer within her heart even the small, dark spot of the doubt that had led her to him tonight. She knew it all. All the secrets. All the fears.

"I should let you sleep," he said, smiling, but instead he lowered his mouth again to hers, which opened, welcoming, as her body had welcomed him. When he had kissed her, he lifted his head to look down again into her eyes. A few strands of her hair were caught against his cheek, and she raised her hand to push them away. Then she cupped her palm to his face, studying his features in the growing light of dawn.

"Go to sleep," he whispered. "We have a long journey tomorrow."

"Not as long as the one we've made tonight," she said, knowing he would understand.

"An interrupted journey."

"And at the end of the trip we begin tomorrow, Nick, you'll finally meet your son."

"Richard," he said softly, the whispered name like a prayer.

Although he had thought he understood a great deal about what she had felt these weeks, he didn't understand why hearing him say his son's name would make her cry. And if the method he chose to comfort her was perhaps unorthodox, it was, nonetheless, effective.

When Pierce came to wake the duke and to inform him about the arrangements he'd made for their journey, he carried into the room, as usual, shaving paraphernalia and a ewer of hot water. Whistling tunelessly between his teeth, the batman set the items down on the table beside the high bed. He had already turned to throw open the draperies to let in the sun when he belatedly realized that the duke's bed this morning, for the first time since he had known him, held two sleepers.

He turned, despite his embarrassment, to verify what he had seen, but what his mind had not yet accepted. Vail's eyes were open, watching his reaction. They filled with amusement at the sudden flood of color into the batman's lean cheeks.

"Go away, Pierce," Nick ordered softly.

"Yes, Your Grace," Pierce whispered, the unaccustomed title more appropriate, somehow, for the occasion.

"You're blushing," Vail said, the smile that had begun in his eyes finally touching his mouth, "exactly like some schoolroom miss. Or like an old maid," he amended.

"I beg your pardon, Your Grace," Pierce said, beginning to retreat backward across the wooden floor. Mary opened her eyes, disturbed by the conversation. "Your Graces," he added.

Her sleepy eyes examined him, as if she could not decide which one of the two of them was out of place in Vail's bedroom. "Is it time to get up?" she asked, her questioning gaze moving to her husband.

"Past time," Pierce said, finding his usual confidence, which the shock of finding them together had momentarily stolen. "If you intend to make any sort of decent time today."

"Thank you, Pierce," Vail said. It was obviously a dismissal.

"I've brought your razor and hot water."

"Later," the duke suggested calmly.

"It won't be hot later."

"Then we shall make do with cold. Thank you, Pierce."

The batman's eyebrows lifted, but at the duke's tone, he apparently thought better of further argument. He turned and beat a hasty retreat out of the room.

"Why did you send him away?" Mary asked, sitting up in bed. With one hand, she held the sheet over her bare breasts. Somehow, despite the intimacies they had shared last night, she was suddenly shy.

"Logistics," Nick said.

"Logistics?" she repeated. Fascinated, she watched as he threw off the covers and got up, standing beside the bed. Her eyes examined his body. A body she knew well now—not visually, perhaps, but certainly tactually. The scars were far less shocking to her now, expected and familiar, even though they were more clearly revealed this morning than they had been in the shadowed firelight last night.

Patiently he waited until her eyes came back to meet his.

"The logistics of getting you from here," he said, looking pointedly at the twisted sheets of the bed they had shared last night, "to there." His gaze moved to the door that led to her chamber. "Without revealing this," he said softly. His long arm stretched out, and his fingers tugged the sheet she had been clutching out of her hand.

The laughter died suddenly in his eyes, and then he leaned toward her, one knee on the mattress between them. "Faster horses," he said softly.

"What?" she asked, as he pushed her down, stripping the tangled sheet from her lower body.

"Pierce will have to hire faster horses. Or else we're going to be very late."

Despite the undeniable quality of the horses Pierce hired from the posting inns as they traveled north, the journey took almost two days. When night fell, Mary refused to allow them to stop, knowing that if Vail were alone, he would drive through. She didn't intend to slow them down, and there was, of course, no one more eager to reach Richard than she.

The structure Smithers directed them to was large, although by London standards, at least, more primitive fortress than dwelling. It was perched almost at the peak of an equally forbidding hill, the site obviously chosen with an eye to defense, rather than esthetics. But the scenery that surrounded the Border stronghold was incredibly beautiful. The view from its narrow windows would be breathtaking, Mary thought, looking at the building through the window of their coach, which had stopped at the bottom of the steep, narrow road that ribboned upward.

"Abigail never talked about her family, not in all the years I lived in her house," Mary said softly, as the coach began the climb. "I assumed she had no one to turn to, no one to protect her from Traywick's abuses. But it's obvious that's not true. And obvious her family has some standing."

"They cut all ties when she married Traywick," Nick said, repeating what Smithers had told him about the situation.

"Then why would he send Richard to them? That makes no sense."

"His idea of revenge, perhaps? Foist on them the care of a child not of their blood, while at the same time successfully hiding the boy from me. If Smithers hadn't told us where he was, Mary, we would never have found him."

"Then...it was an incredible piece of luck he was with Traywick that night."

"Luck?" Nick repeated, wondering who had been more fortunate. He had already told Smithers what he suspected, but he'd seen no reason to tell Mary. At least not before they had reached the boy.

"He was the only one who knew what Traywick was up to, and you found him," Mary explained. "Was that why Traywick was taking Smithers with him? Because he knew everything? Or because he thought he would need him again when he reached the Continent?"

"I don't think Smithers would ever have set foot in France," Vail said truthfully.

"Never set foot... Then...you believe Traywick intended to *murder* him?"

"Two men, alone in a boat, one of them totally unsuspecting of the other's motives. It would have been very easy for Traywick to have gotten rid of him in the dark."

"No one would ever have known what had happened. Or what had happened to Richard," she realized.

The duke nodded.

"Do you think he'll come back, Nick?" she asked.

"Only a fool would return now, and whatever Traywick may be, he's not a fool. I hold his notes and mortgages, and as soon as we have Richard, I intend to do exactly what I threatened to do before—destroy him. There will be nothing left in England for Traywick to return to when I get through."

Not a fool, but a madman, Mary thought, shivering. She felt the coach draw to a stop, and she didn't voice the objection aloud. Nick was right. Once they had Richard Traywick couldn't hurt them any further.

* * *

The great hall into which they were eventually led was cold and dark, despite the enormous fire and the candles that stood on every table. The feeble light they provided did little to chase away the shadows from the stone walls. Mary's first assessment had been correct. More keep than castle, and, given the bloody history of the region it guarded, that was understandable.

The old woman who sat huddled in the high-backed chair was small, almost shriveled with age, but her black eyes, set like obsidian in the seamed face, were as sharp as the occasional draft that penetrated the room, despite the ancient tapestries. She watched, unblinking, as they crossed the floor.

Mary could only imagine the impression the four of them were making—disheveled from two days of travel and obviously exhausted. Only Nick seemed presentable, she thought, but that was due more to the inherent arrogance of birth and training, which made him at ease in any social situation, no matter how awkward. As they approached the old woman, Mary realized for the first time exactly how awkward what they had come to do might be.

Somehow, she knew, it was up to Nick to speak. Rank might have its privileges, she thought, almost amused by the realization, but it also had, of course, its responsibilities. She saw that the jet eyes had already fastened on Vail's face, recognizing him as their leader and waiting for his explanation as to why they had arrived at her door so late at night, requesting an audience.

"Lady Keith, please forgive our intrusion, especially considering the lateness of the hour, but we have come to discuss something that is very important to us both. We've traveled a great distance to—"

"Who are you?" the old woman said, rudely breaking into the polite and polished beginning.

Nick's mouth moved—fighting a smile, Mary thought—before he answered her.

"My name is Vail," he said simply. Automatically he had used his title, although he had not believed it would mean anything here.

"Vail," she repeated, and then: "The Duke of Vail. I knew your grandfather. A scoundrel and a blackguard." The words were almost a challenge.

"But, you must admit, a charming one," Nick agreed, smiling at her. The old man had certainly been both, he knew, but he had also been extremely popular with the ladies.

She laughed, the sound of it rusty, as if it were an activity she engaged in seldom now. The laugh turned into a rasping cough, and when she was again able to speak, her words had nothing to do with his illustrious ancestry.

"You seem to have been careless with one of your possessions," she said, her gaze tracing his features and then rising again to meet the gray eyes.

"Remarkably careless."

She nodded. "I expect that bastard Traywick had something to do with it." Hers had been a generation in which women were allowed—or had simply been brave enough to seize—far more freedoms that those permitted their granddaughters, who were endlessly constricted by the restraints of the beau monde.

"Shrewd, as well as beautiful," Nick said, his face a polite mask as he offered the ridiculous compliment. Surprisingly, he was rewarded with what was almost a simper. "I had worried about how I should explain our mission to you," he went on. "Obviously, I was worried without cause."

"I always knew he wasn't Abigail's, despite Traywick's message. He couldn't be. A more spineless ninny than Abby I've yet to meet. The only time she stood up for herself was when she eloped, imagining she was in love with that toadying merchant. Or rather imagining that he was in love with her. Repulsive creature. Did you by any chance kill him?" she asked suddenly, real interest in her voice.

"Unfortunately..." Vail said, letting the regretful sentence lapse.

"Pity," she said. "The boy looks a great deal like you, you know. *And* like your grandfather. I don't know why I didn't see that before. I couldn't decide who he was. I knew he wasn't Traywick's. Or Abby's. I just didn't know who he was, or why that filthy cit would send him to me."

"But he's safe?" Mary asked, because she couldn't wait any longer for that assurance.

The old lady's black eyes turned to examine her face with the same open scrutiny she had afforded the duke's. "And who are you?" she demanded.

"Forgive me, Lady Keith," Nick answered. "May I present to you my wife, the Duchess of Vail."

"Mary," the duchess added, not yet accustomed to that title.

"You're his mother," the old woman said.

"Yes."

"Then why—" Lady Keith began.

"It's a very long story," Vail said, interrupting her. "And extremely painful, I'm afraid, for us."

Her gaze shifted again to his face, and finally, seeing in his eyes the truth of what he had just said, she nodded before she turned back to Mary.

"Then *you* may tell me, girl, if he won't. A fair exchange, I think. I have ample time to hear a *long* story, and I do so love a good tale. We called them *on-dits*. Everything French. Very fashionable. I had my Season, you know. In London. In my day, the more scandalous the tale, the better we enjoyed hearing it. Is this one…scandalous, my dear?''

Thinking of all the things that had brought them to this isolated location, Mary told her the truth. ''Enough scandal to ruin the child's life if the story's repeated,'' she said simply.

''I'll be dead in six months. My doctors all agree. That's the *only* thing they agree on,'' the old woman said, her eyes shining as if she had just made a great joke. ''Besides, there's no one here for me to tell your secrets to. No one to talk to anymore. I married the Earl of Keith because he was as charming as your husband, and I never went back to London. He didn't tell me before he swept me off my feet that he couldn't bear to leave his beloved Scotland, so I've spent my life here.''

''Without regret,'' Vail suggested softly, clearly reading the echoes of that strong love. The memories of her husband were still in her voice when she said his name, her accent touched now, after all those years, with the soft burr of her Scots servants.

''You *are* a charming rogue,'' she said, smiling at him before she turned back to Mary. ''Your secrets are safe with me, my dear. As was your son,'' she reminded them. ''Will you let your story be the price of my guardianship of him these weeks?''

Recognizing that she really had no choice, Mary finally nodded.

The men had been banished to the dining hall to be fed, and reluctantly Mary had taken her place, as instructed, in the chair that faced the old woman's. Her quiet words had faltered at times, but eventually she had relived it all, sparing no detail of the narrative, unsparing of her own mistakes, and the jet-black eyes had not left her face as she talked.

"And then tonight we arrived here, and...the rest you know," she finished.

"Would you like to see him?" the old woman asked softly.

Because Mary's heart was still lost in the wonder of the small, firelit bedroom of the inn where Vail had destroyed the barriers between them, it took a moment for her to realize the gift that was being offered.

"Richard?" she asked.

"He's asleep, of course, but not far away. I can take you there, if you'd like."

"Oh, yes," Mary whispered.

"Do you want to send for that charming scoundrel you married?"

It wasn't fair, Mary thought, not to let Nick see his son, but for some reason, she hesitated.

"Then come," the old woman said, making the decision for her. "It's best for just women. We won't wake him, and in the morning you will have thought how to introduce him to his father. His da, as they say here. A strange people, the Scots," she said as, using her cane, she made her slow way across the stone floor and through one of the shadowed doorways. "But good men in a fight. Make no mistake about that. Born to be warriors," she said. "And lovers," she added, her voice rich with memory. The dry whisper of her laughter disappeared down the dark hall, and, smiling, Mary followed her to find her son.

She had almost forgotten how small he was. He slept on his side, his fingers curled against his chin, pink and rounded as an infant's. The candle the old woman held high illuminated the guinea-gold curls and the smooth, translucent skin of his cheeks. Safe, Mary thought, feeling her eyes foolishly fill with tears at the realization. Safe. Marcus Traywick would never be allowed to harm him now. Nick would see to that.

"He's a fine boy, Mary," the old woman said, looking down on the sleeping boy. "A son to be proud of. A shame he's not really my grandson."

"Thank you for guarding him," Mary whispered. She touched one of the yellow curls that lay against the pillow. "I don't know how to thank you for what you've done, especially since you felt all along that he wasn't Abigail's. It may help to know that she loved him, as much, I think, as if he had been her son. The first time I met her and recognized her generosity of spirit, I knew somehow that she would. I think that's the only reason I was able to give him to her."

"A silly chit," Lady Keith said, almost harshly, and then she added, spoiling whatever effect she had intended, "Poor, silly chit. Was he at least good to her, Mary? I think if I knew he had been good to her, I would be more at peace with it all."

There was a slight, telltale hesitation before Mary could formulate the lie, the remembrance of the dark bruises that had marked Abigail Traywick's wasted body suddenly vivid in her mind. "Of course," Mary whispered finally, thinking the truth would serve no purpose here. "He was her husband. Of course he was good to her."

Black eyes locked with blue, and then Abigail's grandmother said, "Not so skillful a liar as your husband, my dear, but thank you for trying."

She turned to lead the way out of the room, taking the candle with her. Before she followed her hostess, Mary bent to touch her lips to the softness of the golden curls she could no longer see. As she crossed the floor, the old woman's voice floated back to her, from down the shadowed hall, the candle she carried casting a wavering light over the stone walls. "My poor, sad chit."

When Mary had said good-night to Lady Keith, she followed the serving girl to the bedchamber that, she had been told, connected to the one where her husband was sleeping. She left the girl standing in the dark hallway, assuring her that she could manage her own disrobing. As she closed the door on the last of the maid's protests, she felt a soft flutter of anticipation move through her body.

"Did you see him?" Nick asked. She turned to find him standing by the low fire, and seeing that he was already undressed, she was thankful that she hadn't allowed the maid in.

"Yes," she said, walking across the room to stand before him.

"And?" he asked.

"I didn't wake him."

"What will you tell him, Mary?"

"I don't know. I don't know what's best. Perhaps nothing, at first—except that we've come for him. That we want him to live with us. That Traywick is gone." The inflection was questioning. Now that they had found Richard, it was hard to know how much or how little to explain to a child of his age.

"But not the rest?" he asked. Not the truth of his parentage.

"He's only a little boy. He lost his mother not long ago—the only mother he'd ever known. There was that terrible morning Traywick was injured, and I disappeared from Richard's world, jailed and charged with attempted murder. Then his father sent him to live with strangers. Now we suddenly appear to disrupt his life again. I don't know what to tell him, Nick. It seems too much to ask of him, to accept all the mistakes the adults in his life have made.''

"You don't intend to tell him the truth?" he asked flatly.

"Of course," she said, but then, compelled by his eyes, she admitted what she had already decided in her heart. "In time, I'll tell him, but not yet. He needs a chance to adjust to us. To living at Vail. It will all be so strange, Nick. It doesn't seem fair to tell him that his whole life has been a lie. None of this is his fault."

This, too, was part of the price he must pay for what he had done, Nick thought bitterly, but he knew Mary was right. For Richard's sake, he must wait a little longer. At Vail, at least, the child would be safe. Then, when he was no longer a stranger to his own son, perhaps it would be easier for the boy to accept the relationship.

"Come to bed," he said invitingly, finding a smile for her despite the sudden despair. "You don't have to solve all the problems tonight. After all, we have the rest of our lives to make it right."

She held out her hand, and he took it, holding the slender fingers in his own. Finally he raised them to his lips and brushed a kiss across them.

"You'll have to help me," she said. "Thankfully, I dismissed Lady Keith's maid. I believe you might have given her a shock," she said, her eyes falling provocatively to examine his nude body. "A very great shock," she added softly. As it had in the inn, soft, becoming color had stolen into her cheeks.

"I hadn't realized that the term *blushing bride* might be taken so literally," Vail said. He put his hands on her shoulders to turn her around and then, with a deal of unthinking expertise, he began to slip the small buttons that ran down the back of her gown out of their loops.

"Bride?" she repeated. "Blushing, perhaps, but never a bride."

"I made you my wife," he agreed, easing the dress over her shoulders. He paused to press a small kiss on the soft tendrils of dark hair that floated against the back of her neck. "But you never had an opportunity to be my bride. I'm afraid it's too late to remedy that omission, Mary. The judge's acceptance of the legality of our vows in the courtroom that day would make it dangerous now to pursue a more sanctioned ceremony. It would call into question any claim Richard has—"

"I'm not complaining," she said quickly, turning to face him. She took the gown he'd helped her remove and laid it on the chair before the fire, and then she caught his hand in both of hers. "I had rather be your wife, Nick, than anything in this world. If the beginning of this marriage was wrong, then we'll work harder to make it all come right. In my heart, I have always been your wife. Nothing can change that. Nothing ever has."

He held her eyes a moment, and then, with his free hand, he untied the ribbon that laced the low neckline of her chemise. Finally she helped him slip the garment off her body, so that she stood before him, her body again clothed only with the subtle play of firelight.

He lowered his mouth to kiss the small depression at the base of her throat, and with the touch of his lips, she was lost again in the world that only they possessed. All other considerations disappeared—even, for this brief moment, her concerns for the small boy who slept safely in the stone fortress that surrounded them. Nothing mattered tonight but this. So new and yet so achingly familiar, echoing countless dreams that had haunted her nights, their power unacknowledged in the light of her busy days, desire for him carefully hidden under bitterness and regret.

And now, as surely as his hands were moving over her body, Nick was stripping away all the defenses she had built through the years, replacing the old, dark memories with these. He carried her as before to the bed, and in the gathering darkness, as the low fire burned itself out, he taught her again, with exquisite patience and tenderness, what it meant to be his wife.

The knock in the predawn darkness was very soft, and it was Mary, waking with a mother's concern, who tiptoed to the door. When she opened it, however, only Pierce stood in the hallway.

"Lady Keith asked if you and the colonel would join her," he said.

"Join her?" Mary questioned.

"You need to dress."

"But—"

"And you need to hurry," Pierce suggested.

"Richard?"

"The boy's fine. It's nothing to do with the boy, I promise you, Your Grace. And the old lady's been so kind..." Pierce didn't need to complete the reminder of all they owed to Abigail's grandmother.

"Of course," Mary said softly, and whatever explanation she offered the duke, within a few minutes they were both following Pierce through the silent halls of the Border fortress.

He led them finally to a small family chapel which had, through the long years of religious turmoil, been stripped of whatever ecclesiastical finery had once decorated it. Now the only ornamentation was a small stain-glass window above the stone altar. And waiting in the shadowed dimness was the Countess of Keith and her aged spiritual advisor, his hair as white and his face almost as kind as that of Mary's father.

The old woman walked toward them, but her eyes were focused only on Mary's. "I thought, if you'd allow me..." she began. When she put out her hand, thin and blue-veined, the knuckles knotted and distorted, it trembled, so Mary took it between both of hers. "Not Church of England I'm afraid. Even I couldn't manage that. Not here. Not and keep this marriage a secret. But he's a good man for all that. And he's God's man. We've argued our religions through the years until we've come to an agreement that God isn't so much concerned about our wranglings over doctrine. Only about our devotion. Our love for our fellow man."

"And our intents," Mary whispered, her eyes moving to the dawn light that was beginning to seep in to illuminate the figures in the window.

So at last, with Sergeant Major John Pierce and the Countess of Keith as the only witnesses, the marriage of the Duke and Duchess of Vail was finally officially sanctioned by holy church. Only a renewal of vows that had been made, and had been faithfully kept, so many years before.

Chapter Fourteen

"*Now* you may open your eyes," Lady Keith said.

The small boy whose hand she held obeyed, the curve of golden lashes rising quickly to reveal gray eyes, widened with anticipation. There had been too few pleasant surprises in his short life, but still, with the optimism of childhood, he had believed his great grandmother's assurance that she had a fine, rare treat in store for him, waiting in the great hall below.

He had thought briefly of the wooden soldier Mr. Smithers had burned, and then, realizing that there was no way she could know how much he longed for another, he had banished that thought as being far too much to hope for.

"Mary!" he gasped, breaking from the grasp of the old woman to run across the stone floor to his former governess. He hesitated only briefly before throwing himself into her arms, despite the tall stranger who stood beside her. "Oh, Mary," he whispered, his face pressed to her shoulder as she knelt, both arms locked hard around the small, sturdy body, "I've missed you so."

"And I've missed you," she answered, fighting tears again. For so long she had denied herself the right to cry, and now it seemed that her emotions would no longer be denied expression.

Richard leaned back to see her face. A small thumb wiped away the tear that had slipped out. "Did my father send you here?" he asked, his eyes troubled and full of all the questions her unexpected appearance had created. His gaze swung briefly to Lady Keith and then back to Mary's face. "Did he send you to fetch me back home?"

"Your father...has gone away for a while," Mary said. She had decided to avoid too much explanation. The less said, the fewer lies she would have to tell him. She had never been comfortable, of course, with the lie she lived before, pretending to be her own son's governess, but that was necessary, she had believed, to protect Richard. And protecting him was still her prime consideration.

"Away?" he echoed. "To London?"

"Not this time," she said. Unthinkingly, she pushed the tumbling curls off his forehead, and then, seeing the confusion in his eyes, she smiled at him. "I don't think, Richard, that he will be coming home. At least not for a very long time. So I thought, with Lady Keith's permission, that you might like to come and live with me."

"At my father's house?" he asked, his voice echoing the doubt she had seen. She wondered what explanation Traywick had given him for the scene the child witnessed that winter morning after the merchant tried to rape her. Whatever he had been told, clearly it had not destroyed the love Richard had always felt for her. His greeting had been demonstration enough of that.

"No," she said, glancing up at Vail for the first time. The boy's gaze had followed hers, but she was not aware of the direction of his eyes. They met hers again when she turned back to continue the explanation. "I'm living somewhere else now. With my husband. And we would very much like for you to come and live with us."

"Until my father returns?" he asked.

Unwilling to add another lie to what she had already implied, Mary simply nodded.

"But what about Great Grandmother?" Richard said, turning to look at the old lady, who was still standing, leaning on her thick hawthorn staff, watching them.

"Great Grandmother thinks Mary has a wonderful idea," Lady Keith said. "I'm an old woman, not fit company any longer for a boy."

"But..." the child began, his clear eyes troubled.

"Boys are noisy and impudent creatures, always mucking about with their dogs and their ponies," she added, the jet eyes tender as they lingered on the golden head.

"I'm not noisy," the child protested softly, stung by the unfair complaint. Quick color stained his cheeks. "Or impudent. And I don't even have a pony, or—"

"But you should," the old woman said decisively. "That's exactly the trouble. You *should* be all of those things. Instead you're mewed up here with creaking servants and a foolish old woman who loves to live in the past."

"I like living with you," he said.

"Oh, child," Lady Keith whispered, "this isn't the place for a boy. You go on home with Mary and your—" She stopped suddenly, and Richard's eyes lifted again to the tall man who was still standing beside Mary's kneeling figure. The man who had so far taken no part in this conversation. "With that charming rogue she's married," the old woman amended. "I think he has a pony or two hidden away somewhere. And a dog, perhaps, Your Grace?" she suggested, her eyes still on the boy.

"One or two," Vail agreed.

"Two ponies?" the child asked unbelievingly. His gray eyes, round with amazement, looked up at the duke.

The well-shaped lips of His Grace, the Duke of Vail,

flickered dangerously near a smile at the awe in the childish voice, but he exercised the control he was famous for, and met the boy's eyes, eyes that were exactly like his own.

"And dogs," Vail agreed.

"And I might..." The boy hesitated, unsure how to ask this stranger the question whose incredible answer he thought had been implied. There was a possibility he had been wrong, that the pony His Grace had mentioned was *not* meant for him, but belonged to someone else, to some other boy. It would be very embarrassing to be mistaken about something that important. His eyes sought Mary's for reassurance that he might ask, and only when she nodded did he look up again into the gray eyes. "*I* might have one of them?" he whispered.

"If you care for him as he deserves," Vail said seriously, fighting the pull of emotion at the joy revealed in the child's face. "Horses serve our needs and give us pleasure, but in return, they are our responsibility."

That was the lesson Vail's father had taught him, and his father before him. With privilege comes responsibility, the duke had reminded Nick and his brother, time and again. The greater the privilege one is given, the greater the responsibility. His understanding of that had been the guiding principle of Nick's entire life, he realized, except for the one failure represented by the child who stood before him.

"I don't know how to care for ponies," Richard confessed, seeing that wonderful promise disappear almost before he had had an opportunity to grasp its possibility.

"Then Pierce will teach you," Vail said, glancing at his batman for confirmation of what he had just said.

When he met his master's eyes, Pierce's were as troubled as the boy's had been, but he had seen the sudden flare of hope in Richard's face, and so, despite his doubts about the duke's motive in assigning him the task that should rightly belong to the boy's father, he nodded.

"I'll teach you, lad," he agreed, "and gladly. But you ask the duke to pick him out for you. There's not a better eye for horseflesh in the country."

"Thank you, Pierce," Vail said. His tone said clearly that he knew exactly what his batman was up to.

"Will you do that, sir?" Richard asked. "Pick out a pony for me?" he added.

Vail studied the eager, upturned face a moment. His son. Yet, despite the success of his long search, there must, it seemed, still be barriers between them. He believed Mary was right not to burden the boy with a truth that would be painful and hard even for an adult to understand, but keeping his distance from this child was going to be far harder than he had imagined—perhaps the most difficult thing he had done in his life.

He wanted nothing so much as to kneel as Mary had and gather the child he had deserted, the son he had deprived of his birthright, into his arms. But because he had shirked his responsibility so long ago, out of fear and pride, to claim this boy openly now as his flesh and blood was not yet his privilege. So again, as he had when he first learned of his son's existence, Vail forced himself to keep his distance, his emotions guarded.

"Nick?" Mary prompted, wondering at his hesitation.

"I think we'll be able to find a suitable mount at Vail. The stables are quite extensive."

"But..." the boy whispered, again fearing to confess the truth, lest the tall man find him unworthy to have one of his ponies. "But, sir," he finally admitted bravely, "I'm afraid I don't know how to ride."

Courage and honesty and heart—all those he'll learn from his first horse, Pierce had said. But it seemed to Vail that, without any help from him, his son had already acquired all three.

"Then I suppose I must teach you," Nick said. "If you would like to learn."

"I should like that above all things," the child said. "If you don't mind, sir."

Finally the controlled, almost stern expression of the gray-eyed man relaxed slightly. "I don't mind," Vail agreed, and he was rewarded with a smile, shy and hesitant but unmistakably a mirror of his own.

"And this is the nursery," Mary said, opening the door on the room she had deliberately reserved as the last they would visit on this abbreviated tour of Vail. They had arrived home very late the night before, after the long journey from Scotland, and she had tucked the boy into her own bed. He had been asleep almost before his head touched the pillow, but she had sat beside him for a while before, leaving the door ajar, she slipped into the adjoining room where Nick was waiting.

By tradition, however, this room was the proper place for the heir. Nick had already sent for his beloved governess, who he felt, despite her age, would be willing to help look after the boy until some more permanent arrangement could be made for his education. Although he was almost of an age to be sent away to school, Vail had acknowledged that Mary—with good reason, of course—was not likely to give Richard over to strangers for a long time. And not, he himself had decided, until he could be certain that Traywick no longer posed any threat.

Nick had refused Mary's invitation to accompany them, determined not to force himself on the boy until he felt more at ease in his new surroundings. The spaniels at his heels, Vail had already started down the wide central staircase, late for an appointment with his estate manager, when memory intruded. Perhaps because he had been picturing their entry into the rooms where he had spent so many hours of his childhood, he suddenly remembered the charred fragment of wood in his vest pocket.

Vail didn't know why he still carried the remains of the toy soldier Smithers had been ordered to destroy, but he had kept it with him since he found it amid the ashes that dawn. At first it had been a talisman of sorts, some tangible bond with the child they sought. And now...perhaps now he kept it simply to remind himself that his son was safe, and that never again would he allow anyone to deliberately destroy something the boy cherished.

Turning, the duke retraced his path back up the stairs. He hated making his estate manager wait, courtesy to one's employees another responsibility that had been drilled into his head by his father, but suddenly this seemed far more important.

The nursery door was open, and so he stood a moment, watching his son explore the room. Small fingers touched the treasures he and Charles had collected: the colored rocks; shells that had come from visits to the seashore; a bird's nest, its three small blue eggs still inside, as perfect as when he had found them, almost thirty years ago. The careful fingers were reverently examining them all, trailing lightly over the smooth contours of a stone or holding a feather up to the light.

The child turned to smile at Mary and became aware of the duke standing in the open doorway, watching him. Slowly he laid the feather back on the shelf and put both hands behind his back, as if he had been caught in some embarrassing faux pas.

"Are all these yours, Your Grace?" he asked.

At the question, Mary glanced around to the doorway, her quick smile again inviting Nick to join them. The dogs had followed their master, and seeing the child, to whom they had not yet been introduced, they edged around Vail and into the room. Richard's eyes grew wide as they greeted him with friendly cold noses, making their welcome obvious. Tentatively, he caressed a silken ear. He had apparently forgotten his question to Vail, because he looked up, startled, when the duke answered.

"They belonged to me or to my brother Charles. Except for the shells, they were all found here on the estate," Nick said. "You're free to do your own exploring of the grounds. They're quite extensive." Seeing the sudden apprehension in his wife's eyes, he added, for her benefit, "And well-guarded." That was an order he had already put into effect. "The dogs would probably like to join you."

"I may take them outside?" the boy asked, fascinated by the idea of being in charge of these glorious creatures.

"Their names are Romulus and Remus, and you may take them wherever you wish," Vail agreed, leaning against the frame of the door. "Although I'm not sure it won't be a question of who's taking whom."

"Thank you, Your Grace," the boy said politely, his small fingers gingerly stroking one of the spaniel's heads. The other dog pushed his nose under the caressing hand, provoking a smile from the childish lips.

"This is your home now, Richard. You must feel free to explore it. He'll be perfectly safe, Mary, I promise you," Nick added softly, forestalling the protest he sensed she wanted to make. "There is something here I'd like to show you. Something that I believe you might enjoy."

The duke limped to the far side of the room and opened the door of one of the wall cabinets. It held more of the paraphernalia of his childhood, its disorder still very familiar, somehow, as if he and Charles had played here only yesterday.

Nick pulled out a small wooden chest, its top covered with a fine layer of dust. He resisted the urge to blow it off, something that he would surely have done if he were still his son's age. Instead of rushing to examine whatever the duke had thought he might like to see, the boy simply waited where he was, eyes wide, but revealing no other sign of excitement.

Too subdued, Vail thought. It was almost unnatural. Or perhaps, he thought, it was simply the strangeness of the vast house, and the shocks the boy had endured in the months before his arrival here. Surely this unnatural restraint would pass, and eventually Richard would learn to relish country life with the same exuberance he and Charles had always had. And soon, he hoped, the boy would feel more comfortable in his presence.

Vail carried the box to the nursery table and set it down. He unfastened the latch with his thumb and then lifted the lid to reveal the contents, which were exactly the same as when he himself had put them there.

The pieces of cast metal were unchanged—two small armies, their brightly painted coats only slightly faded by the passage of time. The prancing horses that carried the stiff cavalrymen seemed as alive to him now as they had so many years before, always ready to charge into battle, carrying their fearless, unmoving riders with them. The cannon, too, still looked as capable of puffing smoke and thunder as when he had supplied the battle noises he believed they might make.

One by one, he set the pieces out—friend and foe. He had had more than his share of toys, but these small figures had always been his favorite. He had fought endless battles, and no matter which army won, of course, he had always been the victor.

As the soldiers were lined up on the table, the child eased closer, his fascination apparent. But his hands were still clasped behind his back, tightly held. It seemed he suspected that if he released them, they might, against his will, embarrass him by reaching out to touch the small figures the duke was laying out. When the last piece had been removed, Nick closed the lid of the chest, and only then did he look down into the gray eyes that had watched every movement of his hands.

"I know these cannot replace the soldier Mary gave you, but they were always my favorites," he said. "I would like for you to have them."

There was something in the boy's gaze that he couldn't read, some thought, moving unspoken behind the eyes that had seen too much, that were far too adult for his age.

"Did you want to be a soldier," the child asked, "when you were a boy?"

"I don't think I ever wanted to be anything else," Nick admitted.

"Vail was a regimental colonel," Mary said. "He served under the Duke of Wellington."

"Mr. Smithers fought at Waterloo," Richard offered. He had been forbidden by Traywick to talk to the ex-soldier about his battlefield adventures, but that had not destroyed the fascination. "Did you perhaps..." He hesitated, remembering the merchant's injunction.

"There and in Iberia," Nick said.

Apparently the duke didn't feel that battles shouldn't be talked about, and so the pent-up questions tumbled out, one after another. "Is that why you limp? Were you wounded? Mr. Smithers lost his arm at Waterloo," Richard confided. "Were you a hero, too, like Mr. Smithers, Your Grace?"

He was too young to realize that the questions were not those one asked soldiers, Vail knew. His limp and its history were to the boy simply a matter of great interest, romantic and apparently, he hoped, heroic. "I was wounded at Waterloo," Nick said softly. There was so much more that he would have to explain one day to his son, but now, of course, was not the time. "I hope you enjoy the soldiers," he said simply.

It was an obvious closure to the brief conversation, and

the boy was sensitive enough to recognize it. "Thank you, Your Grace," he said. It was not until the duke had left, late for his appointment, that the childish fingers finally reached out to touch the bright red-and-gold coat of the commander of the British troop.

"Which would you like to keep?" Nick asked a few days later as they completed their inspection of the promised ponies. In the stalls at Vail were four ponies—carefully chosen from the docile and well-mannered animals the district had mustered at such short notice. Vail's instructions had ensured that whichever animal the boy fancied, it would prove to be entirely suitable.

The child's eyes again traced down the line of small, finely shaped heads bobbing over the low doors of their stalls. As the duke and Pierce watched, Richard had carefully touched each nose and looked into each pair of dark, wide eyes. Again Vail had found himself wondering what the boy was thinking. *Too reserved,* he had thought. *At least in my presence. Unnaturally restrained for a child this age.*

"Mr. Pierce said that you might choose for me, Your Grace," Richard ventured finally, looking up shyly at the duke, "if I asked you."

"They're all fine animals. The choice is simply a matter of which one you like best, the one with whom you felt some bond. A good pony will not only be your mount, but your friend, a true companion."

The boy's eyes traced again down the row of stalls. "What will happen to the others?" he asked softly. "To the ones I don't choose?"

Puzzled, the duke shook his head, a small crease forming between the arch of golden brows. "They'll be sent back. Back to their owners."

"To belong to some other boy?" Richard asked, his eyes still focused on the row of stalls.

"I don't know. Perhaps. They've not been mistreated, if that worries you. You have only to look at their condition to know they've been very well cared for." Nick couldn't imagine what was bothering the boy. Given this opportunity, he had thought the child would be more than eager to pick out one of the ponies.

"Do you think they'll know?"

"Know what?" Vail asked.

"That I chose another," he said, looking up finally into his father's eyes. "Will they feel that I liked another better, and that that's why they were sent home?"

"I don't think their understanding is that great," Nick said softly. Unthinkingly, he put his hand on the fair curls, almost a caress, and then he smiled. "Would it make you feel better if I make the choice?"

"Then...might I say goodbye to the others? After you've decided?"

Four ponies, Vail thought, looking back down the row of stalls. Their presence would never be noticed in the vastness of the stables.

"Keep them all," he said brusquely to Pierce, seeing the quick surprise in the batman's eyes, followed closely by what looked like amusement. "I believe there's room," the Duke of Vail added caustically. It was almost an explanation.

"You may, of course, do as you please, Your Grace," Pierce said, his face carefully controlled. "They're your stables, after all." *And your son,* he added mentally, as Vail turned away. Smiling, Pierce put his hand on the small head, exactly where the duke's had rested so briefly.

"Which one shall we saddle first?" he asked the boy.

"I'm to have *all* of them?" Richard asked unbelievingly. "But that's far too many. I didn't mean..." A minute crease appeared between the gray eyes.

"I've found it best through the years," Pierce said, "if

you do exactly what he tells you. Saves wear and tear on the nerves, I've found," he added, as he had said to Mary. His hand fell between the small shoulder blades, directing the boy back down the line of stalls. "And, as he said, there's certainly room for them all." The boy, lost in the incredible joy of the ponies, did not see the batman's satisfied smile.

"How did it go with the ponies?" Mary asked that night.

They were again in the privacy of the duke's bedroom, the first moment they had spent alone during the long day. Vail had been closed in the study all afternoon with his man of business, who had come up from London. The discussion, although he had not revealed that to Mary, had centered around the foreclosure and disposal of the merchant's enterprises.

The duke had also passed on his suspicions that Traywick had been involved with the owlers on the Kentish coast. A word about that in the right ears, and there would be another reason to prevent Traywick's ever being allowed to return to England. The authorities wouldn't turn a blind eye to the freebooters, no matter what the inhabitants of the region felt about their activities.

"He was afraid to choose," Vail said, remembering the worry in the small face.

"Afraid?"

"Afraid that the feelings of the ponies who were not chosen would be hurt because they were being sent back. His sensibilities are all yours, Mary. At his age I would never have considered a pony's feelings about rejection."

"Perhaps because you were never rejected," she suggested softly.

He turned back to the mirror, carelessly tossing the stickpin he'd removed onto the top of the dressing table. Still considering her comment, he said nothing as he untied the intricate folds of the cravat and dropped it to join the pin.

"And he has been?" he asked finally, turning back to face her. She looked up at the question. She was sitting on the bed they shared each night.

"Traywick, whom he believed to be his father, didn't like Richard very much. He wasn't quite so...malleable as he believed he should be." There were so many incidents she could have told him about to illustrate that dislike, but the guilt Vail bore about the child's life with Traywick was already painfully sufficient. There was no need to add to that burden more than was enough to help him understand his son.

"I thought the merchant was the one who wanted a son," he said.

"Not one like Richard. The alienation was not intentional, I can assure you, because the boy was hungry for his father's attention. But...I think Traywick was astute enough to realize, eventually, anyway, that Richard saw through him. The boy may even have known about Traywick's mistreatment of Abigail. I did the best I could to protect him, Nick, but still, somehow, I think he suspected. And knowing that, he couldn't admire the man he wanted so desperately to love. There were times when it was...obvious Traywick knew how the boy felt about him."

"Times?" Nick asked, working to control his voice, to keep the quick rage covered.

She looked up at his tone.

"You told me he likes to cause pain," he said. "Did he hurt the boy?" Maybe that would explain the child's reaction to him—another man to be feared. Maybe that would explain his quiet reserve.

"He...punished him. No more harshly than other boys, perhaps. At least I told myself that. It was always much worse for Richard if Abigail or I protested. Eventually I learned to hold my tongue."

"I should have killed him," Vail whispered. "His threats were hollow. He wasn't in a position to hurt the boy. I should have strangled the life out of him when I had the chance."

"Then we might never have found Richard," she reminded him. "Whatever happened in the past, whatever Traywick did, can be overcome. It may take longer than we had hoped, but eventually Richard will learn that here he's loved and he's wanted."

"And you believe that will make up for all the other?" he asked bitterly.

"Yes," she said, holding his eyes. "Love makes up for a great many mistakes. We have both made our share of those, and yet..."

When she hesitated, he walked across the room to stand before her. "And yet...here we are."

"Together."

"Again," he said softly, and finally he smiled at her.

"Children are far more ready to forgive than adults," she assured him, touching his hand. "To forget the past and accept the future. Our future lies together, the three of us. Eventually he'll understand that—with time and patience. Of which you seem to have an endless supply," she suggested.

"Patience?" he repeated.

"And time." She pulled him down beside her on the vast bed. "We have the rest of our lives, my darling," she whispered as his mouth closed over hers, "to make it all right."

The long days drifted by with an English summer's tranquillity. In a London that seemed far more distant than it was, the Duke of Vail's powerful solicitors began the slow process they hoped would eventually lead to the recognition of his firstborn son's legal rights. The duke's marriage to Mary Winters had already been accepted by the king's justices, they argued, and all that remained was to apply the traditional laws of primogeniture to the son the duke was eager to acknowledge.

The fact that the child had been christened Richard Traywick was glossed over as a terrible mistake, caused primarily, or so the lawyers suggested, by the grievous wounds the duke had suffered while in the service of his country, his young wife's grief over his absence and what she had supposed to be his death, and her own illness after the child's birth.

There was endless gossip and speculation among the beau monde, of course, but on the vast estate, Mary and the boy were as protected from the avid interest of the ton in the legal proceedings as Vail could manage. He had been assured that the case was going well. After all, Marcus Traywick was not in the country to protest, and given Vail's information about his illegal activities, later verified by a close official examination of the merchant's dealings, it would be very unwise for him to come back and attempt to reclaim his son.

Nick could only wish that the battle on the home front was succeeding so well as that being waged in the courts. Despite the almost idyllic happiness he and Mary had recaptured, Richard seemed still remarkably contained for a child of his age, at least in the presence of his father. Indeed, there had been so little relaxation of his demeanor when he was with Vail that Mary had not yet found the courage to broach the subject of his true paternity.

"Just be patient," she had argued softly the last time Nick questioned her delay. "So much has happened to him. He needs time to adjust."

The duke's gray eyes had reflected his bitter disappointment, but Vail had said nothing else, and his manner toward the child had been as patient and accepting as it had from the first. Richard and Pierce had become almost inseparable, and often Nick found himself resenting the easy camaraderie they shared.

The duke, of course, had no way of knowing that most of their conversations regarded his own military exploits. And from Miss Hawkins, his governess, the boy gleaned details of his childhood. The treasures of the nursery, which miraculously, or so it seemed to him, had passed into his keeping, were increasingly valued for their association with the tall, gray-eyed man about whom Pierce, Smithers and Miss Hawkins spoke with such admiration and affection.

So Vail was never aware that during the long summer days and into the coolness of fall, the child's eyes began to follow him about the house and grounds with the same adoration evident in the dark eyes of the two spaniels. The difference was that the boy was careful to hide his feelings, even from Mary. They were too private and too personal, the hope they represented too fragile to trust to any confidante, even one so well-beloved as she.

Chapter Fifteen

In the darkness of the October night, the vast household employed by the Duke of Vail slept soundly, lulled by the midnight peace of the surrounding countryside. The groom who sounded the alarm could never have said what had awakened him—perhaps only the promise of frost in the autumn air. But he was more fortunate than he would realize for a long time that when he stirred drowsily in his nest of blankets, the acrid smell of smoke had reached the place where he was sleeping, and he recognized the scent that automatically stirs panic in anyone raised around a stable.

When he opened the door, it took him only a moment to realize that the fire was beyond his ability to contain it. And only a second more to raise the alarm. The deep note of the paddock's bell—no sound more dreaded to a horseman's ears—filled the night, and almost immediately, it seemed, the yard was filled with half-dressed grooms and sleepy stable boys, running to fight the blaze, which was already brilliant in the darkness. The squeals of trapped horses, almost mad with terror, spurred their heroic and unthinking efforts.

It was perhaps understandable that no one thought to

send for the duke, at least in the first unreasoning rush to save the animals. The footmen from the Hall had readily joined the efforts, but Thompson had delayed awakening his master until he was sure the situation was serious enough to warrant disturbing His Grace's sleep.

In the end, it was Richard who woke his father. The nursery wing was much nearer the paddocks, and the unexpected clang of the alarm bell had startled the child out of sleep and led him to his window. The horror of what he saw sent him at a run to find the man he had come to believe was able to accomplish anything.

Even though he was jerked abruptly from sleep, Nick's understanding of the child's entreaty was much quicker than Mary's. He had pulled on his clothes and boots before she fully comprehended the boy's tearful plea.

"Keep him here," Nick ordered, picking the boy up and depositing him unceremoniously in the bed beside his mother. "Whatever you do, Mary, don't let him outside." She nodded, holding the child's small, shivering body against her own.

"The ponies," Richard said again, the words almost a sob. "Please save the ponies."

There was no way he could promise to do that, Vail thought. He had no idea how widespread the blaze might be. He also knew, however, that the grooms would surely attempt to remove the more valuable stock from the inferno first. Four ponies, virtually worthless in terms of monetary value, would not be a prime consideration to them.

The first thing his son had ever asked him for, Nick realized as he ran, shouting for Pierce. And there was no way to know until he reached the paddocks if he could accomplish the hope represented by that soft, tear-choked plea.

In the quiet bedroom, Mary held the trembling body of her son a long time, slowly rocking back and forth, the rhythm as comforting, she prayed, as when he had been an infant. Through the long, dark silence, however, her thoughts ran with Nick and the others who would be trying so desperately to save the animals they all loved.

"Will he be able to get the ponies out?" Richard whispered at last.

Reassurance, she knew, was what he sought, but Mary's innate honesty wouldn't allow her to promise what Vail might not be able to accomplish, no matter how hard he tried.

"If he can," she said, smoothing her hand over the small golden head. "If it can be done—" she began, and then realized that Nick would never sacrifice the lives of men for those of the ponies—and it wouldn't be right that he should.

"If that can be accomplished without the risk of anyone's life, Richard, then he will. But a stable fire is very dangerous. The animals are panicked. Despite the fact that the grooms try to lead them away from the flames, sometimes they resist. They'll get them out if they can. But...if not, you must remember that they did the very best they could. You know Pierce and Vail would never let anything happen to the horses if they can possibly prevent it."

"I didn't think about the men," Richard said. "I didn't think..." His voice hesitated, and the gray eyes sought hers.

"I know. I know you didn't. Vail will see to it all," she comforted, her faith in Nick again absolute. "It's all right," she whispered, her hand smoothing back the sleep-rumpled curls.

In his mind's eye, the boy saw the leaping flames that had been visible from the nursery window, as well as the tall, gray-eyed man who had given him the ponies and the metal soldiers and everything else that was now his. The sudden fear that gripped his heart was not for the four small ponies who came when he called them and lipped sugar cubes from his palm.

"We can see the stables from my windows," he said entreatingly.

"But there's nothing we can do. I don't think looking at the fire will help. They're doing all they can, Richard, I promise you."

He was the one who had wakened the duke. His was the plea that had sent Vail into danger. Again his small frame shuddered with the force of that fear.

"Downstairs?" he begged softly. "May we at least go downstairs and wait?"

Mary didn't understand the terror that had prompted the request, but she understood the child's concerns for the ponies. Vail had said not to let him out of the house, but taking him downstairs couldn't make any difference. She could warm some milk for him, and they could wait for news together.

"All right," she agreed. "We'll go to the kitchen and stir up the fire and make the duke and Pierce a pot of tea for when they come back. How will that be?" she asked, smiling at him. His eyes were still too wide, and haunted by the images of the burning stable, but he quickly nodded agreement. Mary found her wrapper and then holding her son's hand, she led him from the bedchamber.

When they entered the upstairs hall, it felt almost as if they were the only ones left in the vast house. Mary knew that couldn't be true, of course. Although Thompson and the footmen would certainly have gone to help with the emergency, the chambermaids and some of the kitchen staff, sleeping below stairs, might not have responded to the bell. Perhaps the women had gone outside to watch the excitement, she realized, but surely someone was still here.

Her intellectual argument that they could not be alone did nothing to prevent the tiny frisson of unease as she led the way down the curving grand staircase. There was an almost unearthly silence about the great dark hall below, touched now with no light but moonlight, filtering dimly through the tall windows. The fire, the rushing men, the alarm bell, seemed a world away from the house's unnatural quietness.

When they had reached the foot of the stairs, she hesitated a moment before stepping across the checkerboard pattern of the foyer's marble squares. The deeper shadows looming in the corners seemed threatening. It felt as if she and the child were isolated from every living soul in the world—alone and somehow, she thought, attempting to quell her unreasoning fear, vulnerable.

Even if all the men on the estate were in the area of the paddocks, too distant to hear anything, that did not mean that there was any danger here. There was no danger at all, she reminded herself sternly. But it was not even a surprise when the familiar voice spoke from the darkest part of the hallway.

"Why, Mary," Marcus Traywick said softly, his tone unctuous with feigned pleasure and surprise. "How appropriate that *you* should be the one to answer my summons. I had expected your noble paramour, but the two of you instead are just as rewarding. Perhaps even more so."

"Your summons?" She fought the sick terror that was clawing up out of her stomach and into her throat.

"The alarm bell. There seems to be a problem in your husband's stables."

"You set the fire," she whispered. "But why? What do you hope to gain by—"

"The only thing left to me now, my dear. Just a small revenge."

"On Vail?" she asked. Apparently Traywick had set the fire and then entered the house, probably when the servants left to answer the alarm. He had waited here in the darkness for Nick, but, knowing the house so well, the duke had chosen another, quicker route below, leaving the merchant waiting. That meant, she prayed, that Traywick couldn't know Nick was already outside and that, except perhaps for a maid or two sleeping below, they were alone.

"He's taken everything. Between you, the two of you have stolen everything that was mine."

"I've taken nothing from you—"

"Money, my business and reputation, even my appearance, Mary. You've taken them all. Everything. And now he has made me a fugitive to my own country. I kept our bargain, and you betrayed me."

"Vail offered to pay you for—" Mary stopped. She had been so careful that Richard shouldn't find out the truth in a way that might shock or hurt him. Instead, she understood now, she had waited too long, foolishly trying to protect him from what was about to happen.

"For his bastard," Traywick said viciously. "For his beloved whore's bastard droppings."

"He'll pay you now," Mary whispered. "Whatever you want." She dared not look down at the boy who stood, still trembling, beside her. She could only hope that in his innocence, Richard would have no idea what the merchant's spiteful venom had meant.

"And my life? Can he give me back my life, Mary? Can even Vail restore to me what he's taken?"

"He'll give you enough to begin again. In France or wherever you wish. He'll give you whatever you want," she offered.

"Whatever I want," Traywick echoed, his voice mocking. "You made me that offer before, and even that was a trick. You came to me, Mary, and you offered me your body, but it was all a trick, designed so Vail would find us together."

"No," she said. "I never intended for him to find out. I would never put him in danger."

"I thought he was dead. All those days I thought I had killed him. Despite the fact that I knew I'd have to leave England, I relished what I had done. His death would be punishment enough for you, too, I believed. And you'd never find the boy. I knew that. Except…"

The hateful voice paused, and Mary waited, knowing that the longer she could delay whatever he had planned, the more chance there was that someone would return to the house.

"Except now I know that you haven't suffered at all. You have destroyed my life, and you have everything you ever wanted. It didn't seem fair, Mary, that you should have everything and I should have nothing. Your son. Your husband. All this," he said, gesturing with one hand at the magnificence of their surroundings.

With the movement, Mary caught a glimpse of what he held. A pocket pistol, perhaps the same one with which he had shot Vail. "What are you going to do?" she asked, but because she fully understood now the evil of which he was capable, she believed that she knew what he intended. Her heart turned to ice, and the blood in her veins slowly congealed with that fear.

"What will cause you pain, my sweet Mary? I tried to think, throughout those months in France, watching the pittance I had managed to save from your lover's grasping fingers slowly disappear. The most pain, I thought. What in the world—"

Mary moved suddenly, stepping in front of the child, her body between her son and the madman who held the pistol. And from the shadows she heard his laughter, as chilling as in the courtroom that day.

"Ah, Mary," he said. "Your instincts are, as always, so in tune with those around you. So sensitive. He is, of course, the better choice, but you see, my dear, when I came here, I didn't know you had found him. I thought he was still safely tucked away with that old hag in Scotland. I thought you'd never find him.

"Smithers, I suppose. Another ingrate. I had hoped he'd drowned. He and Vail together, but then, when I tried to contact my bankers, I realized that the duke, at least, had survived the sea and was still persecuting me. But not for long. I don't have to hurt Mary herself, I realized. It will be punishment enough for her to know that she is responsible for the death of someone she loves. The duke, I believed then, but you've made me see the error in that. The boy is so much better for our purposes."

"No," she said. Her hands were behind her, gripping Richard's upper arms to hold him there, safely shielded by her own body.

"His death may even hurt Vail, if he has any father feeling for the arrogant little whoreson. I must confess I never could. Something about his eyes. Too much like his noble sire's, I suppose."

"Vail will kill you," she whispered, her hands urging Richard backward. She felt him take a step up the staircase, and she followed, retreating upward. And then another step. Thankfully, the child had understood her silent communication. There was no other way. To move anywhere else would bring them closer to the merchant, and so she continued, her body always between the dark, unwavering eye of the muzzle of the gun Traywick held and the boy's.

Three steps. Four.

"No, Mary," the merchant said softly.

One shot, she thought. Then he would have to reload. If she took the ball...

"If he shoots, Richard, you must run. No matter what happens, run upstairs. Hide. Wait for Vail to come for you. Do you understand?" Her instructions were very soft—too low, she hoped, for the sound of the whispered words to reach across the foyer that stretched between them. There was no way to verify if the child had heard or if he would obey. No way to know how a terrified child would respond to what she believed was about to happen.

"But your fight, Traywick, is not with them."

The deep voice came from her right, familiar, beloved, and yet unexpected. Vail. Mary had turned automatically at the words, and she could see him standing in the shadows, only the white shirt he had thrown on to rush to the burning stables visible in the darkness. "I'm the one who ruined you. I'm the one you came here for."

"Revenge," Traywick acknowledged, but the focus of the gun did not shift toward the man in the shadows. "And this will be the best way to accomplish that."

"I offered you wealth before, and you refused. You brought about your own destruction. Mary and the boy had nothing to do with that."

"She had *everything* to do with what's happened," Traywick said defiantly. "*She's* the one who broke our bargain. I guarded the boy. All those years I fed and clothed and protected them both."

"You tried to rape me," Mary said. Another step backward. "My body wasn't part of our bargain. And then you brought charges against me because I resisted you."

"I'm the one you want," Vail said again. He took a step forward, moving almost into the moonlight. Traywick's eyes turned briefly toward him.

"How else can I hurt the great Duke of Vail? You have power and money and position, all given to you through an accident of birth. I *made* what I had through hard work and my own sweat, and then you took it away from me because of her, enticing men like a bitch in heat. First you and then me. It's all her fault," he said reasonably. "And she deserves to be punished."

"Can you only fight women and children?" Vail's question was contemptuous. "Why not try fighting someone who's up to your weight for a change?" the duke asked mockingly, taking another step forward, ever nearer the merchant and the gun.

Traywick laughed. "I'm not one of you perfumed fops. You can't goad me with that. I *have* no honor for you to manipulate, Your Grace. I won't meet you between the Elms at dawn. I don't fight by the rules. I make my own rules. You should have remembered that."

As he said the last word, he pulled the trigger, and the sound of the shot echoed through the empty expanse of the marbled foyer. Even as the gun fired, Vail launched his body at the thick figure holding it. The men struggled in the shadows, and Mary could only distinguish which was which because of the white shirt Nick wore. It was so strange, watching the twisting bodies in the darkness. As remote as if they were actors in some play, moving over a stage she could barely see, uttering lines that she couldn't hear for the sudden ringing in her ears.

She sat down slowly on the steps. There was no pain, just a strange weakness. She pressed her hand to her side, which for some reason was hot, her skin burning, and when she raised her palm, even in the moonlight, the thick crimson streak was clearly visible. Against her will, her fingers began to tremble.

"Richard," she said comfortingly, knowing he would be frightened. When she looked up into his face, his eyes were dilated with fear, and she put her hand down, rubbing her palm down the white lawn of her wrapper, trying to wipe away the blood. But the stain it left was worse somehow, more frightening, so dark against the sheer paleness of the fine fabric.

She tried to think what to do, but it was so hard to formulate any thought at all. Her brain wasn't functioning very well. She knew Nick and Traywick were fighting. She could hear them, the sounds seeming to come from a great distance, but she couldn't focus on their struggle, or even on the outcome. There must be something she should do. "Run," she ordered softly, looking up into Richard's eyes. "Run."

He had knelt beside her on the stairs. At her command, he stood, but he didn't climb the stairs as she had intended. Instead, he ran back down the four or five steps she had managed to put between them and the deadly threat of Traywick's pistol.

"No," she said, but the word was only a whisper, her breath stolen by the growing agony in her side. "No," she said again, more loudly now, but the whisper had no effect on the running child.

She pushed up, her hands against the small rise of the step behind her. She could do nothing but watch as everything happened at once. She saw Traywick raise the gun and bring it down on his opponent, the rise and fall of his arm clear even in the shadows. Once, and then again. She couldn't hear the blows. Couldn't hear anything. Vail slumped back against the wall, the white shirt marking him as clearly as if she could distinguish his features in the moonlight.

Traywick moved, his speed once more deceptive in a man of such bulk. He caught the boy before Richard could reach the fallen man. Caught him and lifted him, and then Mary watched as Traywick, carrying the struggling child, disappeared into the shadows from which Vail had spoken.

She lay back against the step, grief and weakness overwhelming her. Their son was once more in the control of that madman, and there was nothing she could do.

"Mary," Vail said. He was kneeling beside her when she opened her eyes, but she didn't understand how that could be.

"Richard," she whispered, reaching up to touch his face. "Traywick has Richard." Still he didn't go. He caught her hand and held it tightly, his strong fingers trembling as hers had when she saw the blood, and at last she understood. She smiled at him. "I'm all right. I promise you, Nick. Go after him. Don't let him take Richard away from me again." And then to make him act, to free him from the paralysis that she knew would hold her were their positions reversed, she whispered. "If you allow him to take Richard, I'll never forgive you. I swear to you, Nick, I'll never forgive that." Her eyes held his, fighting against his natural inclination to stay beside her.

He squeezed her hand, and then he disappeared into the darkness that surrounded her. Relieved, she laid her head back against the step and allowed her eyes to close. All she could do was to trust Nick. All she could do.

It must have taken him only seconds to stagger across the foyer, Nick reasoned as he ran. Less than that to kneel beside Mary and to recognize that what she had said was the truth. He had to stop Traywick. She would never forgive him if he failed her now. Not again, he thought. Not again.

When he burst out into the smoke-filled night through the same door he had entered, his heart lifted. Like a fool, the merchant was struggling to mount Comet. The duke had ridden the charger bareback the short distance from the paddock as soon as he discovered that the stable fire had been deliberately set. He himself had thrown the blanket over the gelding's head to lead him from the burning building, and only his familiar hands and his voice, long trusted for guidance through the noise and devastation of battle, had been able to overcome the horse's terror. The shining chestnut coat had been marked by the rawness of burns. Despite the pain it must have caused, always faithful,

Comet had allowed Vail to slip on his bridle and ride him here.

But not Traywick, of course, a stranger who carried a struggling child. Traywick was attempting to pull the horse to the mounting block. The agony of the burns, the residual terror of what Comet had been through and the harsh jerks on the reins with which Traywick was attempting to control him were too much, even for an animal trained to endure the horrors of battle.

Comet twisted away, rearing against the pull of unfamiliar hands. *Now,* Vail thought, *while he's distracted by the horse's antics.* The attack he mounted this time was not designed to bring down the merchant's bulk. The element of surprise on his side, Vail grabbed the child Traywick was holding. Nick ran with the boy back toward the house, almost throwing him inside the door he had left open. Only then did he turn back to face his enemy, determined to stand guard between the madman and those he loved.

The gelding was plunging wildly, trying to remove himself from the control of the stranger whom he now associated with all his pain. Stupidly, Traywick still clutched the reins, perhaps believing that the horse represented his only hope for escape. Perhaps he was such a poor horseman he didn't realize no one could control the terrorized animal. Or perhaps he held on, jerking the reins, because he had always believed that by causing enough pain he could make anyone or anything do what he wanted.

Vail had not closed half the distance that separated him from the struggle when Comet reared again. The charger was magnificent in his fury and fear, finely conditioned body outlined briefly against the sky, forelegs flailing in the dense, smoke-shrouded air. As the duke watched, one of the gelding's hooves struck Traywick's forehead, and the merchant fell backward like a felled tree.

Comet reared again, but perhaps, even in the midst of

his panic, he had recognized that the thing that lay before
him was a man. The powerful hooves came down this time,
almost dainty in their avoidance of the sprawled body. The
gelding backed away. Wisely Nick didn't try to approach
him. Instead he knelt beside Traywick.

Already the shape of the iron shoe was visible on Traywick's temple. Blood began to seep into the bluing depression in the fractured skull. Nick had seen enough head injuries to know that this one would be fatal. Even if a man
with such a wound lived for a few hours, eventually the
swelling of the brain and the bleeding inside his head would
kill him. Within his heart Vail could find no regret that
Marcus Traywick would die.

If ever a man had deserved death... Nick thought. And
then, leaving the body beside Comet, who was at last quiet,
his reins trailing on the ground, the Duke of Vail ran back
to the house. The child was still standing exactly where
Nick had left him, just inside the open doorway. He had
seen all that had happened—the brutal accidental death of
the man he had thought to be his father. Vail slowed to a
walk, trying to read what was in the boy's eyes as they
lifted to his face, their pupils black and widely distended
in a narrow rim of gray.

Vail had time only to bend and catch the small body to
him as his son hurtled into his arms. Nick held tightly, too
tightly, he tried to remind himself, but for some reason he
couldn't let go—the urge to know that Richard was safe,
the long-denied desire to feel softly rounded, childish arms
fastened around his own neck, a tear-damp face pressed
hard into the crook of his shoulder. Standing, he carried
the boy with him into the house, refusing, despite his hurry
to reach Mary, to let him go.

The doctor had been immediately reassuring, even before
they had carried the duchess to the bedchamber and he had

begun his physical examination. Mary had answered his questions. She was still conscious.

"A flesh wound, we shall hope," he had assured the duke, even as he supervised the careful conveyance of his wife upstairs. "The ball apparently passed through her side, which accounts for the great loss of blood and, of course, the shock and resulting pain. But I believe no vital organ was damaged. Sound and fury, Your Grace, sound and fury. So, at least, we shall hope."

Sending a white-faced Claire to the kitchens to fetch hot water, he had closed the bedroom door in Vail's face. The duke hadn't realized that he was still carrying his son, the warm, solid weight of the small body very reassuring. Comforting. In passing, the maid made a small clucking noise and patted the child on his nightshirt-clad bottom, as she might have given unthinking comfort to one of her half-dozen younger brothers. Richard lifted his head at that to smile down at Claire from the great height at which he was held.

"You may put me down, sir," he suggested softly.

So he could go back to being the child who had lived under this roof like a small, quiet ghost these months, Vail thought. Despite the fact that he and Mary had tried to reassure the boy that his life would always have the stability those peaceful days had provided, tonight had surely undone all the slow progress they had made.

Nick set his son on the floor, and stepped back, looking down only on golden curls. The gray eyes, so much like his own, were directed downward, no longer meeting his with the honesty and courage he had come to treasure.

"He said..." Richard began, and then the childish voice hesitated.

Although Vail had not heard the entire exchange between Traywick and Mary, he could imagine what had been said. They had tried to protect the boy from any shock in learning of his true parentage. Mary had wanted him to come to that knowledge already secure in the love of both of them. And instead...

Vail drew a breath, dreading the disclosure of whatever poison the merchant had suggested. The truth was betrayal enough. But at least the truth was that what had been done, whatever mistakes had been made, had been done in love. His love for Mary and hers for their son. But who could know what damage that truth, distorted through the perverted mind of Marcus Traywick, would do to a child as sensitive as this?

"What did he say, Richard?" Nick was forced to ask finally when the painful silence stretched.

"He said I am your son." The gray eyes lifted, and whatever Vail had expected, he did not find it in the face turned up to his. There was hope there instead. And the same eagerness with which he had heard about the possibility of ponies that day in Scotland. The wordless delight with which he had touched the silken heads of the spaniels, welcoming them as the cherished companions they had become.

Nick's throat tightened with that realization, and for a moment he could not speak, not even to acknowledge what was in his son's face. Tears, unaccustomed and unwanted, burned briefly behind the steady gray eyes before duty and responsibility controlled them.

"You are my son. And Mary's," he said softly. "And we love you more than you will ever be able to imagine. Until," he added, understanding, perhaps for the first time, his own father's demands and endless lessons, "until one day you have a son of your own."

"And I am always to be your son," the child whispered. "Never again to be his."

"A bond unbreakable," Nick promised softly. His father had died coming to find him, to offer what healing his love could give. And even had his father known, had he been able to see all that lay ahead, Nick realized, he would still have come. To the ends of the earth and beyond. As Nick would do for this child. Flesh of my flesh. Heart's blood of my heart.

The door opened suddenly, and they looked up to find the doctor pulling his cuffs out of his recently donned frock coat. The startled physician looked into faces enough alike to leave no doubt as to who this boy was. Strange, he thought, that the duke had not simply marched the child into the London courts and advised them all to look for themselves. But, of course, the nobility was strange, and Vail knew more about his business than he.

"Mary?" the duke questioned.

The flare of anxiety in his face was certainly familiar to the doctor. A love match, then, he thought. Gossip had not lied about that, at least.

"It is as I believed. A very great shock to the system, of course. And given the duchess's condition..." He let the sentence trail away delicately.

"Condition?" Vail repeated.

"But the babe is, I assure you, Your Grace, unharmed. There is no reason to expect anything less than...a very satisfactory resolution." Seeing the confusion in the handsome features, the doctor added, "In due time, of course, a very blessed event."

"Babe?" Nick echoed. "Are you telling me...?" He hesitated because he had never dared to believe that he would receive the news the physician had just delivered.

"Another son, or a daughter, perhaps. In the spring. We may be more certain of the exact date later. You didn't know?" he said. It was obvious that the duke hadn't.

"I didn't know," Vail admitted softly.

"You may visit Her Grace. Briefly, of course. She needs her rest." From his pocket he produced a small glass vial.

"A drop or two of this in a glass of water will allow her to sleep without pain." He held the laudanum out to the duke and had time to wonder at his hesitation in accepting it before Vail spoke.

"No," he said simply.

"The girl can mix the dosage, if you prefer. It's simple enough. The drug will allow Her Grace to rest comfortably. It will also keep her calm. I'm sure you know how women—"

"Obviously—" Nick put his hand on the boy's back to direct him around the doctor and toward the room where he knew Mary would be waiting for them "—obviously, you don't know Mary."

When the two had disappeared into the duchess's bedroom, the physician found himself standing alone in the hallway, still holding out the vial. His brows lifted, and then, shaking his head, he dropped the opium back into his bag and made his way downstairs.

Mary was lying back against stacked pillows. Although her face was very pale, Nick thought she was more beautiful than he had ever seen her. Her hair was loose, the rich, glowing darkness of the spread curls capturing all the candlelight that was not reflected in the softly shining midnight blue of her eyes.

More than either of them had dared hope for, Nick thought, walking slowly to the high bed, his hand still on the back of his son's shoulder.

"He told you," she said, seeing that knowledge, that incredible wonder, revealed in his face as clearly as he had read it in hers.

"Yes," he acknowledged. "I never thought..." he began, and then, unexpectedly, his throat tightened as it had in the hall. "Far more than I deserve, Mary. So much...it almost makes me afraid."

She held out her hand, and he took it into his.

"Fear no longer has a place here, Nick. Finally..." She glanced at the face of the child, standing beside his father. "Only love," she whispered. Her smile for her son was perhaps more tender tonight because of the other life growing sheltered beneath her heart, where she had cherished him.

"I'm to have a brother," Richard told her. Mary's gaze flicked quickly to Nick's, but he smiled at her, and she knew that whatever had been said between them, it was the beginning she had prayed for.

"Or a sister," she said, looking down again at her son.

"Another great responsibility," Nick said.

"Like the ponies?" Richard questioned, looking up into his father's eyes.

"The ponies are fine," Vail finally remembered to tell him. "We got them all out."

"Were they afraid?" Richard asked. "Because I wasn't there?"

"Perhaps," Vail said.

"I didn't want you to be hurt. I was afraid of that. But ponies are a great responsibility," he said.

"As are brothers," Nick agreed. Charles, too, had made that last journey. To the ends of the earth and beyond. "They sometimes need a great deal of care and instruction to learn all that they should know."

It had taken him so long to understand it all. There were bonds that were unbreakable, no matter the circumstance. He had failed these two once before, and they had suffered for that failure. But in the end...

"Nick," Mary said softly, and he cleared the old guilts, all of them, to smile down into her eyes.

If this baby were another son, they would name him Charles, he thought. In love and memory and in honor of all those bonds that had sustained him through the long years and had led him at last to this great victory.

He bent and, holding Mary's eyes, for the first time he kissed his firstborn son.

*   *   *   *   *

still focused on the row of stalls.